Sale

this fire
down in
my soul

Also by J. D. Mason

And on the Eighth Day She Rested

One Day I Saw a Black King

Don't Want No Sugar

this fire down in my soul

J. D. Mason

St. Martin's Press New York

This is a work of fiction. All of the characters, organizations, and events portrayed in this novel are either products of the author's imagination or are used fictitiously.

THIS FIRE DOWN IN MY SOUL. Copyright © 2007 by Jaclyn Meridy. All rights reserved. Printed in the United States of America. No part of this book may be used or reproduced in any manner whatsoever without written permission except in the case of brief quotations embodied in critical articles or reviews.
For information, address St. Martin's Press, 175 Fifth Avenue, New York, N.Y. 10010.

ISBN-13: 978-0-312-32646-3

acknowledgments

Acknowledgments are hard to write because you have to make sure you don't leave anybody out, no matter how unintentional their contribution was to the completion of this book. For instance, my sister wanted props because she said something I thought was funny and told her I liked it and wanted to use it in this book. So, since I did add it, big ups to my lil' sis, Cynthia L. Newsome, for her witty comment, for which she is aware that I paraphrased in this novel.

Of course, as a writer, I absolutely always have to thank my agent, Sara Camilli, for her services and support. The only thing is that she already knows I'm grateful, and I have to wonder if I'm being redundant by thanking her each and every time I write a book. Does it still hold the same impact as it did when I thanked her the first time? And what else can I say about her that I haven't already said? Thanks, Sara, my confidante, advisor, friend, etc. None of that has changed, of course, but I'd hate for her to stop reading my acknowledgments because she's bored by the mention of her name and the use of the same pronouns, nouns, and adjectives to describe what she means to me over and over again. You're great! Enough said.

And I absolutely have to thank my editor, Monique Patterson, especially with this book, which didn't come easily to me. I had a hard time writing this story—I don't know why—but bless her patient heart, Monique, nice person that she is, never once said, "What the hell is this, J.D.?" and I know she wanted to. But instead, she rolled up her sleeves, dug into her stance, and got down to the business of helping me to pull this novel together. If I were a football team, she'd be my coach! She's great, too. I keep saying it, but it keeps on being true.

And then there are the fabulous, fabulous book clubs and all the fabulous members who never cease to amaze me with their love of books and their support of us authors. I've had the privilege of meeting, eating, and drinking with a few of them: Sisters Sippin' Tea, Tulsa Chapter, Circle of Sisters, Kalamazoo, Michigan, Circle of Sisters, Denver, Colorado, and Wits-End Book Club, Denver, Colorado. And a special thanks to the Sistah Circle Book Club for making me an honorary member and for buying me something to eat.

And finally, I'd like to say thanks to family and friends, for your support and, most of all, for just allowing me to be "Jackie," when I'm home on the range, chilling, hanging out, and just being me.

this fire
down in
my soul

prologue

For whatever is hidden is meant to be disclosed, and whatever is concealed is meant to be brought out into the open.
—Mark 4:22

We'd soared so high, but look at where we'd landed. He'd gotten to her before I did. Teddy had killed her, the way I'd planned to. But standing in the midst of that crowd gathered outside her apartment building, no one knew that the gun tucked inside my purse had a bullet loaded in it with her name on it. Not a soul knew the depths to which I'd been driven or that the man I loved, the man I was married to, my life's blood, had lost his mind over this woman.

Sirens screamed in the distance. Lights flashed red, blue, yellow against the pale bricks of the building and stunned faces. A man emerged from inside, carrying a woman, crying and reaching back behind her.

"Noooooooo!" she screamed over and over again. "Please . . . God! Oh Jesus! Noooooooo!"

A sister? Friend perhaps? Hysterical and grieving over the dead woman, it didn't matter to me who she was or that she'd lost someone dear to her.

It was difficult to feel a part of such a scene. My mind detached me from it, and left me on the outside looking in, like I was watching it unfold on a Lifetime movie. But I was as much a part of it as anyone. I belonged there, like the wailing woman, begging for Jesus while wrapped tightly in the arms of a man fighting desperately to keep her from running back inside that building. I belonged there, like that policeman stringing up yellow ribbon, forcing the crowd to move back behind it to protect the crime scene. I belonged there, with the coroner coming out of the building, wearing the remote, grave expression on his face, and with the paramedics trailing behind him, wheeling out the dark vinyl bag on the gurney zipped up, with her lifeless body inside. Finally, I belonged there, the way he belonged there, unable to take his eyes off her, even now, even as she lay concealed inside that bag. He emerged from the building, his hands cuffed behind his back, being led through the door and down the walkway by two policemen. All color had drained from his face. Hollow, empty eyes, glazed over with regret and maybe even sadness focused on her, and then gradually ahead of him.

Traffic was bad this time of day, and I'd been anxious, so I'd taken the highway. If I'd come through the city, I might have gotten there first, and then it would've been me led away in handcuffs instead of him. God knows I'd have shot her, but for some reason, He'd let my husband have that privilege instead. It should've been me to pull the trigger. I'm the one who deserved retribution. Not him.

"I swear, Faye, as God is my witness," he raised his right hand to heaven, and knelt down on his knees at my feet when he confessed. "I'll end it, baby. It's over. Right now. Right now, Faye, just . . . don't . . . don't leave me! I'm begging you. Please! Don't do this to us."

Love is stronger than pride sometimes, and I forgave him. Or at least I wanted to. But instinct took over where trust failed, and I knew deep down inside that she'd gotten to him. I knew it the way I knew my own name. Teddy lied to me. He'd been stung and sprung by pussy young enough to be his daughter and all the faith I had in him faded away.

"Whyyyyyy?" the hysterical woman screamed out as he passed her. "You didn't have to kill her!" She bolted from the man's arms, and ran toward Teddy, my husband, who was oblivious to her and to everyone else around him. The man caught her before the cop had a chance to get to him, and pulled her into his arms again.

"No, baby," he said soothingly. "I got you. He ain't getting away with it. You know he ain't."

"He didn't have to shoot her, T!" The woman collapsed to the ground under the weight of her sobs. "He didn't have to . . ."

"I heard he was married," someone whispered behind me.

"Who is he?" The question came from someone in the crowd.

"Her man, I think." Another woman answered.

"Damn."

"I wonder why he'd do some foul shit like this?"

"Probably caught her fuckin' around."

"That's messed up. He couldn't just dump her ass? He had to kill her?"

Someone chuckled quietly, sending a chill up my spine.

"That's some old school shit right there. Just kill a motha fucka and call it a day."

"That shit's not funny, y'all," a woman standing next to me retorted. "I knew her," she started to cry. "She didn't deserve this. Nobody deserves . . ."

"Yeah," someone else answered. "He's a preacher, too, I think. That's what I heard."

Hope Filled Christian Center was the name of our church. Teddy started it years ago, back when I had more faith in him than I did in God. He started it in a strip mall and, over the years, it had grown into one of the largest churches in Dallas and Teddy's reputation as a profound and charismatic minister also grew. There were offers to take the ministry into syndication, televising it across the nation, reaching hundreds of thousands of people from California to New York City. That was his dream. And his dreams had been mine.

Love. Passion. Obsession. Intoxicating drugs capable of transforming all of us into mindless, sensational, ultrasexed junkies too caught up to recall a higher form of ourselves—until it's too late. Caught up in this surreal moment, I couldn't help but see the illustrations God set before me, leading up to today. Parading caricatures of foolish, impetuous women in front of me that I had the nerve to criticize and even judge. What had once seemed far removed and impossible for me to fathom and relate to had unraveled and become my life. I'd forgotten myself somewhere along the way. I'd gotten swept up in my role as First Lady of one of the largest congregations in the city and separated myself from what it meant to be simply a woman.

Teddy gave me the idea to put my psychology degree to good use and head up the women's ministry in the church.

"Every church needs a good counselor," he'd encouraged me. "Young women need direction and the good sense of someone wise who can guide them, baby, and I can't think of a better role for my wife than that."

They came to me for advice, direction, or just to talk, and I listened, but from my perch higher up than they were because of my position. I was better than they were. Always better and far removed from the problems and issues they'd let themselves become immersed in. My marriage was perfect. My life was perfect. And I existed solely inside the glory of my unblemished world. It wasn't hard to look down my nose at any of them, although I didn't do it knowingly.

"You know you have no business being involved with another woman's husband," I scolded more of them than I could recall. "It's a sin against God, and it's a sin against you as well.

"You deserve better," I'd say, feeling ashamed for them and including them in my prayers at night, because, of course, they were too pitiful and unworthy to pray for themselves.

I'd been blinded by my own self-righteousness. Too blind to see what my man was doing behind my back. Too proud to believe he could ever betray me with another woman. And all along, God had been showing me signs in the women I counseled, enthralled in the sin of infidelity, drowning in it. Different women, cheating for different reasons, all too weak to turn and walk away from their transgressions. Women who were beneath me, pathetic lost souls more in need of my pity and loathing than empathy.

And here I stood, with a loaded gun in my purse, prepared to kill a woman just like them, because my husband had been too weak to walk away from transgressions of his own. This woman had ruled my life and his. She'd affected me more deeply, wounded me more profoundly, and ultimately left me to drown in a sea of desolation because she had the prowess and the power to take from me what I believed could never be taken away. My husband. My dignity.

They folded Teddy into the back seat of the police car. He stared straight ahead, but I know he felt my eyes on him. As the squad car slowly pulled away from the curb, he turned to look at me one last time. Tears filled his eyes and mine, too.

Dear Jesus! We had absolutely destroyed ourselves.

wade in

the water . . .

renee turner

(Laughing) "How come you always look at me like that?"

"Like what?"

"Like you don't know why I keep coming back. Like I don't belong here."

"Is it that obvious?"

"Yes."

"I'm sorry. I don't mean for it to be."

"The church bulletin said counseling sessions were available and open to all women in need of guidance, Dr. Faye. So—come on now. Guide me."

"You don't seem like the type to need guidance, Renee. Confident, ambitious, focused . . . I honestly don't know why you come to see me."

She hesitated for a moment before responding.

"An overachieving, self-assured woman like myself can have

issues like everybody else, Doc. Sometimes, I just need to let off some steam. Sometimes, I just need someone to talk to."

"You're head of the singles ministry, Renee. I'd think you'd have plenty of people to talk to."

Renee rolled her eyes. "My job as head of the singles ministry is to keep lonely people occupied and blind to the fact that they are lonely in the first place." She smirked. "So, who's got time to talk? I mean, *really* talk."

"What about your friends?"

She laughed. "Friends?" Then held up one finger. "I have one friend."

"Raymone?"

"And he makes a joke out of ever fucking . . . I mean . . . sorry."

"No problem."

"I don't always feel like laughing, and not everything is funny. Raymone likes to play that sarcastic queen role of his to the hilt and sometimes it gets on my nerves. I don't think he has a serious bone in his body."

"Why don't you have other friends?"

She shrugged indifferently. "I prefer not to have too many friends bringing baggage and all their drama and chaos. One or two good friends is all any woman needs, but"—her eyes twinkled mischievously—"I think I'm in the process of making another one. Lucky you."

"I'm flattered."

"Don't be. My motivation is purely selfish."

"How so?"

"Ours will be a lopsided relationship at best, Doc. One-sided, and all about me. That sucks, huh?" She didn't wait for a response. “I talk. You listen, maybe nod your head every now and then. A match made in heaven.”

“So, what is it you want me to listen to and nod my head to today?”

Renee smiled. “About—how much I love attending this church, and to ask you where you got those kick-ass shoes, First Lady. Pardon my cussing.”

“That’s par for the course with you, Renee.”

Bohemian—retro—groovy. Say it loud!—bargain basement cheap. Designer label expensive chic. Renee's look summed up in a nutshell. She worked hard developing her artistic, expressive style, in an understated, but definitely enviable and effortless way. Renee Turner climbed out of her black Toyota Tacoma pickup truck, full moon afro first, wearing Jimmy Choo rust leather 'Taris' pumps, 7 for All Mankind Boot cut jeans, a long sleeve, creamy white, V-neck tee that she found on sale at Old Navy, slipping a Dolce & Gabbana camel suede buckle tote over her shoulder. A Tiffany's wide band, eighteen-carat gold ring with ten round brilliant diamonds circled her middle finger, while cheap mahogany carved hippopotamus earrings she picked up at a flea market on her last homage to South Africa, dangled precariously from her ear lobes.

She stared up at the palatial home in front of her. It had that brand-new, old-world, Spanish kind of vibe going, with the stucco exterior, wrought-iron accents, arched doorway of the entry. Given the style and the neighborhood, Renee guessed the price to be between five and six hundred thousand, easily, depending on the upgrades inside. All and all, though—it was cute.

"Trishelle?" Renee smiled at the woman answering the door.

"You must be Renee." The woman smiled back, extending her hand to shake. "It's so wonderful to finally meet you in person," she said, closing the door behind them. "I'm such a fan of your work."

"Thank you so much," Renee responded, making a concerted effort to appear and sound gracious and humble. But her shit was tight, and just about everybody in Dallas, maybe even the world, knew just how tight it was.

Tall woman, Renee thought as she followed Trishelle Stevens. She had to have been at least six feet tall, maybe more . . . . Auburn curls framed her white face and bounced just at the top of her narrow shoulders. Brilliant blue eyes sparkled beneath wisps of bangs. In another life, she was probably a model, Renee concluded. It would have been a damn shame if she wasn't. Trishelle was model beautiful and pliable, almost generic-looking like a mannequin that you could dress anyway you wanted, and she'd end up looking unrealistically good.

"As you can see," she said over her shoulder, leading Renee through the house, "we haven't done anything to the place, except move in," she laughed. "I've never had a house this big before, so I have no idea where to start with decorating the belly of this whale, and I certainly wouldn't want to fuck it up, which is why I've asked you to come."

The kitchen was a chef's and his whole team's dream with granite, slab countertops that spanned for miles, stainless steel, oversized appliances, a huge six-cook top stove, and two baker's oven. An endless array of dark-stained cherry custom cabinets, some with glass-paned fronts, provided space to store enough food and dishes to serve a small country. Canned lighting in the ceilings ran the length of the kitchen, which apparently ran the length of the whole south side of the house.

Trishelle poured two cups of coffee, and the women sat down at a small and oddly out-of-place kitchen table. Trishelle seemed to read Renee's designer mind.

"It's from our home in Seattle," she said sheepishly, lovingly running the flat of her hand across the top. "I'm going to hate to see it go. The truth is, this is a major upgrade for us," she chuckled. "You could just about fit our entire house in this kitchen. My husband called it cramped." She looked at Renee, and smiled. "I liked to think of it as cozy."

So this woman had no idea of what needed to be done to this house. That much was obvious. She was desperate for help and answers and direction. All Renee had to do was rise to the occasion. Interior design was as much psychology as it was art. It was not only a study of space and hardware, but a study of human character as well. If she was going to turn this whale's belly into a home for this woman, then she needed to start her design concept from the center of Trishelle Stevens, and forget all about these oversized walls and the never-ending garish kitchen surrounding them.

"What kind of work do you do?" Renee asked, studying Trishelle.

"I teach." Her eyes sparkled, then faded. "Well, I used to, back in Seattle."

Renee flashed a patient smile. "And what brings you to Dallas?"

"My husband does," she said with pride. "And his new position." That pride faded away quickly.

Mrs. Stevens was here because her husband dragged her here chasing after his career, giving little to no thought to hers. And she loved him just that much to let him. In the short exchange, Renee had Trishelle's life all figured out. That woman was impressed by her new house, but she definitely wasn't in love with it, and she was certainly more than a little intimidated by it.

Dr. Renee Turner to emergency. Stat!

They slowly strolled through the house, room by room, stopping long enough for Renee to record her findings in her microrecorder.

"Color?" she said to Trishelle. "What's your favorite color?" Renee smiled warmly and stared with genuine interest into Trishelle's eyes, as they lit up at the thought.

"I like orange, and plum, and midnight blue." She grimaced. "Sounds like they'd be a mess together. Don't they?"

Renee smiled assuredly. "You'd be surprised."

"My husband, Lewis, on the other hand, prefers neutral colors." Renee hadn't missed that subtle hint of disappointment in her tone. Almost as if Lewis had a tendency to let all the air out of his wife's colorful balloon on a regular basis.

Leave it to Dr. Turner to resuscitate her failing patient, she thought with pride. "Oh, I think we can find some middle ground." She gently touched Trishelle's arm. "Trust me."

Arched doorways and spiraling staircases in this house screamed for attention and dared to be showcased and brought to life. Yeah, when she was finished, this one would go on her Web site and would be a lovely addition to her portfolio for the day she finally landed a meeting with The Donald or Oprah to decorate one of their digs.

Renee was recording her notes in the study, lost in her observations when Trishelle disappeared from behind her. The sound of a man's voice threatened to trample on her creative train of thought.

"Hello," his voice came from behind her.

"Hi, honey," Trishelle greeted him in a whisper, so as not to disturb Renee's artistic vibe.

She finished with her notes, then turned to greet the man who'd be paying for her services. "Hello." She reached out to shake his hand, fighting back surprise. "I'm Renee."

He smiled and gently took her hand in his. "Lewis. Lewis Stevens."

Another one bites the dust. The lyrics rewound over and over again in her head. The brother was nothing short of an African King reincarnated.

"Your home is lovely." Renee hoped she sounded convincing, but she'd seen better.

He smirked. "My home is empty, and I'm hoping you can help make it feel more like we live here instead of feeling like we're taking up space in a warehouse." He looked at the wife he held in his arms, pressed up against the side of him, and gave a noticeable squeeze. "I hear you're one of the best designers in the city."

Something about the look in his eyes almost hinted at sarcasm and cynicism, and Renee knew already that she wasn't digging this caramel-skinned god.

"Yes," she smiled, meeting his gaze with her own. "I've heard that, too."

Touché. He looked as if he thought it, but didn't say it.

"She has some wonderful ideas for the place, sweetheart," Trishelle chimed in. "I think you'll like them once you see what they are."

"I'm sure," he smiled. "Well, I'll leave you two ladies to finish up, and," he gave his wife a quick peck on the lips, while loosening his tie, "I'll be upstairs in the study."

For a second, she felt a twinge of jealousy kick her in the ribs, and a sense of black-on-black betrayal warmed her from the tips of her toes to the top of her head. But common sense rang in, reminding her that he couldn't help who he loved, and when he was looking for a woman, Renee was probably traipsing around Europe with all her belongings in her backpack or some shit like that, which is why she missed him. Besides, she'd never set foot in Seattle, so there was no way their paths would've crossed anyway.

An hour and a half after she'd arrived, Trishelle escorted Renee to the door.

"I have some thoughts," Renee replied, confidently, "and I should have a proposal ready for you in a few weeks."

Trishelle sighed, relieved. "Thank you so much, Renee. I'm so glad to have met you."

"The pleasure was all mine," she said, professionally. "We'll get this place together for you in no time," she winked, and turned to leave.

"Good-bye." Trishelle said one last time. "Oh, and Renee?"

Renee turned to her.

"Remember." Trishelle's expression turned downright menacing. "Money is no object."

tess martin

"*I think he called* himself being in love with this one," Tess Martin said indifferently, sitting at the end of the couch in the office, one leg crossed over the other, her arms folded in front of her.

"You couldn't possibly know that for sure, Tess."

"I've been married to him for twenty-three years, Faye. Women have come and gone, especially when he was appointed to the Deacon's board," she winced. "Everybody else saw that appointment as a blessing, but to me, it was a role that gave my husband carte blanche to do what he did best."

"Tess . . ."

She smiled. "How could I not know?"

The two of them sat silently for several minutes, while Tess quietly reflected on and revisited the past two decades of her life. Recalling the younger woman she once was, filled with ideals and the joy of the life she pictured ahead of her, sadly coming to the realization that she was no longer that idealistic joyful woman. She'd become someone else along the way. Someone she didn't know or even like.

"Men don't know how to leave," she blurted out. "No matter how unhappy they are, or how badly they'd rather be with someone else, they won't leave unless you tell them to. Why do you think that is?"

Faye shrugged. "It's in their nature not to. And I also believe that men want permission to leave so that they don't have to blame themselves or be accused of abandonment."

"I wish he would leave."

"I don't think you do, Tess. I think you're angry and hurt . . ."

Tess shook her head. "No. No, not anymore. I'm tired, Faye. I'm too worn out to care enough to be hurt and angry. I've been hurt and angry for the last twenty years, and—" She shrugged. "I'm done. Emotionally, physically—"

"He did end the affair, though, and at least that's something, Tess. At least you and Jesse have an opportunity to mend and heal and start over from scratch to make your marriage work. If you'll just trust in the Lord and in the love the two of you—"

"Have for each other?" Tess concluded.

"Exactly."

"What if I don't want it to work? What if I'm finally to the point where I want to move on and start over without him, Faye?"

"If that's what you'd really wanted, Tess, you'd have moved on by now."

Tears filled her eyes. "If I knew how—if I had the courage—God knows I would've left him years ago."

Tess stood on the beach, gazing at the ocean in front of her, drinking buckets of the salty air, smiling at the sunrise winking at her from the horizon. If she didn't know better, she'd swear she was crazy. But for the first time in her life, Tess felt more than sane, and for the first time in her life, finally in touch with the true nature of her self. Her surprisingly wonderful self.

She and her husband Jesse had visited St. Simon's Island years ago to celebrate their twelfth wedding anniversary. Tess had always dreamed of coming back. He never wanted to. She used to let things like that hurt her feelings. Now she knew they weren't even worth her time. Jesse stopped being in love with her a long time ago. And Tess had come to her senses, finally, and slipped quietly out of love with him, too.

Lord, forgive me for lying, she thought, smiling at the view. Somehow she knew, she didn't even need to ask. Of course, she was forgiven. A woman's got to do what a woman's got to do. If she'd told Jesse she needed to get away, that she wanted to come back here, he'd have come up with any number of excuses to keep her from going, and she'd fallen for them, too. *Why would he stop her?* she'd wondered before deciding to leave. It wasn't that he liked her company so much, or loved coming home to his good wife and better meal. The answer came to her over time, and it didn't make much more sense than either one of them did. He was comfortable knowing she was in a certain place at a certain time every day. He was comfortable in her predictability. Tess never strayed too far away from the routine of her life or of their marriage, and everyone she knew had expectations of her that didn't include hopping on a plane at the spur of the moment and flying off to some island for no other reason than to catch up with her peace of mind.

The images of the waves, gently washing ashore seduced her. The coolness of the water lapping over her bare feet, tugged at her. Seagulls called to her from the crystal blue sky, serenading her, trying desperately to say her name. She felt sexy here. Sensual. Interesting. Deserving. All the things she never felt at home, in Dallas, in her own house, in her own skin. And if it were up to her, she'd never leave.

She'd lied and told Jesse that a small group of people from her church were going to a retreat to the St. Simon's for spiritual cleansing. She chuckled just thinking about it. Tess had played that man like a guitar and he never suspected a thing. She should've been an actress, Tess surmised, proud in her achievement.

"A retreat would do us good, Jesse," she reasoned, pleading to him with her expression, stressing the importance of his presence at the nonexistent forum. Of course, there was a small chance he'd surprise her and say yes. But it was very small, extremely small, microscopically small. "When's the last time we took a trip together? When's the last time we had a vacation without the boys?"

"Tess," he sighed, pretending to sound disappointed. "You know I can't just drop everything and take off like that."

"It's a weekend, Jesse! One weekend," she protested. Tess sat down next to him on the sofa and placed a tender hand on his thigh. "There's going to be counseling." *Going.* "Prayer services." *Going.* "And even a sunrise meditation service right there on the beach." *Gone.*

The look in his eyes told her everything his mouth couldn't. "Well, which weekend is it again?" He tried his best to sound hopeful.

She smacked him in the face with a wide, toothy grin. "Next month. The fourteenth through the sixteenth. All weekend, honey. Oh, and did I tell you Deaconess Wilson has invited the Anointed Voices Choir of Atlanta to come sing for us at Friday night's reception?" It was the final blow, unmerciful and downright hateful, that sent him tumbling over the edge.

"Oh, that weekend." Disappointment shadowed his expression. "That's the weekend before the inspection, baby. Remember? The VP of Manufacturing is flying in to go over some quality and performance issues at the plant. I'll be tied up all weekend buried under mountains of paperwork, juggling numbers—I'm sorry, Tess. But, why don't you go ahead and go without me?"

Tears. She needed to fake the funk real good for a moment. Tess's eyes needed to water, and damn if they didn't. Right on cue. "You sure?"

He nodded, and patted her hand. "Yeah, sweetheart. You go right ahead, and try and have fun."

The sunlight warmed her face, and Tess inhaled, closed her eyes, and smiled. She said a silent prayer that time would be patient today, and not hurry through to tomorrow. Tess was tired of giving all the damn time. For twenty-three years, she'd given all of her self to her children, marriage, insecurity, and blame. She'd devoted every waking moment of her days to raising her twin boys, who were now men, and out on their own. Now it was her turn. She'd lay prone on her back at Jesse's feet, dedicating herself to being the wife he'd dreamed of, only to have him step over her to get to women younger, sweeter, and more enticing than hers. She'd forgiven him his trespasses time and time again, through tears, threats, and anguish every time one of those little trespasses happened to show up in his funky drawers, or as phone numbers stuffed in his wallet.

Thankfully, for the first time in more than twenty years, he wasn't the center of her adventure. She was.

elise clayton

"*This one is special*, Dr. Watkins. Really special." Elise's smile lit up the room.

"From the look on your face, I'd say he must be."

"I'm learning so much from being with him," she continued.

"Like?"

Elise turned inward for a moment before finally answering. "Like how God's blessings don't always look the way we think they should. And how, if you just open your eyes, and your heart and soul to receive them, He'll answer your prayers every time."

"That's the kind of valuable lesson most people miss, Elise. You should be pleased that you've been fortunate enough to grasp it."

She smiled. "He's everything I could've asked for in a man, only, when he came along, I'd given up, Dr. Watkins. I'd had my share of losers and broken hearts and I was through. I even prayed," she laughed, "and told Him, God—don't worry about me. I'm cool by myself, and if I can't do no better than I have with a relationship, then I don't need one."

"That's how it usually works. As soon as you find yourself at the end of your rope, He comes through to catch you right before you fall."

"And he did, too. Jay is—he's handsome, smart, thoughtful."

"Well, good, Elise. You deserve someone nice."

All of a sudden, her joyful expression faded, and her expression turned grave. "I do. Don't I?"

"Of course."

"So," Elise bit down on her bottom lip. "How come I'm so afraid of losing him? How come I feel like it can't possibly last?"

"Elise?"

"I know, Dr. Watkins," she said, emphatically. "I know I shouldn't think like that."

"No, honey. You shouldn't."

"But he's such a good man." She fought back tears. "We have such a good thing together. It's not perfect, but . . ." Elise shrugged. "Good things never last long for me."

"Why would you think that?"

"Because it's true. That's been the pattern of my life for as long as I can remember, and I'm just afraid that—. Every night I pray, and I beg God to make this work for me. To not take this man away from me. And every morning I wake up afraid that He hasn't heard me."

"He hears you, Elise. And He knows what's best for you. If by chance this relationship doesn't work out, then, it's probably for the best and God knows that."

"If this relationship doesn't work out—I don't know what I'll do, Dr. Watkins."

"You'll be strong and get past it."

Elise shook her head. "That's just it," she said, sadly. "I'm tired of being strong and of having to get past it. This time, I just want things to go my way. Or else—"

"Or else—what?"

"I don't think I'm strong enough to get through it this time, Dr. Watkins. I just don't think I have it in me."

Elise was a full woman. Ample. The kind that had more than enough of everything, ass, titties, love. And she was generous with it, too. All of it. Jay gobbled her up by the handfuls, until he couldn't take another bite. But he always came back for more. And with Elise, there was always plenty.

"Show a brotha some love, baby," was all he ever had to say. Jay didn't have to beg or bargain the way he did with his wife. He just had to be there. He just had to call or stop by, take her out to eat or to a movie, and hold her hand. Elise was his magic and that beautiful thing in his life that always made him feel so damn good. Was it any wonder he couldn't stop thinking about her? Or that he'd spend as much of his time as he could spare with her?

Wherever Elise was, that's where he wanted to be, surrounded with her sweet self, savory and wet, welcoming, and waiting for nobody else but him.

She stroked him with slow, rolling thrusts pushed deep into his lap. Jay's legs were stretched out underneath her, the rest of him, sunk low into Elise's sofa. He leaned his head back and gazed into her pretty brown face, behind glazed-over eyes, lost and caught up in a time warp. Elise's long hair was piled high on top of her head, and ringlets cascaded like a waterfall framing her face. Her eyes were slits, cutting deep into his, then closed completely, when she threw her head back, and whispered.

"That's how I like it, baby! That's how I . . ."

The afternoon sun hung low in the window behind her. A warm breeze parted the curtains and washed through the room. Sweat glistened on her soft skin, making her shimmer like something precious. Jay dissolved underneath her. His mind, sense of reason, and presence liquified, and he lost all track of who he was, where he was, and how he'd gotten there. Elise's juices pooled between his thighs, rolling down his balls. Sex—the smell, the sound—permeated the room, and Jay inhaled as much of it as he could, until he was high as a kite.

She opened her eyes, and looked down into his again, and then asked a ridiculous question. "Do you like it, Jay? Does it feel good, baby?"

He grabbed a handful of her hair, opened his mouth wide, and pulled her lips to meet his, and Jay drank, and swallowed, trying to engulf this woman's soul from her mouth the way she pulled his from his dick.

If some fool decided to come through Millington, Texas, that afternoon and blow it the fuck up, he wouldn't be mad. Jay didn't want it to end. He wanted to die, right here, right now, just like this, with this big, pretty, luscious woman dripping all over him, because he knew that this was indeed—heaven.

Hours later, Jay sat on the side of the bed, lacing up his work boots. He'd slept too long again, but it was all good. He'd just say he'd gotten stuck behind some accident on the highway. Jay had been a truck driver for the past fifteen years, and until recently, always hated every minute of it. But in the last six months, it was a job he'd come to appreciate.

Elise walked in wearing a midnight blue, satin robe, tied loosely around her small waist. Big up top, big on the bottom, all held together by a waist that seemed too small to accommodate it all. He wondered sometimes, why she didn't just snap into two lovely pieces. She sat down next to him and handed him a glass of iced tea.

"You sure you don't want me to fix you something to eat?" she asked sweetly.

Just the offer made him feel cared for. Jay gulped down the whole glass before coming up for air with his answer. "Naw, baby. I ain't got time." He handed the empty glass back to her and then kissed her on the mouth. "But thanks for asking."

She followed him to the door, and Jay turned to her one last time. Elise looked up at him and smiled. He dreamed that smile sometimes.

"As usual"—she nuzzled close to him—"I had a wonderful time. But time always flies when you're here, Jay. And you know me." Her eyes sparkled. "I'm greedy, and you're never here long enough."

Jay draped his long arms over her shoulders, and kissed her forehead. "I'm greedy, too, Lovely. If I could stay, you know I would."

"When are you coming back?"

He shrugged. "Soon. You best believe that. I can't stay away from you too long, girl," he teased. "You know that."

He started to leave.

"You'd better call me when you get there. Let me know you made it."

Jay blew a naked kiss into the air and winked.

"Jay?" Elise called out. "I love you."

He mouthed the words back, then disappeared down the stairs, headed for home.

Jay was less than two hours away from where he lived. Other drivers bragged all the time about how many different women they had in different cities, but he'd never been one for all that. Jay had been a married man for damn near fifteen years, with kids, a house in the suburbs, and shit like that was something the OGs did. Jay just took care of home, and that was it, because for a while, home was good. He and Sherry were good together, and she was all the woman he needed, and loved. And then he met Elise. She changed something inside him, bringing him back to life, when he had never even realized he was dead. Elise had more than enough passion for both of them. She was exciting. New. Invigorating and intoxicating. Yeah, his life with Sherry had been cool, but with Elise, it was on fire, and hot enough to keep him coming back for more.

Jay rolled down the four-lane highway heading east. It wasn't like he didn't still love his wife, because he did. The idea of leaving her, his kids, never set well with him. He had his place in their lives, and they had theirs in his, and the two not being together just felt like an unfinished song to Jay, and maybe to Sherry, too. He felt them pulling him home whenever he was on the road, and he felt himself running as fast as he could back to them. So, home was where he belonged. But another part of him belonged back there in Millington with Elise's fine ass, too.

He'd stopped at Fred's near the motel one night when he was passing through Millington on his way to El Paso. Fred's was a nightclub that never seemed to close and had some of the best hot wings Jay had ever tasted. Jay was sitting at the bar, drinking a beer when he saw her come in. It was around seven in the evening, and he halfway expected her to slide up to the bar and start working on an early drunk like most people who came into Fred's, but Elise walked right past him, and ordered dinner for herself just like he did.

She stood near the counter, and surveyed the room, almost as if she'd never been there before. Pretty woman. He thought it, but never said it. She was bigger than Sherry, but in all the right places, with clear skin, bright eyes, and full lips tinted with some kind of gloss or color women like to wear. She was hard not to stare at. She must've felt him looking, because she looked back at him, smiled briefly, mouthed the word hello, then shyly turned away. She looked like she might've worked in an office or something, wearing tailored slacks that cuffed at the bottom, high-heeled shoes, and a blouse that buttoned up the front and looked like she'd laid down for that pattern to be cut specifically for her. A few buttons at the top had come loose, revealing a pretty crease folded between breasts a man couldn't take his eyes off of.

"Hot wings up!" The cook tapped on the silver bell on the counter.

Jay smiled at Elise when he walked passed her on his way to get his order. "How you doing?"

"Fine. Thanks."

Smells good, too, he thought, passing her.

"Hot wings up!" the cook shouted again.

Jay picked up his order, turned and started to walk away before realizing she was standing right behind him. He plowed into her, spilling his order all down the front of her lovely blouse.

"Oh shit!" someone shouted.

Elise jumped back in horror, and frantically swatted the hot food from her chest.

"Damn! I'm sorry," he shouted, hoping she wasn't burned. "I didn't see you!"

"No, it's all right." Elise's expression told him otherwise. Jay looked helpless at this woman, who finally smiled and seemed to genuinely accept his apology. "Really. It's okay."

He paid for her order, asked for another of his own, and offered to buy her a drink.

The club was full by the time they'd finished eating. Elise and Jay spent the evening talking like they were old friends. He told her how he'd always wanted to be an architect, but the trucking business found him first, right after the birth of his first kid. Elise was her name. She'd never been married, but had been close, and she was beginning to think she was getting too old to ever have kids.

"You're a beautiful woman," he reassured her, because it was the truth. "If some man hasn't swooped down on you yet, he will, and if one never does, it's because you wouldn't let him."

She blushed.

She was a real estate agent. A tough business sometimes, and other times, it was the dream job. Elise hated Millington, but she'd grown up there. She had been giving a lot of thought lately to moving east, Washington, D.C., or Florida, she couldn't decide. And though she didn't mind being single, sometimes . . . just sometimes . . .

"It would be nice to know I had someone in my life. Someone who was crazy about me, all the time," she giggled. "Sex isn't the problem. I could get sex if that's all I wanted, but that's not all I want. Well." Elise shrugged, and rolled her eyes. "Sometimes it is." She blushed again.

He was hard the whole time they sat at that table talking, and Jay let his mind wander this time before shutting it down. He closed the door on the image of Sherry's face every time it tried forming in his mind, reminding him that she was waiting on him back at the house. Maybe it was the beer, but he didn't want to leave this woman to the fate of the world. He didn't want to give some man the chance to see this diamond sitting before him and snatch it up before Jay had had his chance to admire it up close.

He walked her to her car. She smelled like smoke and hot wings, but looked even softer under the glow of the street lamp.

She glanced at her watch. "I hadn't planned on staying out this late," she laughed. "But I had a nice time, Jay. And it was good meeting you." Elise held out her hand to shake.

Jay took it in his, and slowly brought it to his lips, and kissed it.

She'd put a spell on him without even trying, and he didn't want her to take it back. Jay took a step closer, and saw apprehension in her eyes. No. *No, baby,* he wanted to reassure her. *I'm not going to hurt you. I would never do that. Just trust me.*

He leaned in close and softly kissed her cheek. "I would love to see you at least one more time," he chuckled. He expected that he knew the answer already. He expected she'd shake her head no, and remind him that he was a married man, and remind herself that she wanted her own man, not to share someone else's.

Elise reached into her purse and pulled out her card. "Call me the next time you're in town. Maybe we can do hot wings again." She climbed into her car and drove away.

The next time he was in town, Jay did call. They met at Fred's, ate hot wings, drank beers, and talked for hours. He led her to his room, lost himself in the world between her thighs, and made a promise to herself and him, that this was more than just a night. He'd be back. He'd keep coming back as long as she'd let him.

Love at first sight? Jay turned on the radio and smiled. "Hell yeah!" he said out loud. That's pretty much what it was or something pretty damn close.

Teddy's voice bellowed like thunder every Sunday morning when he preached. He held that congregation in the palm of his hand, squeezing them hard in all the right ways, and gently releasing and massaging them, applying just the right amount of encouragement and tenderness. They loved him. But sitting on that massive stage behind him, I found myself staring out into that audience, looking—for her. She was in that church. I felt her, could even almost smell her. And yet, I had no idea what she looked like.

He preached on forgiveness this particular Sunday. My big, brown bear, looking like an archangel himself, pacing from one end of the stage to the other, looking into people's eyes, almost as if he could see their souls.

"To forgive," he said carefully, making sure they heard his message loud and clear, "is divine."

Amens filtered into the air.

"Y'all ain't hearing me," he said adamantly. "I said—that to forgive . . . is divine." Teddy closed his eyes tight, making sure he passed along the Lord's message to everyone in that room, so that each and every one of them not only heard it, but felt it.

"Forgiveness is based not on our own understanding."

"Preach, preacha!" someone shouted.

"I said, forgiveness is based not on our own understanding, but it is

based on our pure faith in the Divine Savior. See—it ain't about you, whoever you are who hurt me. It's about me, and my faith in the Lord!"

The crowd went wild. I shivered in my chair, and I continued to search the room, among the women standing and applauding, for the woman my husband was sleeping with.

Lynette. That was all I knew about her. He swore he'd stopped seeing her, but I knew better. My gut told me otherwise. Teddy couldn't stop seeing that woman, because she'd bore into him too deeply.

"I love you, too, sweetheart," he whispered into the phone late one night after he thought I was asleep. "You know I can't. I wish I could but—. Don't talk like that. You mean the world to me, baby. More than—more than I ever thought any woman could."

"Teddy," I said his name like I would call out to a stranger.

"Faye!" he hurried to hang up the phone. "Faye, I—"

"You son of a bitch!"

"Faye!"

"Son of a bitch!"

I hit him in the face. I cried all night, and the next night and too many more nights after that. And Teddy made promises he couldn't possibly keep, no matter how badly I wanted him to.

I found her number on his cell phone bills he kept in the church administration office. I knew it belonged to her, because of when he called it, late at night, when he was supposed to be in meetings or out of town, or when I was out of town. I dialed that number, and got her voicemail message:

"Hi, you've reached Lynette . . . you know the deal, so leave a message and I'll call you back. Promise."

A light-skinned sistah in the front row caught my eye. Young, pretty, with a brilliant smile and long hair flowing down past her shoulders. She gazed adoringly at my husband. Another woman, the one behind her, nodded her head on cue, smiled warmly at him, rose to her feet, tempting him with her shapely ebony figure. Which one? In a congregation of thousands, it could've been anybody.

"How's this marriage ever going to work if you don't believe me, Faylene?" he'd asked. "How can I be the same man, if you don't trust me?"

"I'm doing the best I can," I argued. But I knew that I wasn't. From the look I sometimes saw in his eyes, he knew it, too.

Insecurity crept over me, growing like a fungus, consuming me. I used to be so self-assured, secure, and certain until I found out about her. Every waking moment became filled with thoughts of this Lynette. Common sense would tell me to leave him, divorce him, and walk away with whatever pride I had left. But thoughts of revenge and anger overrode common sense. I knew that my leaving him would be the easy way out for Teddy, despite what effort he'd put into begging for me to forgive him. But he'd hurt me too much, and I wanted him to suffer the way I'd suffered. And then, there was also the chance that he'd shine for me the way he always had, and he'd wade through my suspicions and feelings of betrayal, proving to me that Lynette had been a terrible mistake all along.

Why the hell should he have to apologize for a view like this? Lewis stood at the large, wall-sized window of his office on the twenty-seventh floor, staring out at the Dallas skyline. From Junior Stockbroker to this, Senior VP of Finance of one of the largest investment firms in the country, and it only took him fifteen years to do it. He chuckled at the thought. It seemed like the whole world was on his side when they found out about his promotion. Well, almost the whole world. Trishelle was happy with it until she found out they'd have to move to Dallas. That's when her enthusiasm headed farther south than they did.

"Mr. Stevens," his secretary buzzed his intercom.

"Yes, Carolyn," he answered over his shoulder.

"Your wife is on line one."

In that instant, he felt himself falling from the twenty-seventh floor, hard and fast back to reality.

"Hello?" He sat down in the massive ebony, leather chair behind his desk.

"Don't forget we have the parent-teacher conference at six," Trish blurted out without bothering to return his hello.

"I remember," he said halfheartedly.

"And did you remember to let those people know that

we've postponed the dinner party—indefinitely?" Those people meaning the CEO and COO of his company.

Lewis groaned. "No. But I'll leave messages with their secretaries this afternoon."

"Do it as soon as I hang up, before you forget, Lewis," she said, agitated. "I don't know what you were thinking volunteering me for some impromptu dinner party when we haven't even gotten the house in order yet."

We've been living in it for three months, he thought, getting more irritated by the moment. *I fully expected you to have it finished by now. You don't have shit else to do!*

Lewis kept his thoughts to himself, clenching his jaws tightly together to keep from breathing out fire to light her constantly short fuse.

"What?" she continued. "Did you expect them to eat off paper plates and sit on the floor?"

"I didn't think about it, Trish," he sighed. "How many times do I have to apologize for that?" *For every damn thing.*

"Until I'm convinced you mean it."

"Look, I've got to go," he snapped back.

"Figures. You always have to go just when the conversation starts getting good." Trishelle didn't bother trying to hide the sarcasm. "And we have to meet with the designer in the morning at ten."

"Can't you go without me?"

"I could . . . but I'm not going to." Just then, he heard the doorbell ring in the background. "I've got to go. I'm interviewing housekeepers to help out around this place."

"Yeah. Knock yourself out," he said, dishing out a little sarcasm of his own. "And I'll see you at the school this evening."

"Don't be late."

He hung up without responding.

The move, the promotion, had taken their toll on both of them. Trishelle never wanted to leave Seattle. Being Canadian, it was close to home and family for her, and she'd put down some pretty deep roots there. Lewis had been a military brat, so there was no such thing as roots for him. When they offered him the position, he took it. When they told him he'd have to move to the Southern Regional office in Dallas, Texas, he never gave it a second thought, and he packed up his shit and his family the way his dad had packed up all of them, his whole childhood.

"Did it ever occur to you that I have a career to think about, too, Lewis?" she argued, when he told her they were relocating.

Trish's job—teaching history at a local community college. No. It never crossed his mind that she couldn't land something just like it in Any-Damn-Where USA at the drop of a hat.

"Don't you think you owed it to me to ask, before blindly accepting an offer to move halfway across the goddamned country?"

"What was there to discuss?" He said it before he realized it. In an instant, his life transformed into a bittersweet kind of fruit. One minute, he was the golden boy of ASAP Investments, courted and celebrated by his peers, wined and dined and initiated into the executive culture of midweek golf games at exclusive country clubs, to Friday night martinis and poker in private Las Vegas suites where anything and everything was possible and forgiven. And when it was over, Lewis wound up sleeping on the edge of the bed, or on the couch somewhere, trying to put aside his own anger and resentment, knowing that his wife refused to see that he wasn't just being selfish. He was being a visionary, and she was really getting on his nerves.

For two people sitting right next to each other, they might as well have been on separate continents. The air between them was thick with dissention and Renee had to triple up on her charm and powers of persuasion to seal this deal.

"The beamed ceilings, hardwood floors, and iron accents just said old world to me," Renee explained to the Stevenses sitting in her studio. Body language between the couple spoke volumes, as they sat leaning in opposite directions of each other. "Old world . . . Tuscany palette is what I've come up with." She pointed to color charts and fabric swatches on the table in front of them. "The rooms in your house are massive and a style like this, weathered and textured, would add warmth, bring the rooms in just a bit, and create a more inviting environment."

Trishelle's face lit up. Lewis just sat there.

"Can we forego the whole floral thing?" he asked, looking indifferently at her samples.

Trishelle tried not to appear annoyed, and Renee, the consummate professional, pretended not to notice.

"Absolutely. We can tone it down using a subtle damask or tweed patterns."

Trishelle interjected quickly. "As long as it's not too masculine. I happen to like the flowers." She smiled.

Okay, so not only did they expect her to make their home a showcase, but they wanted her to balance on her tiptoes on a high wire between them, too?

Money is no object, Trishelle had told her at the consultation. Renee decided to use that as her motivation, and she'd balance the hell out of that wire if she had to.

"Well, we could strategically place floral accents throughout the room for emphasis. Not too much," she looked at Lewis, who shrugged indifferently. "But enough," she smiled at Trishelle.

An hour later, they were gone. Renee dimmed the lights in the house, lit some sage-scented candles all around the room, played her sound of running water CD, sat in her favorite chair, and meditated for about fifteen minutes. The Stevenses had bad vibes crawling all over them, and the last thing she needed was to catch that shit and come down with that pissy vibe in her world.

"What the hell is wrong with you?"

Damn! When did he come in? She opened her eyes and stared up at Raymone, standing across the room in the doorway, with his hand propped on his hip, wearing brown leather clogs, designer jeans, and his favorite baby blue pashmina, wrapped around him like a cocoon.

"You can't knock?" she asked dryly.

"Why I got to knock? I thought we was boos and shit." He swished his flamboyant ass over to the sofa, kicked off his clogs and slung both feet up on the sofa. "What's wrong?"

"What makes you think something's wrong?" she asked, not bothering to hide her irritation.

"Candles lit up, water music playing and you sitting over in the corner praying to Buddha instead of Jesus. You going to hell. I don't know why you don't listen to me."

"Ever heard of meditation, fool?" she retorted. "And instead of worrying about my afterlife, you need to worry about your own. I thought Jesus didn't dig homosexuals."

"Girl, please, that was back in the nineties." He smirked and rolled his eyes. "Now, He almost cool with it." Raymone tossed a throw pillow at her hitting her in the head. "So why you meditating, Princess?"

"Trying to get rid of that badass vibe those toxic people left in my house. Remind me never to get married."

"Marriage, family is the foundation of the world, baby. So not only am I going to encourage your ass to get married, but I'm going to make sure you have a house full of bad kids, too, to complete the picture so you'll know what it's like to put self last for a change."

Renee laughed. "Look who's talking. When was the last time you put yourself last for anybody, Raymone?"

"Two nights ago. I met this fine brotha—"

"You use something?" she quickly interjected before he had a chance to go farther.

He sighed. "Of course. Now can I finish?"

She shrugged.

"I let him cum first, and didn't worry about getting mine until much, much later in the evening. Just before he dozed off as a matter of fact."

"I'm moved." she said dryly.

"Yes, and so was he."

Renee playfully slapped Raymone on his thigh. "Why are you so ghetto?"

"I'm just me, baby. I can't help it if you see me as ghetto. I'm just Raymone.

"You need counseling."

He looked at her like she'd lost her mind. "Just because you're crazy doesn't mean I have to be. So, keep your little shrinky dink to yourself, girlfriend."

"You'd love her, Ray. Patient woman, will sit and listen to anything no matter how crazy it is. Believe me. I've hit her prissy, pious ass up with some shit and the most she ever does is shake her head. But she's cool people even if she is married to a preacher. She might even be able to help you work through some of your relationship issues, bro man. Help you out with some of those self-esteem issues you have," she teased.

"That's all well and good, but, first off, I ain't in no relationship, nor am I trying to get into a relationship. And second of all, I have absolutely no issues with self-esteem or their lack of, so she couldn't do shit for me."

"That's because you're in denial, ho."

"Take a ho to know a ho! Oop!" He put his hand dramatically to his lips. "I'm sorry. You can't be a ho. You ain't had none since God made dirt, so I guess you right." He raised his hand in the air. "I'll be the ho. Tired. Fulfilled. And pass me a cigarette because I just got *another* nut—ho! And I didn't even have to use my own hands."

"Fuck you, Ray!"

"I'm gay, girl. You got to get yours from somebody else."

Of course, Jesse wasn't home when she pulled into the driveway. Tess had chicken slow cooking in the Crock-Pot for dinner. She put down her purse and headed into the kitchen to finish preparing dinner. A few minutes later, a knock came at the door. It was her sister, Juanita.

Contessa was a dumb name. Tess's parents probably thought they were being cute when they gave it to her, but she always cringed when someone called her by it. Thank goodness the years eventually shortened it to Tess, and Contessa was reserved for the name space on her birth certificate and for her older sister, Juanita, whenever she wanted Tess's attention. The age difference between them was as wide as a river—six years—and after their parents passed, Juanita decided it was her place to step in and become the matriarch of the family, despite the fact that it was only she and Tess left, and despite the fact that Tess was married with kids of her own when they died. The truth was, Juanita just wanted to be the boss of Tess.

Juanita followed Tess into the kitchen, went to the refrigerator, and poured herself a glass of lemonade, then sat down at the table. Tess pulled out a bag of potatoes and started peeling.

Small talk bounced back and forth between them for a few minutes, before Juanita finally got down to business and used the C word.

"Contessa," she said soberly. "Is there something going on with you that you want to talk about?"

"Why, yes," Tess started to say. She put down her potato and casually waved her knife in the air at her sister. "If you call me Contessa one more time, I'm going to slice and dice you up like a carrot." Tess smiled and went back to preparing her vegetables.

"I'm serious." Juanita sounded serious, too. Like that should've made a difference, but it didn't. "Jesse told me about the retreat you went on last weekend. And needless to say, he was surprised, that I didn't know about it."

Tess shrugged. "Jesse knows I don't tell you everything."

"There was no retreat to St. Simon's with the church, Contessa," Juanita said belligerently. "I spoke to Debra Hawkins and she told me that the church had already been on its retreat to Philadephia back in November."

"What's even more surprising," Tess interjected, "was that my husband, the good Deacon, didn't know there wasn't one." She sliced a potato and ate a piece. "Don't that just make you wanna scratch your head?"

"Tess." Juanita looked and sounded sincerely concerned about her sister. Tess had been acting so strangely lately. She hadn't been herself, predictable. The last two years, she'd watched her sister wallow in depression over that whole empty nest thing, and wander around like a lost soul in the desert of life, not knowing what to do with herself now that she didn't have the kids to look after anymore. All of a sudden now, the woman was jumping up at the drop of a hat and leaving Dallas to fly off to God knows where on a whim, lying to her husband about where she'd been and why. "Are you thinking about hurting yourself?" Juanita asked cautiously.

Tess stopped cutting and stared back at her sister. "Hurting myself?"

Melodrama shot from Juanita's eyes like darts at Tess. "Why'd you go by yourself, Tess? Why'd you lie to Jesse, and why didn't you tell me you were leaving?"

"I needed a vacation, Juanita," Tess said flippantly. "You know, one of those things people do sometimes to get away from it all."

Juanita looked appalled. "Don't make light of the situation, Contessa. I'm dead serious. If all you needed was a vacation, then why didn't you tell Jesse the truth instead of lying about going with the church?"

"Because he'd have talked me out of it."

"Maybe he'd have come with you."

"I didn't want him to come with me," Tess shot back, seeing Juanita recoil in confusion. "I needed to get away for a while. That's all it was."

"To do what?"

Tess's thoughts drifted back to her trip, and the things she did on it to find the answer to that question. An appreciative smile spread on her lips, and for a moment, she felt herself alone, standing on that beach at dawn, letting the sea air wash over her.

"To get up at dawn, just to watch the sun rise," she said dreamily. "Then stop in some little dive, eat fried fish, grits, and mangos for breakfast, and wash it down with a cool glass of fresh squeezed orange juice, and a cup of some of the best tasting coffee I've ever had."

Juanita stared at her sister in disbelief, as Tess seemed to almost physically leave the room and take herself back to that little island off the coast of Georgia.

"When I was full . . ." Tess moaned and rubbed her stomach. She licked her lips. "I went back to my room, stripped off all my clothes, and lay naked across the bed with the windows wide open, and let the breeze from the ocean caress me."

Juanita blinked in astonishment. She started to say something, but Tess continued.

"I laid there most of the day like that. Lazy and lavish, dozing in and out of sweet sleep, until finally, I had to get up to pee. I showered, and put on a new little sundress I bought just for the trip, slipped into my shoes, and followed the sound of old school soul music wafting in from down the road. I was drawn to the sound of it, opened the rickety door to a sea of brown bodies inside, glistening and swaying back and forth like the waves of the ocean, all dancing like they were one person, and I let my body slip in between them, and I danced, too."

Tess didn't dare open her eyes, for fear that she'd have to leave paradise again, and come back home to a nosey sister, unappreciative and inattentive husband, and potatoes that needed to be peeled.

"I got drunk on gin and juice, laughed with strangers, and let men I didn't know hold me close to them in slow dances. 'You sho' are a beautiful woman,' they told me over and over again. 'Where yo' man? He let you come out by yo'self?' "

Tess sighed, ignoring the urge to feel sorry for herself because her man had been all the way back in Dallas, Texas, with no clue of how beautiful she was, because he'd rather sit in front of the television all weekend, savoring his peace and quiet away from her, than to be in that dark, dingy club, holding her in his arms.

"I ate greasy fried shrimp off a flimsy paper plate; shoveled spoonfuls of coleslaw into my mouth, and finally stumbled back to my room at three in the morning, and passed out cold."

"I don't believe—," Juanita started to say, she didn't believe it.

"The next morning, I sat on the balcony of my hotel room, and stared out at the water. First, I thought about how I didn't get sick from all that greasy food and gin." Tess laughed. "Then I thought about how much I wished I didn't have to go home, and if I did, how I wished I could put that part of that small island and sand in my purse, and bring it with me, and look at it every time I needed to get away."

Tess finally opened her eyes and saw Juanita looking back at her. "Jesse would've told me it was a bad idea and that I shouldn't go. It ain't safe for a woman to be going to places like that by herself. Or, you need to stay home, and we'll go next summer. Just taking it for granted that I wanted to go with him in the first place."

"But you could've at least told me you were going, Tess. I could've gone with you, or—"

Tess put down the knife and went and sat by her sister. "I didn't want to go with you either, Sister." She took her sister's hand in hers, to ease the pain of the rejection shimmering in her eyes. "You wouldn't have eaten in that dive, without seeing a copy of their last health inspection. You'd have complained about the calories and the grease, and how unclean the place looked. You wouldn't have wanted to lay up in the room naked all afternoon. And you certainly wouldn't have wanted to party with a room packed like sardines full of strangers rubbing all up against each other drinking cheap gin and eating greasy shrimp."

Juanita slumped back in her seat, knowing Tess was right.

"I had the best time I've ever had in my life, Sister. And I couldn't have if I'd taken you or Jesse with me. And if I feel the need to go on another excursion again in my life." Tess smiled broadly. "You and Jesse will be the last people on earth I'd ask to go with me."

She got up, kissed her sister's head, and went back to peeling and cutting up potatoes.

Tess had lost her ever-loving mind, Juanita concluded, driving home. Something had snapped in that woman, something sinister and insane. Jesse certainly hadn't been the best husband in the world, sleazing around with this woman and that one, through the years. But he'd been there to take care of Tess and those boys, and Tess had stuck by him, thick and thin, swearing that her marriage would see itself through a host of storms, and it had. Now all of a sudden, she needed to get away. She needed to be free and walk naked on the beach. What kind of mess was that?

Juanita had covered for her this last time, when she'd called the house and Jesse told her that Tess had gone on the retreat, surprised to find out Juanita didn't know about it. "Oh, was that this weekend?" She pretended to sound surprised. "I thought that was next weekend. I tell you, I've been so busy lately, I don't know if I'm coming or going."

Well, the next time, Tess could keep her own damn secrets

from that man. No telling what else that girl had done on that island. Or who, for that matter. An image of Tess, wrapped up around some man, moaning, groaning, sweating, and probably panting, flashed across her mind. Juanita gripped the steering wheel tightly and almost missed her turn.

"But Mom—"

"But Mom nothing, Jasmine! I said no, and I mean it!"

Jay's thirteen-year-old daughter stomped upstairs to her room.

"And don't you dare slam that damn door, Jasmine!" her mother called after her.

Jay was in the garage, working on an old Caprice he'd been restoring for what seemed like forever. Another Saturday morning in the Hunter house. Hell started breaking loose around 8 A.M. and didn't settle down until after noon. He'd done his part, though, mowed the lawn, fixed the garbage disposal, and changed the oil in Sherry's car. All he wanted to do now was blend into the walls of his garage, and pray these people didn't notice he was there.

"Dad!" his sixteen-year-old son, Jayson, called to him as he ran up into the yard. "You got time to take me driving today?" The boy was inches away from getting his license and it seemed like all he wanted to do was park his ass behind a steering wheel.

"Later on," Jay grunted.

"What about now? I'm going to hang with Kevin and Jon-Jon later on. We going to the movies."

"I said not now, Jayson," he told him again.

The boy huffed, and disappeared inside. "I ain't never going to get my license." he muttered.

Jay ignored him, which is a whole lot more leniency than his momma would've showed him, because she'd have swatted the back of his head with that crescent wrench Jay was working with.

"Jay?" Sherry came to the garage, and from the tone of her voice, he had a feeling he wasn't going to like what came next.

"You didn't trim the tree. The Parkers are complaining again about it growing over into their yard and threatening to call the Home Owner's Association." She didn't wait for him to respond. She stormed off, rolling her eyes. He didn't have to see her rolling eyes to know she'd rolled them, because he felt them, all up and down his spine.

"Shit!" he mumbled, grabbing the electric saw from the shelf, and heading to the back of the house to cut the damn tree.

His mind was back in Millington. Baby Girl, in her world, alone without him, made him feel uneasy, thinking about some niggah up in her face talking shit and trying to get in with a good thing. Elise was a damn good thing, and it was only a matter of time before somebody found Jay's treasure and tried to move in on it. It was a feeling he had.

Her butter-soft ass was always in the forefront of his mind. The more time passed, the more he couldn't stop thinking about her: the way she looked, how she smelled, her smile, hair, lips, eyes, hands, and her nakedness. He was a different kind of man when he was in Millington. Jay was just Jay, free and easy and without a care in the world. That was part of the draw, though. All he had to do was sit back and enjoy the ride with

Elise. Not trim trees or deal with unappreciative teenagers. They were each other's number one priority when they were together, and all the bullshit was left on the other side of the door to her place, waiting for him to leave.

Half an hour later, Jay was back in the garage putting his saw away when Sherry came out of the house, and kissed him tenderly on the cheek. "Now," she smiled up at him, "that wasn't so hard. Was it?" She didn't wait for him to respond and disappeared back inside.

Leaving Sherry was never an issue. She was his wife, his lady-love, and he'd promised her his life. He meant it, too. But Elise was just something that happened. He hadn't planned it, or even wanted it really. She'd been like a gift from heaven or something, being the answer to prayers he never thought he had. She kept him coming back for more, counting the minutes until the next time he could spend time with her.

Whenever Jay reached out to touch Elise, she never pulled away, shrugged him off, or rolled her eyes.

"I'm tired, Jay!"

Words like that never came out of her mouth. The distance made it cool. It made her miss him, and welcome him every time he walked through the door. They saw each other maybe once a week or so, and that was enough to keep the fires burning. As a matter of fact, his fire was burning already, and Jay had to adjust his hard-on in his pants.

"Jay!" Sherry called from the back door. She looked disgusted. "I've got to go in to work. Ally called in sick again!" She let the door slam behind her.

Nursing was hard work. He knew it, and what little energy she had went into everything else but him. Jay would spend his

Saturday afternoon barking orders to the kids, running errands Sherry couldn't finish, and wishing he were someplace else.

Sherry had left for work hours ago. Jay's son had taken off for the movies with his friends. His daughter was probably in her room running her mouth on the phone, as usual.

"Hey, sweetheart." Jay smiled at the sound of her soft hello.

He lay back on the bed, freshly showered, cool and naked, underneath the ceiling fan whirring above the bed. "Yeah," he said, putting on his best Barry White impression. "I miss the hell out of you, too."

I want to be living
For the love of you

Ron Isley was summing it up rather nicely in the background, crooning from the stereo across the room. Calling from the house was dumb. He knew it, but didn't care. All of a sudden, he didn't give a damn about anything except hearing Elise's voice on the other end of that phone. Jay closed his eyes, and imagined her warm, soft caramel brown ass all nudged up next to him. His dick stiffened as she spoke.

"I should be out your way on Thursday, baby. It's been too long, already."

She laughed.

He was dead serious. A week was too long between visits. Hell, a day was too long sometimes. "What do you mean what are we going to do when I get there? We're going to do what we always do." Now she was just being silly. Jay wanted to lay up between those creamy thighs of hers and cum so hard he passed out. "Go dancing?" He sighed, holding back his impatience. But what was wrong with a little dancing? Not a damn thing. Especially when he knew what was waiting for him at the end of the night. "All right, baby girl." He smiled. "Yes. I will take you dancing. Ballroom? Or disco?" he laughed.

Jay's hard cock lay long and rigid against his stomach. He wrapped his fingers around it and squeezed, then slowly rubbed up and down, trying not to make a sound while she was on the phone.

"All you have to do is ask, girl. I'll give you the moon if you want it. Just ask."

In his mind, Jay watched Elise's tongue slide slippery wet, up and down the shaft of his dick. He watched her wrap those full, pretty lips over the head, and try to make damn near the whole thing disappear inside her lovely, sweet mouth.

"Yeah, baby. I'm glad you're in my life, too. So much was missing before you came along. And now that I have you, I can't see letting you go."

She talked some more. He sort of listened. Jay responded on cue. Came on cue. Said good-bye, and then lay back, temporarily relieved, but looking forward to the real thing.

Faux leather walls! Some shit just brought tears to her eyes, and this particular paint treatment was one of them. Renee walked into the Stevenses' grand foyer, breathless at the progress Antonio and his crew had made. Artists! That's what they were. Pure and simple—artists!

"It's beautiful, Tony," she gasped, staring up at the walls. Antonio was perched high on a ladder above her, dabbing paint off the portion he'd just finished, over the raised stencil design he'd plastered on and sanded down earlier. "You've finished the entire foyer, already? Damn! That was fast."

"Well, we're using a new process," he said, climbing down from the ladder. "More efficient. Takes less time."

"I was worried the color might be too dark, but it works well in here."

He nodded. "This room gets tons of light, so I think it works well. C'mon." Antonio pointed toward the living room. "I want to show you how much progress we've made in the formal living room."

Voices and echoes of clicking heels bounced off the bare walls like Ping-Pong balls. Lewis's frustration swelled with every sound.

"Why the hell can't you be here to babysit the painters?" he'd asked Trishelle angrily.

Trishelle shrugged matter-of-factly and basically blew him off. "I told you, Lewis. I've got to take my certification exam today, so that I can get back into teaching. Besides, it's your turn to make a sacrifice this time around. All mine are just about used up."

Lewis was already frustrated from spending hours hunched over his desk, analyzing the company's financials from the past five years, having the daunting task of fixing what was broken, despite the fact that he hadn't been the one to break it in the first place.

The sound of a woman laughing grated on his nerves like fingernails scratching down a chalkboard, until finally Lewis couldn't take it anymore, and stormed downstairs into the main part of the house. What's her name? Renee? Renee was hunched over a can of paint running her mouth and laughing her silly ass head off.

"Excuse me!" he said, interrupting them. "But, I've got a lot of work to do here, and I cannot concentrate with all the noise," nostrils flaring, veins swelling on the sides of his neck.

"Oh, I'm sorry. I'm afraid that's my fault, Lewis," Renee said sincerely. "And I apologize. I just came by to check on the progress, but I'll be leaving shortly."

He huffed and turned hot on his heels, disappearing back into his office, and slamming the door.

She looked at Antonio and smiled. "Is it me?" she snickered.

Antonio shrugged. "He's not exactly what I'd call friendly."

"He hasn't been here long enough to understand the meaning of Southern hospitality," she quipped. "But give him time. He'll be a good ol' boy before you know it. Anyway, I think you might need to lighten up on that tint some." Renee pointed at one side of a large wall. "It looks darker over here, than it does on that side. A bit too dark." She was so busy looking up at the wall, that she didn't notice how close she'd gotten to the ladder. "This is perfect. You can see the texture of the . . ." Before either of them could stop it, the six-foot aluminum ladder crashed to the floor, echoing throughout the rooms like thunder. And seconds later, Lewis Stevens burst from his office, mad as hell.

"What the fuck?" Lewis glared at Renee, who was attempting to help Antonio set the ladder back up. He ran down the stairs two at a time, heading straight for her. "Idiots! Goddamned idiots!"

Antonio stammered. "I'm so sorry, Mr. Stevens! I just—"

"No! No! It was my fault!" Renee interrupted. "I'm such a klutz to—"

"I want everybody out," he said sternly.

Renee looked at him. "Fine. I'm leaving. I'm out."

"All of you! Get the hell out!"

"Lewis? Don't you think you're overreacting? I mean, it's not their—"

"Out! I want you and your crew to get your shit and get the hell out of my house!"

Renee had had just about enough of his unreasonable ass. Lewis was overreacting, being a drama queen, and absolutely ridiculous all at the same time. "We didn't break anything, Lewis. It was an accident. These guys have been working hard all morning to get this done on schedule, and—"

He stepped over to her, and stared down his nose at her. "I want you out of my house, lady, and I want you to take these fools with you, or I swear . . . I'll call the cops and have you hauled off to jail for trespassing."

Renee threw up her hands, and started backing up towards the door. "No problem," she said coolly. "We're out. Antonio, have the fellas pack up. We're leaving." She turned and headed straight for the front door.

Lewis wasn't far behind. "I want them to put shit back the way it was before they got here," he demanded. "Beige walls! I had beige walls this morning and—"

Renee spun around, stopping Lewis dead in his tracks. "And . . . I don't have to fix a damn thing," she spat back smugly. "According to the contract, what you see is what you're stuck with, like it or not. You don't like my work . . . you want to terminate, fine. I'm gone. Paragraph 6c. Read it." She stood toe to toe with Lewis Stevens, daring him to say one rude thing to her. "You bought the paint. You own it. It's yours. Now . . . if you want to change it, I suggest you go out and invest in a ladder, a couple of cans of beige paint, and put the shit back on the walls yourself. Because I no longer work for you."

She'd never had a job she didn't finish. Impossible people, with impossible demands and visions, morons, stupid people, mean, tyrannical people—she'd developed a knack of being able to work with them all. And she could've worked with Lewis, too, if he'd have been man enough to listen to reason. He'd been a brat, a baby, throwing a juvenile temper tantrum over something dumb. Renee sat in her living room, lit by candles, letting Kem's soothing voice and melodies set her mind at ease. The wine helped, too.

Renee had taken the phone off the hook, turned off the computer, and closed herself off from her studio. Tonight would've been a good night to have somebody. Some. Body. Just to stroke her, and tell her she was cool, and that crazy had taken over that lost soul called Lewis Stevens. It sure would've been nice to have someone sitting on that sofa with her, rubbing her feet, massaging her toes, wildly exclaiming in that soulful man tone of his, that she was the most beautiful, the most desirable woman in his world.

She sighed and poured herself another glass of wine, then sank slowly into the cushions of her cozy sofa. Renee was horny, pure and simple. She searched her memories for the last time she'd had sex, then frowned, because it hadn't been good at all. Little dick. Little patience. And selfish. Just plain selfish. He looked good, though, but looking good hadn't been enough to make her come. Not for real anyway.

"Was it good, baby?" He had the nerve to be out of breath.

"Yes," she said, then she climbed out of bed, peed, brushed her teeth, and handed him his boxers. "I've got clients coming early in the morning," was all she said, and that was the last she'd heard from him. What was his name?

The Stevens' project would've been a nice addition to her portfolio, but not at the expense of that arrogant motha fucka's nasty attitude. The brotha had forgotten where he'd come from. That's all. He'd forgotten all about the struggle of his people, the bonds that had been broken, and that desperately needed to be mended if the black race in America was ever going to gather itself to itself.

"Amen to that," she muttered, then gulped down the wine in her glass.

Oh well. It wasn't like the old days when she was hurting for work. Shit, Renee had to turn down clients; her time was in such demand. She had projects scheduled from now until this time next year, and was giving herself a headache trying to figure out how in the world she was going to fit them all in.

One less bell to answer. One less egg to fry. One less asshole to deal with. She reached over to the end table and flicked off the light switch. Her couch was much too comfortable to move from. Renee nestled in for the night, pulled that old afghan she'd crocheted back in the seventh grade to her chin, and drifted off to sleep.

God is grace, He certainly is, Tess thought, watching herself in the full-length mirror in her bedroom, doing deep knee bends. Nobody but God could've thought up something as luxurious as stretch denim jeans. Her future daughter-in-law, Keisha, told her about them. She twisted and turned, bended over and squatted, relishing the comfort of jeans that fit like skin on her forty-one-year-old behind. Tess laughed out loud. Damn! she looked good. She had a closet full of sweat pants and suits she'd worn most of her adult life, chasing after twin boys and keeping up with them, too. But the boys were men now, way past the age for their momma to be chasing after them. Tess decided it was about time to put away her Nike's, sweats, and scrunchies, and finally give in to looking like a woman her age ought to look. *Fine.*

Tess slipped on her cranberry colored V-neck sweater, smoothed it down her hips and clasped the gold necklace with the ruby princess-cut stone around her neck. It's amazing what a new hairstyle will do for a woman. Tess admired her cropped cut, smoothing her hand down the nape of her neck, feeling a bit naked without hair there. She'd spent years of her life, fussing and fighting to keep her hair from breaking off because Jesse preferred it long, when they first started dating. One day, it dawned on Tess, she was fighting a losing battle, because Jesse hadn't preferred anything on her in years. And besides, she usually wore it up anyway, in ponytails, or pinned to her head. Two days ago, Tess gave in to the skilled scissors of the able bodied hair technician and felt like she'd been born again. She even let that girl talk her into lightening her natural dark brown hair, adding dark blond highlights that framed her smooth, oval face perfectly. She stood back admiring herself in the mirror. *Is this what a resurrection feels like?* she wondered.

She hadn't noticed Jesse standing in the doorway watching her. Maybe because it was something he rarely ever did. In twenty-three years of marriage, Tess had become like the furniture to her husband, blending into the walls and taken for granted. The furniture had one up on Tess, though. If a piece was moved or broken, he made it a point to notice, even attempt to fix it. Tess was something he never paid attention to, broken or not.

"You going out?" he asked, startling her.

Jesse's big self almost filled the doorway completely. Years and age had added a little weight to both of them. But he was still handsome, and was often mistaken for a retired football player. His dark, brooding eyes studied her in a way she wasn't accustomed to.

Tess pretended to fuss with her hair. "I thought I told you that I was going to the movies with Bev. Remember?"

Of course he didn't. She never told him.

"Oh yeah." He nodded introspectively. "That's right."

Liar.

Lying was second nature to that man. Always had been, and always would be. But Tess had grown used to it, even learned to make the most of it in recent years, and had learned the value of making up a lie every now and then herself.

She sat down on a chair across the room and slipped into her boots.

"You look real nice." Jesse eased into the room and sat down on his side of the bed. "That a new top?"

Tess smiled. His attempt to make conversation was awkward and left her speechless and guarded. She had nothing to hide. Yes. It was a new top, and new jeans, and new boots, too. But it seemed senseless to mention it to him—after all, Jesse really didn't give a damn.

"So what are you gonna see?"

Tess stood up at the dresser and started putting on her lipstick. She watched him from the corner of her eye, trying not to look surprised that she was actually making the effort to wear makeup. She normally saved makeup for church, holidays, or every now and then, a Vicodin and Chardonnay cocktail pity-party she might have by herself when she knew he wouldn't be home until late, finally creeping up the stairs to their bedroom, thinking she wouldn't notice that he smelled like sex or soap.

"That new movie with Jennifer Lopez in it. I can't think of the name of it. Wanna come?" she asked with a mischievous twinkle in her eyes that she knew he'd fail to notice. No, he wouldn't want to come. Thank goodness.

"No." He shook his head. "You know I don't get into those romantic comedies."

Jesse slowly stood and started to leave. He hesitated just outside the room and turned to her one last time. "You do look nice. Did I tell you that already?"

Something had gotten into her. Jesse couldn't put his finger on it, but Tess had been acting funny lately. Funny different, like she was changing. He used to believe he wanted her to, until now. He opened the refrigerator and pulled out a beer. It was the third one he'd had since finishing dinner. He had to be to work early in the morning for a meeting with his boss. His department hadn't been doing so well lately, they'd been missing ship dates on a regular basis, and being the department manager, the burden fell on his shoulders to straighten it out, never mind the fact that he had a bunch of sorry asses working for him. The beer would help him sleep.

Jesse slumped down in his chair in the den across from the television, picked up the remote and started flipping through channels. He was tired. Seemed like he was always tired lately, ever since she quit him. He sipped on his beer and tried not to think about her. *Sandra.* The thought of just her name set his blood on fire, but it was one he'd learned to squelch ever since she left. She said she'd had enough one day. Got mad at him because he wouldn't leave Tess, and said she didn't want to spend a lifetime sharing another woman's man. Women were a trip sometimes, changing their minds at the drop of a hat.

Wasn't long before that when she'd told him, *"I couldn't leave you if I wanted to, Jesse."* She laughed. *"Ain't no man out there who could ever make me feel the way you do."*

He used to tell her he loved her, all the time. But he just said it because it seemed to make her feel good. Deep down, he never believed it himself until she was gone. Then he missed the hell out of her in an ache that never seemed to go away.

"Why do you keep doing this to me, Jesse? Go back to that bitch you've been fuckin' and get the hell out of my house! I don't want you! I don't want your cheating ass anymore!"

It didn't matter what she said, or how hard Tess cried and slapped his face. It didn't even matter that she wanted him gone, and that more than anything, he wanted to leave her. He never could bring himself to do it. In his mind, he'd left that woman a thousand times through the years. Tess had always been a boring, predictable woman. When he was younger, he thought predictable was what he wanted in a wife, but through the years, long years, it became harder and harder for him to stay interested or even get excited by her. Tess fit nicely into a place in their lives, and he needed more than that. He searched for it, too, every time something sexier or prettier came along. Every time some woman swore to him that she worshipped the ground he walked on, he swore this was it, and that he was leaving Tess, but something always kept him there—the kids, the money, and just the simple fact that he had loved that woman once, enough to marry her, and to swear to her that the only thing that would ever part them was death.

Sandra's brown eyes sparkled every time he walked through her front door. She'd throw her arms around his neck, and smother him with buttery tongue kisses until his knees were weak and he could hardly stand. She made love to him like it was the first time, the last time, and the only time, leaving him full and greedy for more. He couldn't get enough of that woman, and he never wanted to. Since she'd been gone, Jesse didn't know what to do with himself, except to suck down beers, and flip through two hundred channels of satellite television, not watching a damn thing.

Tess came downstairs, and picked up her purse and keys just in time for her friend Beverly to honk her horn outside in the driveway.

"What time you be back?" Jesse sat up and asked, surprised at himself for caring.

Tess's wide hips swayed back and forth carrying her to the front door. She did look good though, he thought somberly. It had been a long time since she'd looked that good, or just a long time since he'd noticed, and it stirred something familiar in him.

She turned to him before leaving and shrugged. "We might go get something to eat afterwards," she said indifferently. "Don't wait up."

Both of them knew he wouldn't.

She closed the door shut between them, and all of a sudden Jesse realized how lonesome he was.

Long John Silver crawled on all fours across the crowded floor where the frantic wave of howling women parted like the red sea to let him through to get to his destination. One of his wild, dark eyes twinkled in anticipation, the other was covered behind the black sinister patch, and he licked his lips at the sight of Bev, sitting, tantalizing, in her seat. The music thumped ferociously in the background, sounding animalistic and feral, driving this untamed beast to his prey. He stalked her, slowly climbed up her legs to her lap, straddling her, thrusting his tight ass to the rhythm that drove him. Bev was slick, though. The five-dollar bill she'd been waving in the air at him since he'd come out on stage, she tucked securely in the crease of her cleavage, deep enough until only a corner of the bill was visible. Bev was a DD cup, at least, and somehow, she'd managed to push all that flesh up and out into a enticing mound that must've looked delicious to Long John, because he dove in without hesitation, burying his nose in her ample bosom until his whole head nearly vanished. Bev threw her arms and head back, closed her eyes, and let the heaven of this delicious man's lips press against her wanting and hungry flesh, and steal her away from a roomful of screaming women. He found his treasure, and carried it from its prison between his teeth. Bev nearly fell over backwards in her chair, but her savior, Mr. Silver, caught her before she did. And just like that, he was whisked away from behind, by some other savage female, dangling a ten-dollar bill over his head.

Tess had strayed away from their table, up to the front of the stage, swinging her hips and waving her arms, shrieking every time something male set foot on stage. She was high—on life, and on the orange martinis she'd been drinking all night. Tess gulped down what was left in her glass, and flagged down the waiter to bring her another one.

"I can't believe I let you talk me into going to some mess like this," she'd told Bev in the car on the way to the club. They'd found the flyer on the shelf in the beauty shop, and Bev begged and pleaded for Tess to go with her until Tess reluctantly agreed. She damn sure was glad she did, too. How in the world had she missed something like this in her lifetime? Women were wild and free here. They were open and hungry and feeding on man-flesh like it was all the meat there was in the world. Pretty man-flesh, young and firm, and eager to please, for the measly price of a dollar. Muscles rippled, dicks hung low and hard, thighs bulged.

Tess had tucked herself away for too many years, thinking she was doing the right thing, only it never really did feel right. Not as right at this. Not nearly as right as half-naked men, bumping and grinding up to her, sucking down martinis, and coming together with a pack of other deeply deprived women, letting loose of every single inhibition she'd ever had, and feeling naked like she was the one running around with a g-string on.

"I sure wish my tubes weren't tied," Bev said to Tess, as she finally sat back down. "I'd have all kinds of kids for a man like that."

Tess laughed. "From the looks of him, he isn't much older than one of your kids."

Bev shook her head and dug around in the bottom of her purse. "I don't give a damn! Just call me Mrs. Silver, girl. I wonder if he takes credit cards?"

"Where you going to swipe it?" Tess and Bev stared at each other, and then burst out laughing.

The female MC's voice came from a dark booth behind the crowd and permeated the room. "And now, ladies," she said huskily, "the moment you've all been waiting for, and dreaming about. Our next performer is your hero." Whoops and screams filled the air. "He'll avenge your love and your lust, your desire, and that sweet-hot craving for what a real man should be." More screams and hollers. Bev and Tess looked at each other, beaming. A funky bass sound seemed to rise up from the floor, shaking beneath their feet, vibrating all the way up to the tops of their heads. "Ladies!" the MC shouted above the music and screams. "The Masked Avenger!"

The tall man in black wasn't a dancer. He sauntered out onto the stage, with deep emerald green eyes sparkling from behind his mask, wearing a long cape that swept the floor when he walked. One sistah standing next to Tess started jumping up and down, putting her hands to her mouth, trying to control the fit that was about to take over her body. Tess just shook her head, and tried not to laugh. This woman obviously did not get out enough. But then, the masked man began removing his clothing, one article at a time, making a point to stand at the edge of the stage, in front of a particular woman here and there. He'd reach out his hand to her, and just before she could take it, he'd slowly pull away, and find some other female to tease and tantalize. When he was naked from the waist up, Tess could finally see what all the commotion was about. His broad, bronze chest was wider than her king-sized bed. The Masked Avenger's long limbs seemed to go on forever, flexing muscles and tendons to the rhythm playing in the background. He was beautiful, and Tess didn't realize she'd stopped breathing. He stood near two women and jutted his pelvis out to them, encouraging them to remove his tear-away pants. Grand, hard, perfectly proportioned thighs shimmered under the flashing lights, and those women fought over those pants, until they each had a section clutched tightly to their chests. Tess had spent her remaining dollars on the last dancer, but deep in her purse, there was her emergency money. The money she kept just in case the car broke down and she needed to call a tow truck. Or, the money she'd use if she just needed to get away from Jesse, and spend the night in a hotel room somewhere. She found a one-hundred dollar bill folded perfectly in thirds. Hypnotized by this masked man, strutting his stuff on stage to a sea of intoxicated, horny women, Tess made her way through the crowd to the front of the stage, waited for him to make his way to her, and held up her money. Tess was oblivious to everything in the world but him. She couldn't feel her legs, couldn't hear her own thoughts, and never once heard her friend Bev scream out, "Tess! That's too much damn money to give that fool!"

The Avenger looked down at her and smiled brilliantly, then held open the front of his g-string, wrapped his long fingers around Tess's small hand, and shoved her entire fist down the front of his draws. *Goodness gracious!* Tess nearly passed out. She felt it! She felt all of it, and it was huge, for real! The masked man never let go of her hand. Instead, he pulled her up on stage, motioned for someone backstage to bring up a chair, and sat down in it, pulling Tess down onto his strong, virile, ample lap. He put his hand under her chin, then turned her face to his. "What's your name, dear?" His voice was deep, and she detected a slight accent.

Tess had to catch her breath before answering. "Contessa," she said, breathless, and out of character.

His green eyes locked onto hers, and he nodded. "Of course it is."

He turned Tess away from him, until her back was to him, then seductively grinded his hips against hers, until either real or feigned, Tess felt like she was about to explode. Every manner of sexual fantasy she could conjure up was being fulfilled in that moment. Tess savored every inch of his hardness wedged against her, imagining the two of them naked, hot and sweaty, drowning in each other's juices.

"That's it," she mouthed, afraid she might've said it out loud. But so what if she did? "Right—right there." She fell helpless back against him, and he wrapped both his strong arms around her, then kissed the side of her neck. Tess had died. That's all it was. She'd had a heart attack and died in this man's lap, and it was all good.

He lifted her up, then slid out from under her, and let her rest in the chair. Then he turned to her, and whispered close in her face. "Wait here, Contessa. Daddy has to go make some money."

Tess watched limply, not sure of whether or not she was conscious, while this masked man made his way around the room, from one woman to the next, filling his fists, mouth, and g-string with money. She wanted to get up and off that stage, but Tess was afraid that if she stood, she'd fall back down again, because she didn't think she had the strength. She heard Bev laughing, maybe even crying. Finally, the Masked Avenger came back to Tess and helped her to her feet. He lovingly cradled her face between his big, perfect hands, then kissed her, first one cheek, then the other. "You have truly made my night, beautiful Lady Contessa."

Before she even realized what she was saying, Tess blurted out, "I love you."

He smiled. "Yes."

The masked man helped her back to her seat, bowed deeply, waved to the crowd, and headed backstage.

"Girl?" Bev leaned across the table, staring concerned at Tess, and drying tears from her own eyes. "You all right?"

Tess shook her head no. "I'll never be all right again, Bev. I swear I won't."

Jesse was asleep by the time she made it home. Tess was drunk, on martinis and masked men and life. She made her way upstairs, peeled out of her clothes, and decided to forego the shower. The last thing she needed to do was pass out in the tub and drown. She crawled into bed, and sank down into the cool sheets, with a smile on her face. Briefly, she turned and looked at her husband. The thought crossed her mind to wake him, but why? She needed the kind of loving he'd never been willing or able to give her. She needed the kind of loving she knew he lavished on other women. How come he couldn't have made love to her like that, she questioned herself time and time again. The answers were never good ones. Tess craved nasty, sloppy, unorchestrated sex, primal. The kind she imagined she could get from the Masked Avenger. She closed her eyes and saw the two of them together, with him braced behind her, and Tess balanced on all fours, hungry and hot for him, anxious to be fucked hard and furious. He grabbed a handful of her hair, and forced his dick deep into her dripping pussy, thrusting with full force hard enough for it to hurt, to lurch her forward, but she'd hold on.

"Give it to me!" he'd command. "Gimme my sweet, hot pussy!"

"Take it, daddy!" she'd grunt. "It's yours! It's all yours!"

Just thinking about it was enough to make her moist. Jesse stirred, but Tess lay still to keep from waking him up. Sex with Jesse would just piss her off and leave her stranded in frustration the way it always did.

She recalled emerald green eyes shimmering at her, as she

closed hers to sleep. Tess fell in love tonight, and it felt good. She was seventeen the last time that happened. Every woman should fall in love at least once a year, she thought, trying not to laugh out loud, even if it did cost her a hundred dollars. It was worth every penny. The Masked Avenger was worth every red cent. *Contessa.* The way he said it, made it not sound so dumb after all.

Downtown Millington. What the hell did Jay know about downtown Millington? He paid a five-dollar cover charge at the door of Lady Blue, the club Elise insisted on meeting him at.

"I swear, Jay, if I didn't know any better, I'd think this whole relationship was only about sex to you," she argued over the phone.

No. It wasn't *only* about sex. But that was a big part of it. He thought it, but dared not say it out loud.

"You come into town, stop at my place, and we spend the whole time in bed," she scolded him softly.

"I didn't know that was a problem," he gently retorted over the phone.

"It isn't," she sighed. "But there's more to a relationship than sex. You ought to know that."

"I do know that." He loved how uncomplicated Elise could be. But at the moment, she sounded like a woman about to complicate the hell out of the situation.

"It's not like you have to worry about running into anybody you know. We can go out, have a good time, and relax, honey. Just let our hair down and cut loose. Shit, Jay. I'm walking around here telling everybody about the new man in my life, but they all think I'm lying because every time I am out, I'm by myself."

Out? Jay felt the sting of jealousy. Out where?

"I'd love to show you off, baby." The sound of her voice sent a shudder through him and landed in his lap. "Or are you ashamed to be seen with me in public?"

The place was a dive, but Elise had insisted that it was the place to be. Lady Blue's wasn't much bigger than the walk-in closet in his master bedroom. Jay waded through the thick crowd, packed shoulder to shoulder, cutting his way through cigarette smoke, heavy perfumes and aftershaves, and glares from a room full of people who instantly recognized him as new meat in the joint. They were sharks and he felt like some dumb-ass, pitiful seal caught smack dab in a school of them.

Usher played in the background, and across the small room was an even smaller dance floor packed to capacity with asses bumping and grinding all up against each other, and dark-skinned bodies glistening under the glow of sweat and Long Island Iced Teas.

He finally spotted her, backed into a corner, up against a wall by some brother, leaning a little too close, trying to get his mack on over the music. Elise's long hair was set free and hanging down past her shoulders, straightened, and looking like she'd just gotten it done. She wore a low-cut purple blouse that exposed way too much of what he knew was his, and this brother standing over her was no doubt getting an eyeful. The blouse was tucked into a form-fitting, knee-length skirt, capped off by some black stiletto pumps that made those sexy thick calves of hers flex every time she so much as inhaled. She sipped on something, batted her pretty brown eyes, and laughed like this motherfucker was a goddamned comedian.

"What did I miss?" Jay asked, making sure the son of a bitch standing over Elise knew he was playing with another man's fire.

Elise stepped toward Jay. "I didn't think you were coming. I thought you might've just kept going since you weren't here at—"

"I said I was coming." Jay glared at the man, then looked down at Elise. "When have I ever said I was coming, and not shown up, Elise?"

Elise looked stunned at the tone of his voice. Jay was more stunned at how pissed he was at this whole scene. He clenched his jaw at the man standing behind Elise who was either too dumb or thought his ass was too bad to step off.

Elise gently took Jay's hand and led him to the other side of the dance floor. "We were just talking," she tried to explain. Jay snatched his hand from hers, then made his way to the bar and ordered a beer. It was bad enough she had to drag his ass out here to this hole in the wall, knowing he'd been on the road for two fucking hours. But then she's got to be all up in some knucklehead's face, flashing titties like Jay was a figment of her imagination and not her man. What the hell kind of shit did she do when he wasn't on his way down? Jay wondered.

Elise squeezed up close to him, and kissed his cheek. "I missed you, baby."

He gulped down half his beer and ignored her. His woman. Right or wrong, Elise was his woman. He'd climbed mountains to get to her on a regular basis, lying and cheating, and fucking going out of his way just to make sure he passed through this pisshole called Millington, Texas, all for the sake of seeing her. And this is the kind of crap she pulls?

"We were just talking, Jay," she leaned in close and told him. "He's looking for a house, and I was telling him about some places that have just come on the market."

Jay looked at Elise, then down her blouse. "Any of those places happen to be down there?"

At first, she thought he was joking, and Elise laughed. But it wasn't long before she realized he wasn't.

"I know you didn't come all the way here just to argue," she snapped.

Jay finished the last of his beer, then ordered another one.

"What right do you have to be jealous, Jay? You told me you'd be here at ten, it's eleven thirty? I didn't think you were coming."

"I said I was coming," he muttered.

"Well, how was I to know you didn't get held up by the wife brigade? How was I to know you didn't change your mind and decide you didn't want this anymore?" Elise didn't bother trying to hide her anger. She pointed her finger at Jay. "You're the one who's bound by commitment, Jay! Not me! I don't have a ring on my finger and since I don't, I don't have to answer to your married ass, and who I talk to is my fucking business!" Elise turned, winding her way through the crowd and out the door.

Man-beast instinct quickly kicked in, and Jay hurried to pay for his drinks, then chased after her. He caught up with her just in time to see Motherfucker blocking her way between the club and her car.

"I don't want to talk right now!" she shouted at the man.

"You can't give a brotha your number, sweetheart? I just want to call you and—"

"Elise!" Jay shouted

She turned to him, rolled her eyes, and pushed past Motherfucker. "Fuck you, Jay! Go home!"

"Hey, brotha!" the man made the mistake of grabbing Jay by the arm. "I think the lady wants you to leave her alone."

It all happened too fast and before anyone had a chance to stop it, Motherfucker lay flat on his back on the ground. Jay stood over him, breathing fire through flared nostrils, and Elise stood across from both of them, her eyes wide in astonishment, staring at Jay like he'd lost his damn mind.

"That's my woman, mothafucka!" Jay's chest heaved up and down. "Don't ever try and keep me away from my woman!"

He'd never known this side of himself existed. Jay felt prehistoric and invincible. He looked over at Elise, his prize, knowing full well, that the sex was going to be off the fucking chain tonight! "Let's go home," he commanded.

She nodded, meekly, took hold of his hand when he held it out to her, and followed him to the car.

"Jay! Oh, Jay!" Elise's thick legs were wrapped tight around his waist, as Jay drilled as far down into her as he could. He refused to let her turn off the lights. Jay made angry love to this woman, branding her and owning her. Elise's once bone-straight hair, was frizzed and tangled all over her head, matted to her face by sweat.

"That's good, girl!" he said, clenching his teeth. "Oh damn! This is some good pussy! Good—my pussy, baby!"

"It's yours Jay!" She pulled his face to hers and slid her tongue into his mouth. "It's your pussy, baby," she said, breathless, between kisses.

Jay nodded, and pushed deeper into her, claiming his territory with every thrust. Hell yeah! It was his!

Afterward, Elise lay stretched out next to him. Jay was too damned exhausted to be mad anymore. "You didn't have to hit him, Jay." Elise rested her head on his chest, and traced figure eights on his chest. A cool breeze from the open window filtered through the room, gently blowing through the sheers.

Jay raised his hand and flexed his fingers. "Yeah," he said lazily. "My hand still hurts."

"Why'd you have to hit him?"

Shit. Why did he hit him? Jay couldn't put his finger on a good solid reason. Feelings welled up in him like a toilet overflowing and just spilled out all over the place.

"I don't know. I just—"

Just lost control of himself. Jay hadn't hit anybody since high school. He hadn't lost his temper like that in years. He'd erupted for no better reason than jealousy and now it embarrassed the hell out of him.

"It's not like I can't take care of myself," she said smugly. "If I thought he was being a problem, I'd have slugged him myself. I didn't need you to do it."

Elise was independent like that. She was self-sufficient like that. She was capable of not needing him and that's what bothered him most. After all, what did he have to offer a woman like this? She was like water he was trying to hold on to. Her beautiful self was everything he craved. She was the root cause of his insatiable appetite and the one thing he could never get enough of, no matter how many nights he spent at her place.

"I know you didn't need me to do it, Elise," he sighed, then realized the truth. "But I didn't do it for you."

She balanced herself up on her elbow and stared into his face. "So, just good old-fashioned jealousy made you do it? Don't tell me you thought you were doing him a favor?" she teased.

Her soft, round face melted a space inside him. Jay touched her cheek, then traced a line down to her lips. It was hard to feel what he felt for this woman, knowing he had one at home he loved. But Jay couldn't help it. He didn't want to. Elise had the power to turn him into another kind of man altogether. One who could knock another brother out with a punch, then stand over him beating her chest like Queen Kong.

"I did it for me, baby," he said sincerely.

She smiled.

"I did it because I don't want another man to put his hands on you, or—to take you away from me." Jay said his words carefully, so that she'd understand each and every one of them. "I don't want you to leave me, baby girl." He swallowed hard and locked his gaze onto hers. "I'd be empty inside if I ever lost you, Elise."

The trip seemed longer than usual. Jay headed to Lexington, Kentucky, to drop off a load of shipping pallets. He almost didn't recognize himself sometimes, especially lately, since he'd met Elise. He'd been faithful to his marriage to Sherry. Every now and then, temptation threatened to get the best of him, especially when he was out on the road. With Elise, it wasn't about regretting a damn thing. It was about finding ways to get back to her because when they were together, she was his world. Love? Was that what it was? No. It wasn't love he felt for the woman. It was more, maybe. Or just different. Whatever it was, it was stronger than he was. It was consuming and desperate. Whatever it was had a grip on him so strong, he wondered if he'd ever be able to break free of it, even if he wanted to.

Elise lay across the bed naked, letting her thoughts slip into Jay. Lately, that's where they always seemed to be. She never dreamed she'd end up like this, in love with a married man. It wasn't like the opportunity never presented itself before, and Elise always turned away from it. But for whatever reason, she hadn't turned away from Jay.

She was thirty-three years old, and damn if she didn't want to hurry up and get married. All he'd ever have to be was single, and she'd ask him to marry her, buy him a ring and everything. She smiled at the image of her getting down on one knee in front of him, sliding a ring on his finger, and him gawking down at her with that "what the hell do you think you're doing" expression thick on his face.

Jay hadn't said it yet. But it was on the tip of his tongue. She tasted it there every time they kissed. She heard it in his voice whenever he called. And last night, she saw it pissed off and balled up into his fist when he laid that brotha out in the parking lot. Butterflies tickled her insides, and Elise closed her eyes bringing his full image into view behind them.

Jay was that common kind of handsome, unextraordinary until you looked long and hard at him. That's when you saw it: strong and rugged handsome, hidden in dark penetrating eyes, a square chin, and broad nose. He might've been considered "cute" when he was in junior high school, but not fine. But she was never into fine because she never thought of herself as fine. She was pretty, on a good day, and unassuming on the rest of them. For some reason though, Jay's eyes lit up every time he saw her. He loved to just stare at her, and went overboard telling her how beautiful she was.

The ceiling fan whirred over her bed, and Elise could almost swear she could smell his scent stirring around in the room. Why'd he have to be married, God? She thought sadly. Jay was the man of her dreams, every inch of his six-foot-one-inch frame. He was the one she'd dreamed about, who accepted her fully and unconditionally, and appreciated all of who she was. What kind of woman had managed to snag a man like that, and keep him? What kind of woman had been the one he'd proposed to and had kids by? And why hadn't Elise been on time to have been that woman?

The phone rang, startling her. Elise rolled over on her elbow, and looked at the caller ID. It was him. It was her baby.

"Hello?" she nearly whispered into the phone.

"Did I wake you?" he asked quietly.

She smiled. "No. I was just laying here, thinking about you, as a matter of fact."

"Oh really?" he asked, sounding like he was hoping she really had been.

"Really, really."

"Then, that must be why I called."

"Kismet?"

"Among other things."

She wanted to ask what other things. But Elise held back, preferring to believe that she knew what he meant, what he was hinting at, even though he wasn't ready to say it yet.

I love you, too, Jay, she said in her heart. One day, he'd say it out loud. Until then, she'd wait. Jay was worth waiting for.

She walked into Renee's studio wearing wide-leg, cuffed, eggshell-white slacks, a pink, off-the-shoulders cashmere sweater, and bone-colored, buckled, low-heeled shoes. Her auburn hair was slicked back off her face, highlighting classic cheekbones, and stunning eyes. Renee answered her door barefoot, in tattered jeans, and a man's white cotton, button-down shirt.

Trishelle's expression screamed apology. "My husband is a brilliant man, but he has a tendency to do dumb things."

"Sounds like a lot of men."

Trish laughed. "Probably. But I can only speak for my own." She turned to Renee and smiled. "I'm sorry."

"Why?" Renee walked past her and sat down at her drafting table. "You weren't the one who fired me. So, why are you apologizing?"

Trish sighed, then sat down in one of the leather chairs across from Renee. "Technically, he didn't fire you, either."

"Sure sounded like it."

"Well, he's good at sounding like a lot of things he doesn't mean. But he's all bark," she shrugged.

"Bark or not," Renee leaned forward, "I don't take kindly to being thrown out on my ass."

"Which is why I'm here. I don't want you to go, Renee. I love your ideas, and I love what you're planning on doing with my house, and I don't want you to go."

Of course she did, Renee thought staring at the desperation in this woman's eyes. It was hard not to gloat or to feel smug, so, she didn't try hard to hide it.

"Can you please finish this project? You'll be dealing with me, and not Lewis, I promise. He only did what he did because he was angry with me. He's been angry with me ever since we came here, and to be honest—" Trish looked like she'd crossed a line, told too much, said things she had no business telling Renee, but she needed to convince this woman to stay on and to finish what she'd started. "—This move has been hard on both of us." She feigned a smile. "And I'm not too happy with him either. Unfortunately, you fell in the crossfire of that, and that's what I'm sorry for."

"Then that's what I'll accept your apology for."

"I really want you to finish, Renee," Trish pleaded. "That place is like a tomb, empty and cold, and I need you to make it feel like home."

She's good. Renee stared at her, impressed by Trishelle's dramatic plea. But she wasn't impressed enough to give in too soon. And it wasn't Trishelle she wanted kissing her ass and begging for a reprieve. It was Lewis.

"I'll have to think about it," she said apologetically, escorting Trishelle to the door. "We can talk tomorrow. I'll call you."

Of course, she'd go back. Renee never met a project she didn't finish, and she'd be damned if she started now. But let them sweat just a little longer. Waiting had a way of building character, and if there was anything Lewis Stevens lacked, it was certainly character.

If he expected Renee to bow down and wash his feet with her tears and hair, he might as well hold his breath, and wait. Because it just wasn't happening. Over the past week, since his little temper tantrum, Renee had brought the crew back in to finish up the custom paint treatment in the foyer and formal living room, which looked fantastic. She'd stopped by today because the newly upholstered sofa and chairs had arrived and she wanted to ensure the work had been completed to order.

Trishelle had rushed out to pick the kid up from school, and for some reason, Papa Bear had decided to come home early.

"The painters did a good job," he said, clearing his throat.

Her first thought was to ignore him, make a wish, and hope that he'd go away in a puff of smoke. But she was a better woman than that, and just because he had to go around acting like he was twelve, didn't mean she had to.

"They always do," she said, examining the direction of patterns on the chairs.

"I uh . . ." Lewis stood in the arched doorway of the living room, with his hands in his pockets, looking as if just talking to her were painful. "I want to apologize about . . ." He shrugged, looked at her, and faked a smile. "You know?"

Okay, so maybe she wasn't such a good woman, or better human being. The man was almost groveling, and when was the last time she'd had a good-looking brotha grovel to her? Business or pleasure? Something evil welled up inside her, that wouldn't just let bygones be bygones, slap him a high five, and get on with life.

"No," she said smugly. "I don't know." Renee stopped what she was doing, stood in the middle of the room, and crossed her arms over her chest. Lewis stared at her with a wicked look in his own eyes, pissed and stunned that she had the nerve to put him on the spot like this. "Tell me."

He hesitated, unsure of what to say. "Well . . . about the other day, when I . . . I um . . . ."

"When you went off on me and my crew like some toddler throwing a fit?" she spoke softly. "Is that why you're apologizing, Lewis?"

Lewis didn't appreciate the tone or attitude she'd taken with him. Trishelle might've been one to put up with this decorator's shit, but Trishelle had also been the one to sign that ridiculous contract without even reading it or letting him look it over first. The contract that left them stuck with a bill whether they liked what she'd done or not. The one that required an astronomical deposit before she'd even started working on the house. The one for which he'd have to pay a huge penalty for, should he cancel her services right in the middle of a remodel. Trishelle had put him in this position, feigning ignorance. "Oh Lewis!" she gasped, "I had no idea." But he knew better. She knew better, and this whole situation was just another way to punish him.

He stared hard at her. "Yes. That's why I'm apologizing."

Let's see. Renee studied him for a moment. Did she have time to get him to wash her feet with his tears and dry them with his hair? Probably not. Oh well.

"Apology accepted." She picked up her bag, and started to leave. But she stopped and stood next to him and smiled. "If we all play nice from now on, everybody can walk away happy."

"You screwed us with that contract, and you know it," he said coldly.

She smiled. "It's my standard contract, and it's always open for negotiation, and at the top, it clearly states, 'Please Read in Its Entirety.' If you had a problem with it, all you had to do was say something."

"Trishelle signed it."

"If she had a problem with it . . . all she had to do was say something."

"Well, I'm saying something now. I want to renegotiate." His request was a joke, and he knew it.

Renee patted his arm. "Signed, sealed, and delivered, baby," she winked. "I'm all yours."

She headed for the front door. Lewis called out to her. "If I were a different kind of brotha, I'd tell you to get a lawyer."

She turned. "Please. You don't give yourself enough credit, Lewis. I can't say I've ever met a brotha more different than you." Renee waived her hand casually. "Ciao!" and left.

She was impertinent, and overstepped her bounds on the whole first name thing. She was flippant, and in her own cunning way, a con artist. He looked around the room, admiring the work she'd had done on the walls. She was good, he thought, awed, despite his frustration. But not that damn good.

Brandon was the younger twin, idealistic and romantic to a fault. Tess saw images of her younger self in him sometimes. He thought he wanted to get married, and maybe he really did. But Brandon was basing his idea of marriage on a fantasy he chose to believe his parents lived. Jesse and Tess had given up trying to talk him out of it. He was twenty-three years old. That was plenty old enough to screw up his life. It was past old enough.

"I love my mom to death, but sometimes, I just wish she didn't want to help plan this wedding," Keisha, Brandon's fiancée, said, exasperated. Tess and Jesse smiled from across the dinner table. Dinner was Brandon's idea, or so he said. Tess figured that it was probably really Keisha's, and she just told him to say it was his.

Pretty girl, shorter than Tess, butterscotch brown, with wide-set eyes, and a perfect teeth commercial smile. Brandon was fixed on that smile most of the night, holding on to the girl's hand, rubbing his shoulder against hers. Tess and Jesse both leaned in opposite directions from each other the whole evening.

"Sometimes," Keisha continued, playfully berating her mother's efforts, "I have to wonder if this is my wedding or hers."

Brandon rolled his eyes and shook his head.

"Let her have this moment." Tess reached across and gently tapped the girl's hand. "You're her only daughter, Keisha. She won't get to do this again."

What she really wanted to say was, *Better her than me,* but Tess held her tongue.

"And I told your mother the last time we spoke, that if there was anything I could do to let me know."

"Well, she loved the caterer you suggested, Miss Tess. She couldn't say enough good things about him."

Miss Tess. Sort of made her sound like she should've been sitting on the porch in a rickety old rocking chair, smoking on a corncob pipe, with stockings rolled down around her knees, calling out to the field for Sounder to bring his ass home.

"Is your daddy going to be able to make it to the wedding?" Jesse asked, trying to contribute to the conversation. Keisha's mother and father were divorced, and her father lived in Atlanta.

The girl's smile lit up that whole side of the restaurant. "Yes, sir. He's coming, and he's going to give me away."

They made it through dinner, and Jesse and Tess rode home in silence. Without realizing it, both were traveling back in time to when they were younger and about to get married. Tess had just turned eighteen, graduated from high school, and starting to show. She'd fallen in love with Jesse on sight, watching him saunter up to her and his girlfriend in the park, looking like some kind of All-American wearing a University of Southern California football jersey, jean shorts, and white sneakers.

"Girl, he's coming this way," her best friend at the time, Rhonda, mumbled, pretending not to notice him walking in their direction, and adjusting her skirt. "Don't say nothing stupid, Tess," she commanded. "I'll pinch you hard if you do."

Tess ignored Rhonda's threats, her mouth fell open, and she never took her eyes off him.

"Hey, ladies," he said, smiling hard and staring right at Tess. "I saw y'all from across the park and figured I should come over and introduce myself."

"I'm Rhonda," she said, sticking out her chest and then her hand for him to shake, and to get his attention directed at her. Rhonda cocked her head quickly in Tess's direction. "This is my best friend, Tess."

Jesse's broad shoulders cast a shadow as big as that shade tree they were under. Sweat glistened on his dark brown skin, and muscles bulged in his calves. His lazy eyes made him look half awake, like you were the first thing he saw in the morning. Jesse spread out on the blanket they were sitting on and threatened to charm Rhonda right out of her panties. But it was Tess he could hardly take his eyes off of.

"So, *Best Friend*," he teased. "Why you being so quiet, girl?"

"I'm not," Tess spoke up before Rhonda had a chance to. "I'm just—"

Rhonda shot an evil glance her way, and Tess almost gave in to it, but then she looked back at him, and all that best friend stuff disappeared in a puff of smoke. He was too fine, and it was every woman for herself as far as Tess was concerned.

"Just what?" he asked playfully.

"She was just about to leave," Rhonda interjected. "Ain't that right, Tess?"

Jesse grinned. "Oh, say it ain't so, Best Friend. Not when we were just about to embark on a meaningful relationship."

"Don't you have to leave, Tess?" Rhonda asked frantically.

Tess shook her head no and locked eyes with Jesse. "Nope. But you can go if you want. I'm fine right here."

Needless to say, Rhonda did leave and took her half of the best friend collaboration with her.

"So what brings you up here?" Tess asked the question.

"The military. Army."

"How long you here for?" Tess asked.

He shrugged. "I'll be here for three and a half years. Then, I don't know what I'm going to do."

He never left. And here the two of them still were, acting like strangers most of the time.

She used to sneak out of the house to see him. Tess lied to her parents, sisters, and some of her friends just so that she could get away with spending time with him. Back then, he was full of sweet talk, sweeter actions, and the sweetest love. Three months after they met, Tess found out she was pregnant, and shortly after she graduated the two of them went to the justice of the peace and got married.

Tess's thoughts drifted back to riding in the car next to him, passing familiar streets on the way to the house.

"What's on your mind?" he asked quietly.

She sighed. "Nothing much."

Jesse chuckled. "Liar. And not a very good one either."

She looked at him. "What's that supposed to mean?"

"I recognize that look on your face." He glanced at her and smiled. "You were thinking back to when we got married."

Tess was shocked but not surprised. That's how it was sometimes between them. Jesse would instinctively know her and she would know him, and every now and then, it mattered. "That was such a long time ago."

He nodded. "It was, and it wasn't."

Tess went back to staring out the window. "So much has happened since then."

"Yeah." Jesse took a deep breath, and then he did something he hadn't done in years. He reached across to her lap and fondly held her hand in his. "But not all of it has been bad."

It's hard sharing a bed with someone without touching each other. Jesse reserved his side nearest the door, usually sleeping with his back to Tess. Tess's side was closest to the bathroom. On the ride home from the restaurant, there was a connection, unnoticeable, unavoidable, and from an emotional distance, maybe even welcomed.

Tess and Jesse lay in bed, staring up at the dark ceiling. Would anybody make the first move, or would someone eventually tire of waiting, and turn their back to the other, quietly retreating to what had become the norm for them?

Sandra's name was the thick air between them, and always stuck in the back of Tess's throat, ready to spit out at him if he did one wrong thing, or said a wrong word. Sandra was gone, though. He'd backed off when she told him to, and all that was left was Tess, his wife, laying here next to him, sending out vibes that she wanted him to make love to her tonight, just for tonight. They'd been married long enough for him to just know some things.

Jesse turned on his side to face her, and warily placed his

hand flat on her stomach. It was a move, a first move, and he ought to know in a minute if she'd accept it or not. Tess waited for a moment, then placed her hand on top of his.

"It's been a long time," she whispered, then looked into his eyes.

Inside Jesse, relief set in, and he moved closer to her. "Too long, honey."

Jesse slid his hand from underneath hers and pushed it under the covers. He found the hem of her gown, and slowly slipped his hand up her thigh, past her panties, and followed the trail to her bare breast. He hadn't touched that breast in forever, he thought, fondly, for a moment. It wasn't as big as Sandra's, or as firm, but he knew every inch of it, how it tasted, how it responded to his touch. Jesse grazed his thumb over her nipple, slowly, back and forth, feeling it swell hard and round. Even with that, Tess moaned, and reached for him to climb on top of her. He helped her out of her panties, then slid out of his shorts, quickly, surprised to see how hard he was, and wondering when that might've happened.

"I need you, Jesse," Tess was breathless, and convincing, and all of a sudden, intoxicating. He realized that he needed her, too.

She was waiting for him when he rolled on top of her. Tess's thighs were spread wide, her back arched. It didn't take long for him to ease into her, and when he did, both of them seemed to breathe a long awaited sigh of relief from having waited so long to do this. There was nothing in the world better than sweet-hot pussy, he thought, closing his eyes, and nestling deep into this place that belonged to him. No man had been here but Jesse. He was Tess's first, and he'd be her last. Pride swelled in him at the thought.

T*hat's it, baby,* she said, softly in his ear. Jesse felt her fingers dig into his broad back, her legs wrapping around his to hold him in place. *Put it right there. Right there.* And he did, too. He put it there, then lay still, savoring the victory of her pulsing against him, getting wet all over him. *Don't you dare hurry, Jesse,* she commanded seductively. *Take your time with me. Take your time, until you hear me scream.*

He looked down into her eyes, staring up at him, and even through the darkness, they sparkled, inviting him to see her passion. The kind he'd never known in another woman, before. The kind—he'd never known at home.

He wanted to say her name, but he'd learned not to. *Sandra* raised the roof in his world. It tore holes into his foundation and wreaked hell in his house, so he learned never to say her name, when they made love. But he wanted to, so much sometimes, he nearly choked on it.

Sandra made slow, wide circles with her hips, forcing him to move before he was ready, but she felt so good, he couldn't help himself. She put her hand on the back of her neck, with the other, she gathered her full, round, brown titty. A dark brown, almost black, nipple jutted up at him and made his mouth water. *Sandra* pulled his head to her breast, and filled his mouth with it. Jesse sucked, licked, flicked his tongue back and forth against it. He pushed slow, and deep in and out between thick thighs, relishing in the juices spilling out from this woman, making him wet all the way up to his stomach.

Oooooh! She moaned, her eyes, closed, her head back, hips pushing back against his. *That's it! That's it, baby! Awww Jess—! Oh Jesse! Oh—Jess!*

Jesse felt himself swell even more inside her. His cock felt like a rock, solid and stiff, engorged with the sensation of her, of all of her—her scent, her touch, her nipple, her hair, her voice, the sound of her voice—

Oh Jesse!

Sandra!

Jesse—yes!

Sandra, baby!

Jesse! Don't stop! Please! Don't—

Tess? Jesse suddenly came to his senses, and realized, that it was Tess's voice he heard call out his name. It was Tess's pussy he'd lost himself in, not Sandra's. Tess's legs were wrapped around him, and it was her small breast, not Sandra's, he'd been sucking.

Jesse's pace quickened. He could feel his hard on shrinking, taking his desire right along with it. He'd wanted Tess. For sure, he'd wanted his woman, but even now, Sandra snuck in, and put herself between them, and had taken him away from his wife.

Jesse raced to finish, hurrying to meet his small orgasm before it was too late. He shuddered, and wearily lifted himself off of Tess, rolled over to his side of the bed, and shut his eyes.

Drive-by sex. What started out as a passionate and heated session of love making quickly crashed and burned into nothing more but a pathetic orgasm for Jesse. Tess lay stunned that in a matter of minutes her husband had transformed from the lover she needed into a man who had no interest in her whatsoever. She'd have had to have been deaf, blind, and crazy to have missed it.

Tess quietly climbed out of bed and went to the bathroom to wash up, feeling like she'd been pissed in. She stared at her reflection in the mirror, and saw dissatisfaction staring back at her, and knowing, instinctively, that for a moment, he'd forgotten who he was making love to. For a moment, he'd looked at her, the way she always wanted him to, like she mattered. Like her needs mattered, too, and like it was his mission in life to satisfy those needs. Recognition filled his eyes, like he'd just woken up from a dream, and resented that it was only a dream.

Tess came out of the bathroom in time to hear him lightly snoring. She slipped into her robe, went downstairs to the kitchen to make a cup of tea, and cried.

"*You want to talk* about it?"

He'd almost forgotten she was there. Sherry rode next to Jay in the SUV, staring out the passenger window. Rain came down in buckets, and he wasn't in the mood to go to any housewarming parties.

"Talk about what?" he answered halfheartedly.

"I know you don't want to go to this thing. But Reggie's going to be there, too, and other women are bringing their husbands along."

"So?" Jay remarked flippantly.

She looked at him for a moment, then rolled her eyes back toward the window. "So—the least you can do is fake the funk when we get there, Jay. Don't act like I dragged you out kicking and screaming by your heels."

"I told you I don't mind going," he snapped.

"Please," she sighed. "You've had a bug up your butt ever since I mentioned it. Come to think of it," she muttered, "you've had a bug up your butt longer than that."

"What's that supposed to mean?"

"It means," she said definitively, "that your attitude is beginning to show, Jay."

He looked at her. "No more than yours."

Sherry smoothed her long locks back behind her ears. She was such a beautiful woman, with pretty, smooth, dark skin and exotic almond black eyes. Sometimes, it was hard not to stare at her. And not just for him, either, but most people stared at Sherry, especially when she was dressed up. Tonight she was casual, but she'd opted to wear something besides a pair of faded jeans, and he couldn't remember the last time he'd seen her in anything that wasn't big, baggy and hospital pink.

Sherry wore a black skirt that came down just below her knees, some low-heeled mules, and a fitted orange low-cut blouse. He always liked her in bright colors. She'd always been shapely, but slim. The biggest thing on her was her ass. Titties weren't much more than a thought on Sherry.

"We've been working too hard," she mumbled indifferently. Jay wasn't sure if she was talking to him or not.

She looked at him when he didn't respond. "Maybe we should take a vacation. Just the two of us. Leave the kids here."

Jay's mind had wandered off to Millington.

"We keep saying we need to get away for a few days. We could drive down to the Gulf for a few days. It's not much, but—"

He'd left several messages for Elise, but she hadn't called back. He'd left them at her apartment, on her cell phone, at her office.

"We could see if we could find something cheap in Mexico," he heard her say. Jay felt himself shrug.

"Yeah, we should check it out." His voice came from some faraway place outside that car.

Where the hell was she? He wondered, growing angrier and more worried by the mile. It wasn't like Elise not to call him back. Unless . . . unless something was wrong.

"The kids could stay with Mom and Dad for the weekend."

"They hate staying over there."

"Well, we won't ask them to stay, we'll tell them they don't have a choice but to stay," she laughed.

He nodded and smiled.

A vision flashed across his mind of the brotha at the bar that night, all up in Elise's face. Before Jay'd arrived, she'd been enjoying his company, much more than she let on. What if . . .

Jay clenched so tight to the steering wheel his palms started to sweat.

"It's hard sometimes, Jay," Elise's soft eyes watered. "I wish we could see each other more."

Me too, baby, but . . .

"I get so lonely when you're not here."

I know baby, but . . .

He hadn't seen her in a week. Plenty of time for brotha man to . . .

In his mind's eye, Jay saw the whole thing unfold: the brotha leaning in close, holding her hand in his, smiling that Kool-Aid smile, wearing his cheap-ass suit, and saying all the right things. Elise smiled back. She pressed her full breasts against this dude's arm. Brotha got an eyeful, and smacked his lips. Then he'd say something dumb and ghetto like "Why don't you and me hook up and do something boo?" Smack his big nasty lips, and rope her in with them, lapping her up from the inside out, with his hungry tongue.

"Jay? Did you hear me? Babe?"

"Huh? What?"

Sherry sucked her teeth. "Never mind," she said frustrated.

"I'm sorry, baby. I just . . . my mind was somewhere else."

"Yeah, lately, it always is, Jay. Anyplace else besides where it needs to be." Sherry sniffed, and he could tell she was trying not to cry.

Instinctively, he reached over and took hold of her hand laying in her lap. "I'm sorry, baby."

"I just feel like we're drifting apart, Jay." She turned to him and he saw the tears pooling in her eyes. "I don't want us to fall apart, Jay. We need to pay attention, baby, the way we promised we would when we first got married. Remember? We said we'd always work as hard at our marriage as we did at anything else."

A warm feeling washed over him. Jay gently squeezed his wife's hand, then lovingly brought it to his lips and kissed it. Okay, now this was real, he surmised in himself.

"You're right," he said sincerely. He looked at her and smiled. "You know I'm a bonehead sometimes, girl," he said apologetically.

"Well . . ."

"And you know how to snatch a black man up when he needs it. Got to do that every now and then."

"And I'm doing it now."

"Good," he reassured her, and kissed her hand.

"*Elise—call me, baby*. I've been trying to catch up with you."

Elise listened to the message on her cell phone, then folded it and slid it back into her pocket.

"This house has a fourth bedroom," she said to the couple touring the new development. "It's not very big, but it would make a great nursery or office."

The couple looked at each other and nodded approvingly.

Her phone vibrated against her hip in her pocket, but Elise ignored it. She knew who it was. He'd been calling since last night, and most of the day, sometimes leaving messages, other times, he'd just hang up before her voicemail answered.

"The laundry room is just off the kitchen, and it does include the washer and dryer."

"Are they leaving the refrigerator?" the woman asked.

Elise nodded and smiled. "I believe so. Yes."

Jay needed a lesson on boundaries.

He was married. She wasn't.

He was pressed under somebody else's thumb.

She didn't have to be.

A sense of defiance ballooned inside her. At first, she'd missed his call because she'd had a late showing to go to. The message he left caught her off guard when she listened to it.

"Where are you? You need to call me back when you get this."

It was his tone, irritable, and his mood, aggravated, that she didn't approve of. Who the hell did he think he was talking to like that? Last she looked, she wasn't wearing his ring, or carrying his baby on her hip. And he sure as hell wasn't paying any bills on her behalf. So no. She didn't need to jump to attention and call him back as soon as she got this.

"The backyard is huge." She held the door open for the couple and led them out back. "As you can see, it's very private, and large enough to add a pool if you wanted."

The couple laughed.

Her phone vibrated again. This time, Elise pulled it out of her pocket and checked the number.

"Do you need to take that?" the man asked.

Elise looked at him and smiled, then put the phone back in her pocket. "It can wait."

She wasn't his property or his ho. Jay had no room to make demands on her time. He needed to realize that. She'd call him back when she was ready.

"Elise, baby. I need you to call me back. I'm worried about you."

And that was a good thing. She smiled, waved to the couple pulling out of the driveway, and then went back to the house to make sure everything was locked up tight. He needed to be worried. It meant he cared. It meant he realized that she wasn't a woman to be taken for granted.

"Where were you?" he said into the phone, trying to keep his voice down. An hour after they'd arrived at the party, she finally called him back. Jay wanted to kiss her and cuss her out all in one breath.

"I'm sorry, baby," she said innocently. "I saw that you called, and I got your messages, but I've been so swamped lately. I've got a dozen clients pulling me every which way but loose, and by the time I get home, all I want to do is crawl into bed."

With whom? he started to ask, but this wasn't the time or place to get into that conversation.

Elise smiled. "I've missed you."

It was shit like that he needed to hear. And it was the way she said it that he needed to hear most of all, like she meant it.

He sighed. "I missed you, too, baby. But you had me worried. I thought something had happened to you," he lied.

"Awww, honey. I'm fine, but it makes me feel good that you were worried. Sounds selfish, huh?"

Jay felt relieved. "No. It doesn't sound selfish at all."

"Am I going to see you soon? Please say yes! Please! Please!" she laughed.

"Ain't shit going to keep me away from you, love. It's been too long."

"It's been a week."

"A week too long."

"You'll see me day after tomorrow." Jay didn't have a run to make, but if he had to pay someone to take theirs he'd do it.

Someone knocked on the bathroom door. "I got to go," he whispered then hung up.

He flushed the toilet, ran water in the sink, then opened the door. Sherry was standing there wearing a radiant smile. "Hi babe. I was afraid you might've fallen in."

Jay laughed with her, put his arm around her shoulder, then went back to the party to rejoin everyone else. He felt a whole lot better now. All she ever had to do was call. That's all.

renee

"Cruise. Cruise. Cruise." Renee's annoyance was obvious. "Ever since I took over this singles ministry gig, the C word comes up at every meeting. How come people can't think more creatively than a cruise?"

"Cruises are nice, Faye said. "Or haven't you ever been on one?"

She sighed. "I've been on plenty—but you been on one, you've been on them all."

"So, a cruise it is, then?"

Renee shrugged. "We voted, and I was outnumbered. So yeah. Cruise. Next August. Galveston. Be there or be square."

"You're a good director, Renee. That ought to solidify you a spot in God's good graces." The sarcasm didn't go unnoticed.

"Personally, I think I've earned my wings or something by now, Dr. Faye," Renee said coolly. "It's been close to nine months since I've had sex, and I know that's got to earn me some brownie points for a get-out-of-hell free card. What do you think?"

"I think you should be proud of yourself, Renee. Abstinence in this day and age isn't easy."

"Yeah, but it's not about abstinence, Doc, or even about being a good Christian girl."

"Then what's it about?"

Renee thought reflectively for a moment, before responding. "It's about quality. It's about not going through the motions of wasting my time or my body on any old schlep just because he's good-looking or buys me a drink. Hell, I'm good-looking and I can buy my own drinks, and I can do myself better than any of them." Renee laughed. "I'm just messing with you, Doc. But you've got to admit, I got you with that one. Didn't I?"

"You sure did."

"The last couple of times I messed around, I ended up with the short end of the stick. I mean, nothing. No orgasm. No hurt feelings. No nothing. I was bored and couldn't wait to get it over with."

"Do you pray?"

Renee stared back blankly. "Why would you ask me that?"

"Because—some of the things that come out of your mouth, Renee, I have to wonder if you're serious or if you're just trying to shock me for kicks."

"A little of both, I suppose." She laughed. "I do get a rise out of you, though."

"Pretty much."

"I'm just saying what I feel and what's real, Doc. Don't tell me you never think about things like good sex or bad sex even. I mean, is it always good with the Reverend?"

"I wouldn't tell you if it was or wasn't."

"Well, I wouldn't expect you to. But, I talk to you woman to woman, Doc. Not woman to preacher's wife. Women need to vent sometimes to other women because we've all been there, and we all can relate. Or, am I barking up the wrong side of the tree with you?"

"You just catch me off guard sometimes."

"Then your life must be perfect."

"I never said that."

"You don't have to, Dr. Faye." Renee stared intently. "It's written all over you."

"You turned your back on this marriage long before we got here, Lewis! You lost sight of this family as a unit, and decided all on your own, that the only thing that mattered was what you wanted!"

"I did this for us! I took this job so that I could give my family more, Trish! More of everything! How the hell does that make me wrong?"

"You didn't do it for us. You did it for you, Lewis. You wanted this, and you went for it, and—"

"And you encouraged me to it!"

"Because I thought we were in it together! I thought you'd ask me, rather than tell me, that we were moving!"

"Semantics, Trish. Fuckin' semantics! I did what I thought we both wanted. I got the promotion; I bought you this house . . ."

"No, you brought you this house, Lewis. I never had a say in that either."

"What's wrong with the house, Trish?"

"You just bought a house, Lewis. You never even consulted me on it. Here, Trish! This is where we're going to live. Never mind what I might've wanted."

"I wanted to surprise you, baby. I wanted to make it up to you."

"Don't give me that crap. Just like everything else these last six months, you took it upon yourself to make all the decisions for the rest of us without even consulting me, your wife, because it wasn't on your

agenda to do so. What you did was selfish and disrespectful! You didn't give a damn about what I wanted, about my career, about Tray having to change schools in the middle of the school year!"

"You can get another job! The boy can go to another school! Why the hell do you insist on making me the villain in all this?"

"Because you are!"

"Because you've lost your fuckin' sense of reason somewhere along the line."

"No, Lewis. Because I lost my partner. I lost my husband and I lost my best friend, somewhere along the line."

He was her best friend as long as he was bending over to kiss her ass. Trish called their marriage a partnership. That's what it had been as long as he'd gotten her permission for something as simple as taking a dump. Lewis sat in the corner of the bar a few blocks down the street from his office, drowning himself in vodka tonics. At work, he was the sunshine boy, grinning, slap happy, dancing a jig, and maneuvering himself into a position at the top of the corporate ladder reserved for colored folks.

A black man's got to work ten times as hard to be considered half as good. His grandfather planted that mantra in his head back when he was a kid, and Lewis's ass had taken it and run with it all the way to Executive VP of Finance in some company that only gave a damn when it came to showing off the fact that they'd filled a quota, and tokens needed love, too.

What should've been a dream come true, was biting him hard in the ass. The side glances and abrupt endings to conversations that came at the office whenever he walked into the room were hard enough to deal with, but he'd dealt with them, because he'd been conditioned to in his life. The side glances and conversations that came to an abrupt end at home, whenever he walked through the door from Trish, were harder to ignore. Seemed to him, she was pissed about nothing, except that he hadn't asked her permission to accept this position and move to Dallas, buy the goddamned house, or make a helluva lot more money than either of them had ever made with both incomes. Trish was the one being selfish and inconsiderate. And he was growing wearier by the day, of trying to make it up to her.

"Lemon Drop Martini, please," Renee said to the bartender. "And make sure you use Grey Goose. That cheap shit gives me a headache."

"Aren't you a lovely sight for sore eyes," a man behind her said. Renee looked up into the face of Andrew Littleton, a former client and an almost lover from an assignment she worked on at least a year ago. He sat down next to her and motioned for her to put her money back in her purse, then handed the bartender a twenty-dollar bill.

He was still a beautiful man, with a head full of thick, white wavy hair, dark heavy brows, and a lovely salt-and-pepper goatee framing surprisingly full lips for a white man. Andrew wore his age like an Armani suit, with class and elegance, and without a drop of remorse. He owned several restaurants all across the Front Range, and Renee had created the décor for all of them, in what had been her biggest, most lucrative assignment to date. He loved her—so he said. "Truly, baby. I do." Good thing she wasn't dumb enough to fall for a lame line like that. As it turned out, Andrew loved a whole lot of women, all at the same time, too.

"I've missed the hell out of you, Andy," she smirked and sipped on her drink.

He winced. "How many times do I have to scold you about calling me Andy? You make me want to spank you when you call me that."

She smiled. "Don't I know it. Another time, another place, and . . . daddy, you could've spanked this ass as often as you liked."

"Now you're just teasing me."

"That's how this game is played between you and me, Andy. I tease, you threaten to spank, and it just goes on like that indefinitely until one of us finally gives up."

"Or in?"

"You're a player." Renee chewed on an olive. "And I don't do players anymore. Got too much shit going around for that."

"That's what condoms are for. Besides, I get tested regularly. Wanna see my results?" He reached for his pocket.

Renee laughed. "I believe you."

"I love black women, Renee. And I love you most of all." His sky blue eyes twinkled.

Fatback's "I Found Love" filtered in through the speakers, and tickled her groove bone. "That's my song, Andy." She got up and grabbed his hand. "Come on and dance with me."

He stood his ground, kissed her hand, and shook his head. "You know I don't dance, but I have no qualm standing here watching you dance, Love."

She smiled, and sauntered off to the dance floor by herself. Ooooh! It felt good to close her eyes and release the stress weighting her down. Renee worked too hard and played too little. She was so good at filling her needs and desires with work, projects, clients, more work, that she sometimes forgot what it was to free her mind and body until it was all void of everything except her soul.

I played around with love before
I was silly and you know that I played the fool

She danced herself into a trance, and floated off someplace far away, guided across the parquet wood dance floor by her hips, shoulders, snapping fingers, and the need to fly and feel sexy. Sexy most of all. She glanced to where Andrew was standing, watching her, licking his lips, every time the hem of her skirt licked her thighs. She'd never been into white men. Thought about it, though, especially with men like Andrew. Renee was hot and so horny she could hardly stand it. He'd wanted to do her, asked her a million times, but she'd said no so often, she wondered if she even knew how to say yes to him. Andrew looked like he had skills, though. Maybe the next time he asked, she should change her mind, and say yes. Maybe she should take him back to her place, and ride high and tight, fast and furious, until there was nothing left, but sweat, cum, a limp dick, and a limp Renee.

Andrew seemed to read her mind, and he made his way to her through the crowd, wrapped his arm around her waist, and led her back to the bar. "Finish your drink, and we can leave," he whispered in her ear. "I really need to get you home, Lovely Woman."

Renee fought the urge to take his hand, and slip it up her dress in between her thighs. She swallowed down her martini in gulps, as anxious to get to him as he was to get to her. She had condoms and he had verification from the health department that he'd been tested. She had verification, too—somewhere. She doubted he'd ask to see it, though.

"Andrew," a woman's voice wafted over to the bar where they were standing. "Andrew?" A petite blonde made her way to him, then looped both her arms around one of his. "I thought that was you I saw," she laughed, and gazed up at him like she was gazing at the stars. "Did you get my message? I called last week. Did you get it?"

He looked at Renee and shrugged.

She looked at him, rolled her eyes, and ordered another martini. That kind of evil can kill a wet dream in a matter of nanoseconds.

Lewis leaned over her shoulder and paid for her next drink, ordered another one for himself, then carried them both over to the table he'd been sitting at for the last hour. Renee followed, no questions asked. It was a moment between them that didn't seem to need words or smart-ass rhetoric or anything to ruin it. So she swallowed her pride, and took her seat next to him.

"Long day?" he asked matter-of-factly.

She sighed. "Yep. Long year."

"Yep." Lewis raised his glass in the air, Renee raised hers, and clinked it with his. They both took long sips, then sat quietly for a few minutes, staring out into the crowd.

She broke the ice first. "So. You come here often?"

"I come often enough. What about you?"

"Same. They make a mean Lemon Drop Martini."

He frowned. "Never heard of a Lemon Drop Martini until now."

"You should try one. They're delicious."

He shook his head, and scoffed. "Sounds like a woman's drink."

"That sounds like a chauvinist comment," she muttered.

"Old-fashioned," he muttered back.

"Same thing," she shrugged.

"Not even close."

Before they could get a good argument started, the DJ decided to spin Maxwell's "Dancewitme," and Renee suddenly reached over and put her hand on Lewis's arm. "Oh, I love this song, Lewis," she gasped, her face lit up. "Let's dance." Renee stood up, but Lewis just shook his head.

"I haven't danced in ages," he said apologetically. "I'm sorry, but no."

Renee looked disappointed, then determined. "Lewis Stevens, if you don't get up off your long, skinny ass and dance with me, I'm going to stand here and scream until they call the cops to come in and drag me out by my heels. Now c'mon!" She pulled at him and pulled at him, until finally Lewis gave in and followed her out to the floor.

"Is that all you got?" she asked, embarrassed that this brotha was barely moving and doing some little two-step thing.

He nodded. "I tried to tell you."

"The good Lord gave you hips, man." She placed her hands on either side of his hips. "Shake 'em! Make 'em work, Stevens! See, like this."

Renee swayed her hips from one side to the other, then turned her back to him, and rolled them around in circles, every now and then, rubbing her behind against his thigh.

It took him a minute, and those vodka tonics had started to

kick in somewhere between sitting at the table, and Renee's full behind rubbing up against him. Something tribal clicked on inside Lewis, and the thumping of the music took root and brought him back to his cultural senses. He placed his arm around Renee's waist, lowered his stance on his knees, and moved his hips, as best he could, to the rhythm of Maxwell's bass. Lewis couldn't help it, he laughed at himself. He couldn't remember the last time he'd danced like this. Or the last time he felt the music coming up through the floor and into him. Renee spun around, raised her hands in the air, and gyrated closer to him. Lewis grabbed her hips, and marveled at how smooth she moved, and how her body seemed to liquefy in his hands.

One song led to another one, and then another, until finally, they both stumbled exhausted off the dance floor, hot and sweaty, over to their seats, where, simultaneously, they both finished the last of their drinks.

Renee dabbed her face with her napkin. "That was fun," she said, breathless. "I haven't danced like that in ages."

"That makes two of us."

"You're pretty good." She smiled at him. "Better than I thought you'd be."

He looked at her. "What's that supposed to mean?"

"It means I didn't think you could dance, and for a second there, you had me worried."

"Well, I thought you didn't like me."

"I don't."

He laughed. "So why'd you ask me to dance?"

"Because they were playing my song, or one of them, and because you needed it as much as I did. I could see it in your face."

"I look that bad?"

"Do I?"

Both of them laughed.

There was no denying she was a pretty woman. He'd seen her come in, and from the moment she'd sat down, men stood around gawking at her, wishing they knew what to say, knowing they didn't have a clue. It was the whole package with women like Renee, he surmised, studying her. She was attractive because she'd convinced herself that she was, long before any man ever opened his mouth to say it. The natural, was a statement of who she was down deep, black and a queen. Her eyes never faltered, should a man dare to venture to lock on, and he'd better be strong enough not to blink first. Lewis made it a point not to stare at the soft mounds of cleavage spilling out from her blouse. She had some pretty titties. He could tell from dancing with her. He'd always had a penchant for breasts, full ones. And that ass of hers practically melted in his hands on the dance floor. Lewis adjusted his collar, and glanced uncomfortably at his watch.

"Wow. I didn't know how late it was."

"Really? What time is it?"

"Almost eleven. I need to be getting home."

Renee gathered her purse and wrap. "Come to think of it, so do I."

"Early meeting?"

"Yeah," she smiled. "You?"

"Yep."

"Do you think we work too hard? I mean, after all, tomorrow's Saturday."

Lewis laughed. "I think we work too damned hard."

On the way out the door, Lewis stopped. "Hey, do you think we can keep this . . . tonight . . ."

"I won't say a word to Trishelle if you don't."

"Thanks. I appreciate it."

"No problem."

"Now about that contract—"

"Good night, Lewis."

tess

"*He didn't call out* her name, but he might've well have," Tess told Faye, sitting across from her.

"You don't know he was thinking about her, Tess."

"I've been with the man more than half my life," she said somberly. "I know." Tess fought back tears because she was tired of shedding them over Jesse. "I keep questioning myself. What's wrong with me? Am I too fat? Too old? Maybe I'm not pretty enough."

"Tess. Beating yourself up isn't the answer. Sounds to me like the inadequacies are in Jesse. Not you."

"I wish that were enough to make me feel better. I have never been with another man, Faye. Never really even thought about it. He was always it for me. The only one I wanted."

"So much has happened between the two of you—it's going to take time to make it right again."

"I don't think it was ever right in the first place." Tess was caught off-guard by this sudden revelation.

"Of course it was. It must've been right at some point."

Tess slowly shook her head. "No, Faye. I don't think it ever was. I think I wanted it to be. Maybe he did, too, but—I was pregnant when we got married. And I wonder all that time, if he didn't just marry me because of that."

"He didn't have to."

"I think he did, though. And I think I knew it at the time, somewhere, in the back of my mind. But all I cared about was having him."

"Did you get pregnant on purpose?"

She took some time before answering, but then Tess nodded. "Yes." A tear streamed down her cheek. "I was so young, but I wanted to be pregnant and I wanted him to marry me. He was in the service and I didn't want him leaving without me." She stared at Faye. "I was such a fool."

"You were young and in love, Tess. Young women tend to do foolish things."

"I wonder if I'm being punished."

"No."

"Not by God, but by Jesse. Maybe even in some subconscious way, by myself."

"I don't think that's the case."

"I trapped him, Faye. He knows it. And maybe that's why he hasn't been faithful. Maybe that's why he's never really been interested in me."

"Tess. You're not making sense."

"I'm making sense, Faye. Jesse doesn't love me now, because

he never did love me." She sobbed quietly. "I trapped him in a marriage he probably never wanted and I used my kids to do it."

"If that's the case, then what about now? The kids are grown, Tess. If he wanted to leave, there's nothing keeping him there now."

Tess shrugged. "Habit. The worst ones are the hardest ones to break. And our marriage is a terrible, terrible habit for both of us."

Jesse's gaze followed plump asses across the floor, and the rhythm of bouncing breasts. Nobody seemed to notice but Tess. The Deacon was drunk, standing in a circle of other drunk men, competing in a visual game of Who Can Spot Fine on a Woman First. Tess sipped on her champagne, and shook her head, disgusted.

"Hey beautiful!" Her son Brian slipped up behind her and kissed her cheek. Brian was the older of the twins. The one who thought Brandon was an idiot for marrying the first girl he'd fallen in love with, and the one who vowed not to get married until the world was almost ready to end. He'd been Brandon's best man, though, standing at that alter next to his identical self, as tall and proud as if he were the groom himself.

"Let's dance." Brian spun his mother around, took the champagne glass from her hand, and led her off to the dance floor to drown in the sea of the dance that never died—the Electric Slide. Brandon and Keisha had gotten caught up in it, too, and waved enthusiastically at Tess, as she found her place in the rhythm.

Brian put on his cool suit, and strutted around that dance floor, trying to impress the young women he suspected were checking him out. Woman Magnet. That's what he called himself, entirely too cocky and self assured. The two were identical twins, but for some reason, handsome looked different on Brian than it did on Brandon. Brian flaunted his good looks, wearing an air of confidence so thick it spilled over into conceit. But Brandon had always been the shy one, the reluctant hero so to speak, preferring to shine the light on the substance inside, instead of the layer of skin covering the outside of him. They were as different as night and day, and as connected as Siamese twins.

Jesse's boisterous laugh from across the room caught Tess's attention. She looked over to see him talking with Brandon and Keisha.

"Twenty-three years." Keisha shook her head, smiling, then wrapped both her arms around one of Brandon's. "That's unheard of in this day and age. Everybody's so quick to get divorced." Keisha gazed lovingly at Brandon. "I hope we can make it at least that long."

"Well, you got to know the secret, sweetheart," Jesse bellowed proudly. Tess watched his mouth move, and saw rivers of bullshit spilling out of it onto the floor.

He counted on his fingers. "Mutual respect, communication, and trust. Love ain't enough. Right now you might think it is because you just starting out in your marriage," Jesse slurred, "but when you've been together as long as your momma and me, son, you learn it takes a whole lot more than love to hold a marriage together. Love is glue. That's all it is. The rest is work."

Tess stared in awe, wondering how in the world he could possibly believe what he'd just said, after all the mess he'd done.

Tess expertly maneuvered her way out of the lineup and sat down at an empty table.

"Whew!" Tess was startled back to reality by a man sitting down at the table next to her, looking like he'd had more than his share of alcohol, too. He glanced at Tess and smiled. "Mind if I sit here?"

Tess shrugged indifferently, suspecting he was one of her new relatives she'd gained this afternoon. "Not at all. I'm Tess." She reached across the table to shake his hand. *Good-looking man,* she thought, studying him. Not overly handsome, like someone she'd stop and gawk at walking down the street. But the kind of handsome she had to pay attention to notice.

"Gregory. I'm Keisha's uncle."

"I'm the mother of the groom." She raised her glass in toast.

The man stared at her for a moment, then chuckled. "Ain't that some shit?"

Tess looked stunned. "I beg your pardon?"

"You don't look old enough to be that man's mother," Gregory said casually.

Tess laughed. "Well, I am that man's mother, but thank you nonetheless."

"You're welcome."

Tess had the advantage of being able to look at him without his knowing. He was a long man, had to be at least six-two, maybe even six-four, she surmised. Lean, bordering on skinny, but not quite, with broad shoulders. Clothes obviously were not big on his list of priorities. The navy blue suit he had on was outdated, and looked as if he'd pulled it out from the bottom of his closet and tried to iron it. She glanced at his hands, and noticed that he wasn't wearing a ring, but that didn't mean he wasn't married. She'd learned that from Jesse.

"Makes you wonder, don't it?" He stared straight ahead and spoke almost as if he were speaking to himself.

"Wonder what?"

He turned and looked at Tess. "Why the hell they feel like they've got to get married. Especially now."

"Is that bitterness I hear talking? Or that bourbon you're choking down?" Tess had also been drinking all afternoon, but it wasn't until her flippancy started to show through that she realized she was drunk, too.

He laughed. "Shit! A little of both."

She stared at him, trying to guess his age. "You're not married?"

He shook his head.

"Divorced?"

He lifted his glass to his lips. "Unhappily."

"How old are you?" She wasn't worried about offending him.

"Thirty-six. Why? I look older?"

Tess smiled. "No. I was just asking. You're way too young to be so turned off by marriage."

"You married?"

"Yes."

"Happily?"

She didn't answer.

"I rest my case."

"I didn't say I wasn't happy," she exclaimed.

"But you didn't say you were either. Happy people can't wait to tell everybody how happy they are. You hedged too long."

She shrugged, and gave in to his argument. "Yeah, well . . . I'm not as happy as some, and not as miserable as others."

He turned to face her, resting his elbows on the table and leaned close to Tess to look deep into her eyes. "Now, what the hell kind of answer is that? You think it's a good one?"

She peered back. "It's the only one I have."

He leaned back in his seat. "Well, it's not good enough. Pretty woman deserves more than to be standing halfway on the line between happier than others and not as unhappy as everybody else. Or—whatever it is you said."

Tess felt herself smile. "You think I'm pretty?" Now she knew she was loaded.

He nodded, without looking at her. "Good-looking woman. Is he here?"

Tess almost didn't hear the last part of what he said. "Who?"

"Your man. Your husband. Father of the groom?"

"Yeah," she said unemotionally. "He's here."

"If I were to jump across this table and kiss you, would he give a damn?"

Tess laughed out loud. "He probably wouldn't even notice."

Gregory laughed, too. "Then don't tempt me. Because I'm drunk enough and you're pretty enough that my ass might just do it."

She shook her head. "You can't kiss me. We're family."

"Yeah . . . right."

Keisha floated over to where they were sitting in her billowy white dress looking like a big, puffy cloud. "Hi, Uncle Greg," she sang, then plopped down in the chair next to him. "You having a good time?"

He took her hand in his and kissed it. "I'm having a ball, Love. And did I tell you how happy I am for you? But if that boy ever does anything to hurt you, I'll kick his ass."

Tess grunted and rolled her eyes. "Hmph! You'll have to get past his momma first."

Keisha nearly fell out of her chair laughing. "I think we need to turn off the champagne machine. My relatives haven't been relatives more than three hours and already talking about feuding." And just as quickly, like a butterfly, she flitted away, and off to another family to light on.

Gregory slowly stood up. "Well, as lovely as it's been talking to you, Miss Lady"—he couldn't remember her name—"I need to get somebody to call me a cab to take my drunk ass home so I can pass out as dignified as possible in my own spot," he turned to Tess and bowed graciously. "Maybe we'll meet again at some family reunion or something."

"Looking forward to it," Tess said, as he was leaving.

Gregory searched the room for someone who would be so kind as to call a taxi for him, or even give him a ride to his house. Nice lady, he thought, leaving Tess behind. She reminded him of someone. Good-looking woman, whose husband took her for granted and didn't appreciate what he had wrapped up all nice and waiting for him. Ah yes! The answer came to him. His ex-wife. She reminded him of his ex, and the unappreciative asshole he'd been to her, just before she told him she wanted a divorce. That's who she reminded him of.

Tess sat back in her seat, and watched him swagger away. Bad suit or not, he'd been full of compliments, and flattering conversation. Every now and then—she thought smiling—she wondered what it would be like to be with someone else other than Jesse. Every now and then, she wished she knew how to do that, just to see. Loyalty ran too damn thick in her blood sometimes, and she wished it could be thinner like Jesse's.

Jesse had gone beyond just fucking around. He'd fallen in love with Sandra. Even if he never said it, Tess knew it. She saw it in his eyes that night she found out and told him to get out. A spark flickered that looked a whole lot like emancipation—and fear. That night she knew, he wanted to be set free, but he didn't know how to be, and she didn't know how to free him.

So here they were, living in a shell of what used to be a marriage, with no memory whatsoever of what it was to want each other and nobody else.

"Who was that?" Juanita slurred, sitting down next to Tess. "He's kinda cute."

Tess shook her head. A little booze and Juanita never did mix, turning her older, responsible sister into a sniveling mess most of the time. Tess studied Juanita, realizing that she was about two drinks shy of a breakdown, sniveling and falling into a heap somewhere talking about "Nobody loves me! I just don't understand why nobody loves meeeeeee!"

"That's family," Tess said incidentally. "One of Keisha's people."

Juanita's gaze stopped on the bar across the room. "I'm thirsty." She stumbled away from the table.

Tess watched her disappear through the crowd. The room was filled to capacity with people, dancing, drinking, and celebrating the union of the young couple. But Tess suddenly felt alone, isolated, and separate, like she was on the outside looking in. She'd let so many years slip past her, watching life unfold from a distance, burying herself in responsibilities longer than she should've. There were so many other things she could've done with her life. She could've gone to college, or started a career for herself. She could've taken art classes or joined the choir at church. She could've done a lot of things besides checking her husband's pockets for phone numbers, driving across town to catch the sale on washing powder and bleach, loading up on that shit like she'd be snowed in all winter. Tess had spent too much time looking for recipes for fancy meals, standing over a hot stove cooking all day, just to have the men in her house turn up their noses and ask her if they could have cereal instead. It had been a lame life—boring, predictable, with every spectacular event being contributed to someone else: little league baseball championships, job promotions, graduations, and weddings. But where were her victories?

Sadness crept over her as she searched her memories for them, but Tess came up empty, just like she knew she would.

There's a spark of magic in your eyes
Candy land appears each time you smile

Jesse held out his hand to her and smiled. "Can I have this dance?" he asked sincerely.

Tess stared up at him, her vision clouded by tears pooled in her eyes. Damn! She stood up from the table, and picked up her glass. "I'm thirsty," she said, then turned and walked away, leaving him standing right where he was with his outstretched hand. Rejection was a motherfucker. Now he knew it, too.

elise

"*It takes me almost* two hours to come to church every Sunday," Elise smiled.

"Well, that's a compliment. But wouldn't it be easier to attend a church in Millington?"

"It would be easier, but nobody preaches a sermon the way Reverend Watkins does," she said, proudly. "My cousin brought me here the first time, and I've been hooked ever since. And I like being able to come talk with you, Dr. Watkins."

"I enjoy our talks, too, Elise. And we certainly are blessed by your gifted voice. You must've brought at least a dozen people to the altar with your solo last Sunday."

"If I were to go talk to someone at the church near where I live, everybody would know my business. Millington is a small town and every body knows everybody or someone who knows someone who knows you." She laughed.

"I know what you mean."

"Jay lives about forty-five minutes from here, I think."

"You think? Don't you know for sure?"

"He lives in Prairie View. I've never been there, though," she said sheepishly.

"You've never been to his home to visit?"

"Not yet," she smiled nervously. "I just haven't had the time."

"How are things going between you and Jay?"

"Oh, better than ever. He told me he can't live without me," she said excitedly.

"Oh, my."

"I could hardly believe it when he did. You could've knocked me over with a feather," she laughed. "But I loved hearing him say it. You know? I knew he felt it, but he took his time actually saying it."

"Obviously, you love him?"

"With all my heart."

"Marriage?"

The smile faded from her face. "I hope so. I would love to marry Jay. I think—no, I know—we'd be good for each other."

"If he's as wonderful as you say he is, then I'm sure you would be. So, I take it you're not afraid of losing him the way you were early on?"

"I'm not going to lose him, Dr. Watkins. He cares so much for me, that it's mind-boggling sometimes. He tells me all the time that he wouldn't want to live without me and how he'd go crazy if he ever had to. I pray for us constantly and I think it's working."

"Prayer and faith, Elise, together work miracles."

She laughed. "Reverend Watkins says that all the time."

"Where do you think I got it from?"

"I see the way you look at him when he's preaching." Elise had a distant look in her eyes. "I love the way he kisses your hand after every sermon. It's so transparent how much he loves you, and you him, Dr. Watkins."

"We've had many wonderful years getting our act together, Elise. And it takes work, like anything else that's important to you. Love is a job."

"Oh, I know. I work hard with Jay, and I know he does the same with me, which is why this relationship is so special and different from any other that I've ever had. In the past, it's been me doing all the work, and one person can't do it by themselves."

"No. One person can't."

"I want what you and Reverend Watkins have. That bond that stands the test of time and that can't be broken."

"Prayer and faith, Elise."

"Prayer and faith, Dr. Watkins," Elise nodded assuredly. "I've got plenty of both."

Jay reached across the table and laced her fingers into his. "What are you thinking about?" she asked. Elise's brown eyes sparkled under the light of the candle on the table.

"You," he answered without hesitation. "And how good I feel when I'm with you."

She smiled. "I wish—" Elise stopped short, shook her head and sipped from her wineglass.

"What, baby girl? What do you wish for? Maybe I can get it for you." He laughed.

She looked thoughtfully at him for a long time without saying a word. Whatever it was she wanted, if it was within his power to get it for her, he would. Jay would swim through lava for this woman. All she had to do was ask.

"I wish I'd met you first," she said softly. Elise swallowed. "I wish you could belong just to me, Jay."

Jay sighed, and leaned back in his seat. He could give her the sun and the moon, but he damn sure couldn't give her a single him. More and more she'd been bringing up the fact that he was married, and making it clear that she was having problems with it.

"Let's not do this tonight, Elise," he pleaded. "We don't

have much time alone together as it is, and the last thing I want to do is tiptoe my way around an argument."

"I'm not arguing." Elise pulled her hands away. "I just said what I felt, Jay. That's all. Why do you have a problem with it every time I do that?"

"Because I can't do anything about it." He leaned forward, and tried to keep his voice down. "Things are the way they are, Elise. You knew that going in, sweetheart." Jay softened his tone, to keep from sounding defensive, but that's exactly what he was.

"My feelings for you were different then, Jay. Things have changed, here"—she pointed to her heart—"inside, and I can't keep acting as if it doesn't bother me. Do you think this is what I dreamed my life would be like when I was a little girl? Do you think I grew up thinking that I wanted my prince to be married to somebody else? This isn't easy for me."

"You think it's easy for me?" Jay rubbed the tired from his eyes and tried to hold on to his composure. He'd been trying to make sense of his feelings for this woman for the last eight months to no avail. He'd been wrestling with the obligation and love he still had for Sherry, while working hard to hold on to what he had in Elise, knowing full well his greedy ass needed to cut someone loose.

"If something were to happen to you, Jay, I'd never know. Nobody would call me up and tell me that you're sick or in the hospital. I couldn't help take care of you if I wanted to."

"Hospital?" He looked confused. "What in the hell does that have to do with anything?"

Elise rolled her eyes in frustration. "It's just an example.

You see me once a week, maybe. But your life is with another woman, Jay. I'm a by-product. An afterthought."

"That's not true."

"Well, that's how it feels to me," she reasoned. "In the grand scheme of your life, I'm nothing but a fly on the wall, at best, and that bothers me." Tears pooled in her eyes.

Aw shit! What the hell? Was she going to cry? Jay shook his head and tried not to look at her. Damn if he wasn't a sucker for tears.

She reached across the table and held out her hands to him. "All I ever want in the world, is you," she whispered.

He held her hands, and leaned in close. "You have more of me than you know, sweetheart." Jay felt his heart melt like the butter on the table he'd spread on his dinner roll earlier.

"Sometimes"—she bit down on her bottom lip—"it's not enough."

Panic shot through him all of a sudden, as Jay strained not to hear what he felt like she was about to say. "What's that supposed to mean?"

Elise paused dramatically, then squeezed her fingers around his. "I don't think I can keep doing this, baby." She lowered her eyes and slowly pulled her hands from his.

"What?" he asked, dumbfounded.

"I need more, Jay." Elise gazed into his eyes. "I need all of somebody. Not just what he can spare, because I want to give him all of me."

No. No, this wasn't happening. She was not cutting him loose all of a sudden. Or, was it all of a sudden? Yeah. It was all of a sudden.

"I don't want to spend the next twenty years sharing a man, when I know damn well that I can get my own. You have a family that loves and needs you, and it's not right for me to tread on that, Jay. It's not right for you not to honor it either. Instead of sitting here with me tonight, crawling into my bed, you should be with your wife." Elise sniffed and blinked. A tear streamed down her cheek. "My conscience can't take it anymore. I'm sick of feeling guilty. I'm sick of wanting something I can't have. I'm sick of counting away six days until I see you again on the seventh."

"Elise," he started to interrupt.

"I'm lonely, Jay. And being with you makes me realize even more, how lonely I am. Because you are exactly what I've been praying for in a man. You are the man of my dreams, and you are the love of my life, Jay."

Jay stared at her with his mouth gaping open.

"There," she said, with finality. "I've said it. I've been wanting to say it for months, but I held back because I didn't want to have to say it or feel it. And I damn sure didn't want you to know it." She sighed. "But it feels good letting it out, and letting it go. I feel like a huge burden has been lifted off me, and now I know that it's all right for me to let go."

If he didn't know better, he'd swear she'd memorized this shit from some chick flick. It wasn't that he didn't believe her. But the whole thing just sounded too damn cliché. Elise had played a role, whether she knew it or not, whether she intended to or not. And Jay had a part to play, too, or else he'd spend the rest of the evening watching this lovely, delicious woman slip through his fingers. He felt like a man drowning in a sea of his wife, kids, a house in the suburbs, his job, none of which he wanted to give up.

Elise made his dick hard. She made his heart soft. She made him feel like he was the kind of man he always wanted to be, but it just never quite fit into the kind of man he'd turned out to be. She was his lifesaver. And every drowning man desperately needed a lifesaver.

"I love you, Elise." The declaration came from some faraway place behind him, and didn't even sound like his own voice. But hell. He was drowning. Wasn't he? He was inches away from losing his hold on her.

She blinked in astonishment.

"If I lose you, I don't know what I'll do," he spoke calmly, deliberately, making sure to enunciate every word correctly. "You are the love of my life, too, baby. Please." He felt a lump form in his throat. "Please, don't do this to me. Please, Elise. Don't push me away, sweetheart."

It wasn't as if life at home was unbearable. For the most part, he was pretty damned content. He had some good kids, and a beautiful, loving wife, when she wasn't overworked and overwrought. But life with Elise made him feel like he'd smoked some of the best weed this side of Jamaica. He floated when he was with her. His feet hardly touched the ground, and admittedly, he was about as bad as a crack addict when it came to that woman. He'd lie, cheat, steal for her, if it meant keeping her in his life. Come to think of it, he'd pretty much done all of those things already.

He held her in his arms all night. She seemed to need him, too. In the morning, she made his favorite breakfast—homemade pancakes, bacon, eggs, and coffee.

"I'll call you as soon as I can," he promised on his way out the door, but not before giving her his patented kiss on the tip of her nose.

"I love you, Jay," she said, one last time.

Jay blew her a kiss, winked, and waved good-bye. "Love you too, baby."

It was easy enough. Harmless. It was enough to make her smile and promise to hang in there with him for as long as it took. And he meant it. In so many ways, for so many different reasons, he meant it.

Her best friend Daria called herself being jealous over this new love Elise had stumbled into.

"I got to admit," she said enviously, "I wish I had a man like that. Somebody who was as into me as this brotha is into you."

Daria had no idea what Elise was into. She still hadn't told her that Jay was married. It's hard not to tell your best friend everything, especially when it was something important enough to split you into two pieces. But secretly, Elise loved being the one, this time, who had something to be envious of. Daria was the one who always had a man around. Elise was the one on the outside looking in, pretending not to be fazed by the attention her friend always seemed to get. But at what cost?

She'd meant what she said to him earlier at dinner. Elise had no business being with a married man, and she'd had every intention of walking away from him that night and moving forward in her life and in her search to find Mr. Right, who happened to be everything Jay was, only single. He'd reeled her back in, though. With words she'd least expected him to say, he'd hooked her like a fish, and Elise wondered if she'd ever be able to get away from him now.

I love you.

How sweet the sound. What he said was sweet, and desperately needed, and undoubtedly painful all at the same time. What in the world was she supposed to do with words like that, from a man like him? To turn her back on them and run from them just didn't seem possible. Not now. And besides, what was so wrong with wading into them and bathing into them, just for a little while at least, until she came back to her senses.

Heartache waited for her at the end of this road, no matter how long it took her to get there, and no matter how many detours she took along the way. The truth was, he'd hurt her in the end. That's how it always turned out. But in the meantime, she wouldn't let it. Until that time came, all she wanted to do was savor every last drop of this man until he was empty and she was too full to care about losing him.

"You said yourself, Jay, you had no intentions of ever leaving your wife," she said earlier.

And he just looked into her eyes, for what seemed like forever, and with a straight face said, "We don't know what's going to happen, Elise, or how this will end up. Let's just take it one day at a time, sweetheart."

He almost had her believing that it was possible. That she wasn't crazy for loving him and that maybe there was more at work here than just fate or heartbreak in the making. Jay had twisted this fucked-up relationship into something beautiful and sparked hope in Elise. Maybe not all the time, but sometimes she had hope that theirs was the exception, not the rule. That it was possible that there was more here, and that God could've had a plan to do the unthinkable and make right what was wrong between them.

We hadn't danced like this together in ages. Teddy held me in his arms. We danced slowly, gliding across the floor like air.

"We needed this tonight," he said softly, gazing down into my eyes.

"Yes," I agreed. "We did."

This was our favorite restaurant. It had the best food, drinks, music, and here was the place we'd both always felt our most romantic.

"But do you think it's enough, Teddy?" I asked, trying to ward off my insecurities enough to enjoy the evening.

"It's a beginning to being enough, Faye," he assured me. "I can only regain your trust one step at a time, and you can only let me—"

"One step at a time," I finished his sentence for him.

Once back at the table, he pulled two airline tickets from his breast pocket and laid them down on the table in front of me.

"What's this?" I asked, opening one.

"Tickets to St. Croix," he smiled. "I think we're about due for a vacation. Don't you?"

"Next weekend?" I couldn't hide my surprise if I wanted to. "But Teddy, that's such short notice. What about the sermon next week, meetings . . ."

"I'm trying to save my marriage, Faylene Watkins. I think the church will be fine one weekend without me."

It still felt odd sitting across from him after all that had happened.

We'd come through a storm and the effects of it still lingered on us both. I'd promised him I'd try after he assured me he still wanted to. But it still wasn't easy putting the affair behind me and acting as if it never happened. I'd asked him once, why he didn't leave me for her. After all, we have no children, and both of us are self-sufficient enough to support ourselves.

"Because you're my wife, Faylene. I made a terrible mistake in judgment when I slept with that woman, but that's what it was. A mistake. Losing you would be like cutting off my right arm and I'm right-handed."

Teddy and I were a team. One without the other just didn't feel natural. We'd been broken, but now it was time to mend. And it would take both of us to make that happen.

"I'm excited about going if you are," he smiled.

"Of course I'm excited," I smiled back, elated at the thought of getting away from everything for some fresh air, blue water, and alone time with my husband.

Instinct is more powerful then we are sometimes. Like animals, some processes are automatic and played out subconsciously. Marie, our housekeeper, had been given the day off. Teddy was at the church, making last-minute changes to his schedule to free up time for our trip, and I was home alone, sorting through a load of laundry to wash. I thought about the upcoming trip and of all the things we'd planned to do while we were there. I recalled our romantic date the night before, where Teddy held me in his arms, and our bodies automatically fell into the rhythm of one while we danced.

Darks in one pile.

Whites in another.

"It was a fling, Faye. Not much more than a one-night stand. I don't know! I don't know! It just—happened."

And without even thinking, I find myself sniffing my husband's dirty drawers, one after another. I smell my husband in his dirty underwear, and then—I smell someone else, too, mixed with him. And it's not me.

That mothafucka lied!

who are all
these children
all dressed
in red?

The truth is, I don't know why I'm so mad." Trishelle and Renee were out on a shopping excursion looking for artwork to hang in the formal living room. They'd spent all morning down in Lamar Square, perusing art studios and designer furniture stores for something that worked well with Renee's old-world theme, but that was eclectic enough to stand out and draw just enough attention to itself to start a conversation.

Trishelle had been venting all morning, going on and on about everything from what she thought of Dallas to how much she missed Seattle, to the state of her marriage. "It just seems like, the moment he was offered this job, Lewis changed. He transformed from my easy-going, low-key, happy-go-lucky spouse, to some pompous, pretentious stiff-necked executive who'd somehow forgotten how to laugh at himself. He turned into a drill sergeant right before my eyes, barking orders, and demanding Tray and I drop everything to follow his agenda. I've been a pain in his ass ever since," she looked at Renee and laughed.

"Is that why you signed my contract without reading it?"

"Oh, I read it," she said indifferently. "And yes, that's why I signed it. To get even, in my own little way."

And brothas had the nerve to accuse black women of being trifling? Renee just shook her head.

"Right now, I think this whole thing has gone to his head. You know? Head of the entire finance division, Mr. Vice President, that whole thing. Back in Seattle, he was the division manager of the 401K department. He was good at it, and it kept him in touch with everything around him. He thinks I don't want this for him, but that's not it. I've always known where he's wanted to go in his career, and I've supported him. And he used to support me in mine. All of a sudden, Executive VP outshined Community College professor and my career became something that could just be ripped up from the ground on a moment's notice, and planted somewhere else later on, when it was convenient for him."

Renee listened quietly as Trishelle continued her rant about life in the interracial couple fast lane. "Skin color has never been more than something interesting to look at to me. When I first met Lewis, I saw a black man, but I fell in love with a man—period. The rest of the world sees a black man with a white woman, and between them, they have a beige son. That's not what we see when we look at each other."

Bullshit! Renee held her tongue. How could they not see it with the rest of the world pointing fingers at it and whispering about it all time? The two of them were swimming hard upstream in the river of de-Nile.

"You can't help who you love, and you shouldn't have to apologize for it either. I can imagine the conversations black women must have about us, when they see me with a man like Lewis. Or what white men must be thinking. Everybody thinks we're wrong for being together. They condemn us even before they've gotten to know us, believing that something as simple as skin color should make a difference in the grand scheme of things. It means nothing."

"I don't agree," Renee finally interjected, relieved to have finally opened her mouth to say something, instead of just letting this woman ramble on and on about shit she didn't know anything about. "Being black, I know the impact color can have in a life. Skin color can be the difference between getting a job, and not getting one. It can affect how you're treated by the police, or scrutinized when you walk through the door of Lord & Taylor's. Skin color, in this country, drew a definitive line in the sand in this country less than fifty years ago that each of us can still slip and fall into sometimes."

"But that shouldn't be the case," Trish retorted. "It's ridiculous."

"Sure it is, but it is the case, and as ridiculous as it may be, it's something that myself and even Lewis has to deal with every single day of our lives."

Trish looked sad, and she shook her head. "Sometimes I hate America."

Well then, take your ass back to Canada, Renee thought privately. She placed a comforting hand on the woman's shoulder and tried her best to look sympathetic, when in all actuality, it was Trish who should've been comforting her.

"Roses." Lewis stood in the living room entrance, frowning. "I told you I didn't want to do the flowers thing," he said irritably to Renee, who was busy rearranging pillows.

"Oh, stop it," she fussed halfheartedly. "It's only a few flowers. Stop whining."

He chuckled. "Whining? Is that what you think I'm doing?" When did he start caring what she thought? "You think I whine?"

Renee caught a hint of playfulness in his voice. "Like a baby."

Lewis had been hovering around acting like a man-child lately, finding opportunity to talk to Renee, looking for some sort of confirmation from her that he wasn't such a bad guy after all.

"Where's Trish?" he asked.

"She said she had to run to the store to pick up something for dinner."

His mother told him something when he first told her he'd asked Trish to marry him. Something he found ridiculous at the time, but now—

She told him, "I can't tell you who to marry, Lewis. But I know one thing. One of these days, you gonna miss a black woman."

He looked at her like she was crazy. "I'm in love for the first time in my life, Ma. It doesn't matter to me if she's black, white, purple, or plaid. There is no other woman for me."

"You gonna miss laying next to black skin, kissing black lips, talking black talk, and a full nappy head of hair. Mark my words, son. It's just in you."

There was something comfortable about Renee. Even when she gave him a hard time, it was familiar, and he understood where it was coming from, and why. More and more, he'd found himself thinking about her, remembering her scent the night they danced until they were exhausted and sweaty, and wondering—too many thoughts he had no business wondering.

"You leaving soon?" he asked nonchalantly on his way across the room, to the stairway that led upstairs.

"Yep," Renee picked up a ring of fabric swatches, and her purse. "I spend way too much time in other folks' house, and hardly any in my own."

Disappointment shot through him. Lewis felt like a kid who had a crush on the girl who lived on the corner. He hated to see her leave, but just then, Trish walked in carrying groceries, with Tray by her side.

The boy whisked through the living room, and past Jay, on his way upstairs to his room. "Hi Dad! Hi Renee!"

"Hey Junior," she responded indifferently.

He was gone before Lewis even had a chance to answer.

"You're home early." Trish stopped to kiss his cheek on her way to the kitchen. She turned to Renee. "Renee? Would you like to stay for dinner?"

"No." Renee smiled. "Thanks, Trish, but I have to go."

Trishelle smiled. "Big date tonight?"

"Yeah. Big date."

With the remote control, a Blockbuster DVD, microwave popcorn, diet soda, and maybe Raymone if he wasn't out running the streets. "I'll see you in a couple of days." Renee headed for the front door. "We'll be starting on the master next week, y'all. So, you'll have to find another love nest for a while, but in this place, I'm sure that won't be a problem. Ciao, people!"

Lewis and Trishelle lay stretched out in bed next to each other.

"Dinner was good," he said quietly.

"Thanks. New recipe."

They'd been angry with each other for months, distant, and unforgiving. The wall between them had grown too tall and wide for them to even acknowledge each other anymore. Trishelle missed her husband, though. Lewis missed her, too.

"The house is coming along nicely," she spoke softly. "It's going to be gorgeous when Renee finishes. I'm so glad we—"

She stopped short, when his fingers brushed against hers.

"I think it's going to turn out great," he said.

"When was the last time we made love, Lewis? Do you remember?"

He shook his head. "No, baby. I don't."

Trish rolled over. "Then that's too damn long."

She dipped her tongue into his mouth, and found a flavor she'd gone too long without—Lewis mixed with Colgate . . . mixed with her. It tasted good.

Trish slung a long leg across him, and then sat on top of her husband, peeled out of her nightgown, and grinded herself against his hardening dick.

"My boxers, baby," he laughed, tugging at his underwear.

Trish smiled and slid off him. "Oh, let me do it." She slid his shorts down his legs, to his ankles, and finally threw them across the room. Before he could say a word, she'd taken his swollen penis in her hands, looked up at him and winked, climbed in between his long legs, and engulfed him into her mouth.

"Oh, shit!" he gasped.

Nobody gave head like Trishelle gave head. His eyes rolled, and Lewis's hips lifted up, then down, pushing himself into her mouth. She flicked the tip with her tongue, licked the length of his shaft, rubbed her hand up and down the foreskin, spitting and stroking, and sucking, have mercy! Sucking the life out of him, rubbing his balls, beating his throbbing dick against her tongue, making love to him the way no other woman ever had or could.

One more lick, stroke, tap, thrust, and he was going to cum. Lewis reached down and grabbed her underneath her arms. "I'm about to cum, baby," he grinned. "You need to stop."

"I want to get on top." She crawled up the length of him, and straddled him, slowly easing him inside her. Trish gasped, and rolled her eyes. "Oh yes! Yes! Yesssssss!"

She rocked slowly at first, finding her rhythm, her groove, adjusting her position until it was finally perfect. Trishelle bucked! She bucked again, hard and deep, arching her back, and thrusting her hips forward against him.

Lewis willed his orgasm to stall. He tried not to cum, but, it had been so long that . . .

"No!" she looked at him. "Not yet! Lewis!" It was too late. Trishelle collapsed on top of him and sobbed into his shoulder. "It's not fair!"

He held her and laughed. "I couldn't help it, Trish. I swear I couldn't."

She glared at him. "You owe me."

He stared quizzically at her. "I'll make it up to you."

"You certainly will," she smiled mischievously. "Right now."

Trish climbed off him, went over to her lingerie drawer, and pulled her purple people eater from the back. She turned to him and flicked on the switch, grinning victoriously at the buzzing sound, her eyes staring in awe of the small extended piece coming from the side of the dildo, twirling in a circular motion.

Lewis had never seen that thing before. "What the hell is that?"

Trish crawled back into bed next to him. "It's what keeps me sane when I'm pissed off."

"What am I supposed to do with it?"

Trish lay back in bed, and handed it to him. She closed her eyes, and smiled. "Use your imagination, baby. And make it good."

"A job?" Juanita turned up her nose. "Doing what?"

Tess looked offended. "Doing what?"

"Is there an echo in here?"

"You make it sound like I don't know how to do anything."

"You don't."

"What the hell ever," Tess said irritably. "I've been working taking care of this house, my family, for twenty-three years. So don't you dare try and sit there and tell me I don't know how to work."

"It's not the same thing, Tess," Juanita tried reasoning. "Who do you think is going to hire you? The last job outside of this house you had was at Dairy Queen, filling ice cream cones in the tenth grade, girl. Maybe you could go back to them. They might hire you." Juanita huffed, and rolled her eyes.

Tess rolled hers harder. *Fuck you, Juanita,* teetered on the tip of her tongue, but she swallowed it before saying it. The thing was, Juanita was right. Earlier that morning, getting a job sounded like a fine thing to do, an admirable thing. Tess had worked herself up into a wonderful frenzy imagining herself all decked out in a business suit sitting behind a desk somewhere making important decisions that saved businesses at the end of the day. Juanita had a way of putting things back in perspective, and Tess suddenly saw her limitations glimmering in her sister's squinty eyes.

"You should've gone to college," Juanita muttered.

How come that woman had to shoot down every idea Tess had? And she always came back with some bullshit, too, to just rub it in, that Tess was an idiot and had no business breathing the same air she did.

"I was too busy raising kids to go to college," she spat back smugly. "In case you hadn't noticed."

"Those kids haven't been kids in years, Contessa. And if you'd gone to school like I kept telling you, you'd have at least an associate's and could go out there and find a little piece of job for yourself."

A little piece of job? Who in the hell wanted a little piece of job? Tess wanted to rule the world, have a secretary, and manage people. Not settle for *a little piece of job.* Juanita was out of her ever-loving mind.

"So I didn't go to college. Lots of people didn't go to college and they have jobs. Jesse never finished, and he manages a whole department. You need to listen to Kanye West's CD," she snapped. "College ain't everything."

"Can you rap?" Juanita asked matter-of-factly.

Tess stared blankly back at her.

"Kanye West can rap, Tess. He doesn't need to go to college. You can't rap, baby." She flipped her hand in the air, emphasizing her point.

"I can do other things, Juanita."

"Like what?"

Tess drew a quick blank.

"You might be able to get a job in retail." Juanita came to

her rescue. "You won't make more than minimum wage, but it's a start."

Tess felt herself shrivel. "Thanks for the vote of confidence," she mumbled out of earshot of her sister.

"And Dairy Queen is always hiring. If I remember correctly, you make a damn good soft swirl." Juanita laughed so hard she had to swerve to keep from rear-ending the car in front of her.

"Look out!" Tess shouted, as Juanita swerved the car, just missing the man on the motorcycle in front of them. He jerked to the right to keep from being hit. The back tire skidded out from under him, sending him crashing to the ground, bike and all.

"Oh, no! Oh, no! Oh, my God!" Juanita stopped in the middle of the street, and hurried out of the car to check on him. Tess followed after her. Impatient drivers behind them honked their horns, yelled obscenities from their windows, and gawked in curiosity.

Tess and Juanita made it over to the man in time to help him to his feet. "Are you all right? Mister?" Juanita tried to help dust him off, but the man slapped her hands away.

"Are you fucking crazy?" He removed his helmet, then shook his head, nearly losing his balance. "Look at my damn bike!" He bent over the machine, and tried to lift it off the ground himself.

Another man came out of nowhere to help. "You all right, man?"

Between the two of them, they managed to lift up the motorcycle, allowing the man to brace it up on the stand.

"I don't know what I—" Juanita stammered and wrung her

hands together the way she always did when she was nervous. "I didn't see you, and—"

"And you damn near killed me," he snapped over his shoulder at her. "That's what you fucking did!"

Juanita looked as if she were about to cry. "And we're sorry for that," Tess interjected, trying to calm the situation. The man had every right to be upset, but he had to see how sorry Juanita was about the whole thing. That had to count for something.

The man turned his anger on Tess. "Sorry. You're sorry." He glared angrily at her. "Sorry almost got my ass smashed into the pavement!" he spat back. "Sorry is going to cost me a couple of hundred dollars to get my shit fixed." He pointed to the damaged motorcycle.

How come he looked so familiar? Tess had seen this man somewhere before, but it took her a moment to place him. "George?" she asked, staring quizzically at him.

The man stopped his tirade for a moment. "What?"

"No," she said, suddenly remembering him from the reception. "Greg! Gregory!"

"Yeah?" he asked hesitantly, uncertain of how she knew his name.

Tess beamed. "From the wedding! A couple of weeks ago?" She pointed between her and her sister. "My son married your niece, Keisha. I'm Brandon's mom!" she said excitedly.

Juanita's tears dried up instantly. "Was he at the wedding?" she asked Tess.

Tess nodded. "We spoke briefly at the reception. Remember? You sat at the table I was at and—"

"Yeah." He sort of remembered.

"So, we're family?" Juanita suddenly wrapped her arms

around his waist, and apologized some more. "I'm so sorry, George."

"Gregory," Tess corrected her.

"Gregory. I'm so sorry." She let go long enough to try and examine him. "Are you sure you're all right? Do you want me to take you to the hospital just to let them look you over or something? Really. I don't mind. And I can wait for you, too, if you like, give you a ride home or—"

"No, really," he said, trying to reassure this fool. "I'm fine."

"I'll pay for the damages, of course," Juanita promised. "Oh. Let me give you my insurance and contact information," she hurried back toward the car to get her purse.

"No, it's cool," he called after her, but it was too late.

"You sure you're all right? Maybe you should let us take you to see a doctor."

"I'm fine." Gregory examined his bike, then determined that it was probably all right to ride it and at least get it home. "Look, I need to get going."

"You sure you want to do that?" Tess asked, concerned. "It might not be safe."

"I'll be all right. Tell . . ." he nodded his head in Juanita's direction.

"Juanita. My sister."

"Tell her it's all good. Don't worry about it." He started up his bike.

"No car insurance?" she asked, knowing the answer to the question already.

He shrugged. "Only a fool would pay for shit nobody expects you to use." Before Juanita could make it back over to the scene of the accident, Gregory sped off on his motorcycle.

"Where's he going?"

Tess looped her arm in her sister's and led her back to the car. "He said to tell you thank you for your concern, and that he was fine, and not to bother yourself with something as miniscule as fixing that old sorry motorcycle of his."

"He did not. Did he?"

Tess nodded. "Something to that effect."

Aw shit! Jay's knees nearly gave way as soon as he walked through the door. Anita Baker's voice filtered through the whole house. *Anita Baker!* A trail of candles lit the way from the foyer and guided his path into the living room. A bottle of wine chilled in a silver bucket of ice, and two tall glasses shimmered against the light of candles flickering on the coffee table.

"The kids are gone," Sherry said softly, seeming to emerge like a ghost out of the shadows, wearing a lacy white bra-and-panty set, underneath a sheer short mini robe that wasn't designed to cover up a damn thing. "When's the last time we had the whole house to ourselves?" she asked, smiling, and sauntering over to the table to pick up the glasses.

She looked damn good, but Jay knew he was in trouble. She handed a glass to him, then stood on the tips of her toes and kissed his lips. Sherry gazed deep and hard into his eyes in a way she hadn't done in a long ass time. "I've missed you, baby," she whispered.

Get hard! Get hard! Please goddamnit! Get hard! He pleaded silently to his dick. Jay forced a smile, hoping it didn't look forced and took a drink of his wine. He cleared his throat. "I've missed you too, love."

Sherry giggled, took his hand in hers and led him over to the couch.

"Sweet love," she sang along with Anita, "Hear me calling out your name, I feel no pain I'm in love."

A rock swelled in his throat, then slowly slid down his esophagus and landed with a thud in the pit of his stomach. She wanted sex. He knew that Anita Baker always meant sex for Sherry. But Jay was bone dry. Empty. He had absolutely nothing left to give because he'd spent it all on Elise who'd ridden him like a horse on her couch just before he left to head back home.

Jay sat down next to his alluring wife, fighting to hold back the tears of disappointment filling up inside him. Candlelight glowed off her beautiful skin, sparkled in her eyes, and made her full lips look delicious. That bra she was wearing was barely big enough to hold her shit in, and Jay could see glimpses of her areolas peaking out over the top, flirting with him, taunting him, and daring him to be man enough to swallow them bad boys whole if he could.

Sherry leaned against him, and held his hand, intertwining her fingers with his. "I know things haven't been all that great lately, Jay," she spoke softly, sweetly. Jay could feel the warmth flowing from her to him. "It seems like work has taken over both our lives, and between that and the kids, we haven't had much time or energy left for each other." She pressed her lips together the way she always did when she felt vulnerable.

Jay silently willed an erection, refusing to give in to a battle he knew he'd probably lose.

She took his hand and placed it flat on her thick, firm thigh. "Marriage needs work like everything else does. Don't you think?"

Jay smiled. "Of course it does."

She slid his hand across her lap until it rested on the inside of her thigh. "When was the last time we made love, Jay?" Sherry stared intently into his eyes. "I mean, really made love, the way we used to?"

Jay swallowed a whimper. "It's been a long time," he said weakly.

She smiled. "Too long."

Sherry straddled her husband, and sat on his lap, then slowly began unbuttoning his shirt. She leaned in close, and gently pinched his lips between hers. When was the last time she'd kissed him like that? he wondered, savoring the familiarity of her. She helped him out of his shirt, and pressed her hips into his. "I need you, Jay," she sounded desperate, and like she meant it.

Fuck! Why the hell couldn't he get his shit to work? Just this once. Please!

She slid the robe down off her shoulders and let it fall to the floor between his legs. Then one by one, she slipped each bra strap off her shoulders and pushed herself up on her knees until her breasts were millimeters away from his face. Jay freed her breasts from the confines of the cups, then flicked at her nipples with the tip of his tongue until they swelled. Sherry was breathless. She always did have some sensitive nipples.

"Oh, that's nice, baby," she moaned. Her hips seemed to take on a life of their own, and started to sway from side to side against his stomach. He reached up and grabbed a handful of bare ass, hoping that would be enough to stir up some heat in him too.

His mind was willing, but . . .

Sherry slid back and began unbuckling his belt. She smiled mischievously at him. "Remember when we first moved in here and we christened every room?"

"Every last one of them," he laughed, remembering that night they fucked from the kitchen to the living room to all the bathrooms, even the kids' rooms, finally ending up on the floor of their bedroom. "Did we do the garage?"

She laughed. "Of course we did. Right on top of the washer and dryer."

"The dryer was on."

"It sure was," she said sensually.

Sherry helped Jay to slide out of his jeans, then his underwear. She stared quizzically at his limp penis.

"Baby," he interjected. "I'm funky, and I need a shower." A reprieve was more like it. Even if it was only for a few minutes.

"No you don't," she said, standing up and sliding out of her thongs. Sherry didn't hesitate to crawl back onto his lap. She kissed him passionately.

Jay gently pulled her back. His mind was running circles around this moment. His dick was soft. His wife was on fire. And somehow, someway, he had to fix this before it blew up in his face. "Wait a minute," he said, trying to sound calm. "I know what you need."

He slid out from under her, then lay her back on the sofa. Jay got down on his knees in front of her, spread her legs wide, then looked up at her in time to see a smile spread across her lips.

"You serious?" she asked.

He nodded.

"But, you haven't done that in ages."

A sense of calm filled him. "Then I'm long overdue, baby."

He buried his face in the hot wet spot between his wife's thighs, and made it a point to give her the best oral sex she'd ever had. She squirmed and moaned and damn near cried. She held on to the back of his head, and bucked against his face so hard, at one point, he thought for sure he'd pass out from lack of oxygen.

To his own satisfaction, getting her off was beginning to get to him, and Jay felt his erection slowly begin to take shape. It wasn't much, but at least, it was something. He hoped like hell he could muster up enough of one to stick it in if he had to. Then he wondered if it was possible for a man to fake an orgasm and have a woman believe it. Just in case . . .

"No!" she almost screamed, pushing his face away from her. "You're going to make me cum, baby."

"That's the point," he said.

"Not yet," she was out of breath. "It's too soon, Jay." She closed her legs and pushed him back. "We've got all night, honey." She pushed him down onto the floor, then got on top of him. "All damn night!"

His hard-on slowly evaporated and melted into a soft lump between his legs. Jay was doomed, and he knew it.

"*I told you, I'm* just tired, baby." Jay lay next to his wife on the floor of their living room, flat on his back. Sherry lay flat on hers. "Driving takes a lot out of me sometimes. That's all."

"Didn't used to," she said, disgusted.

He'd done the best he could. He'd thought of his best nasty thoughts, prayed to God, and even conjured up images of himself with Elise. Impotence was a bitch! That's for damn sure.

And so was having too many women, he concluded. Greedy men needed Viagra. Jay would have to check into that shit.

He reached over to touch her hand, but she moved it away. "Is there someone else, Jay?" she asked abruptly, then looked at him.

The question sent a shock through him. "What?" he asked, surprised. Did she know? Had he slipped up some kind of way? Jay studied her face looking for an answer. "What do you mean?"

Tears welled in her eyes, and she pressed her lips together before probing further. "Are you cheating on me?" Sherry's voice cracked.

Jay turned over to his side, and felt himself slipping into survival mode. He had to save himself or lose everything that meant anything to him. He had to swim or drown, climb or fall, fly or die, man. He had to lie his ass off and hoped like hell he was convincing.

He put his hand underneath her chin, then leaned over and kissed her with all the passion he could regurgitate. Then he stared into her pretty eyes, and swore from his soul. "I would never do that to you, Sherry. You are my life. This family . . . I wouldn't put it at risk like that. No other woman would be worth it, baby."

"Sometimes I just get this feeling, Jay, that something is going on with you I don't know about," she sniffed. "Work's been keeping me so busy lately, and I'm not able to spend time with you and the kids the way I'd like, and I know it must seem like I don't care, but—"

"That's not it, baby." He kissed her softly. "Hell, Sherry, we're only human. We've both been busy lately, but that's not reason for me to go out fucking around. I love you," he said, full of sincerity. He was crazy into Elise, but it wasn't the same as what he had with this woman laying naked on his living room floor.

"I don't want to lose you," she whispered.

He traced the outline of her lips with his finger. Jay's heart opened up to his lady love the way it had the first time he realized she was the one, and every other thought and memory and hint of the rest of the world, faded into the background.

"Will you please let me finish what I started?" He smiled down at her, knowing instinctively that she'd understand what he meant.

She blinked away her tears and laughed. "I was hoping you'd say that." Sherry turned her body to him, and spread her legs.

Jay winked, then assumed the position, determined not to stop this time until the sweet juices of this beautiful woman's orgasm filled his cheeks and he choked.

"*I called you and* told you they were coming," Lewis couldn't believe she was doing this. Not now. Any other time she could disappear from the planet if she wanted too, and it would've been cool, but dammit! Not now!

Trish sat on the side of the bed, tying her sneakers. "You told me, Lewis," she spat back. "That's the problem. You never asked me if it was all right. You didn't even stop to think I might've made plans of my own tonight!"

He was outraged. "Well, what the hell do you normally do on Wednesday nights?"

Trishelle stood toe to toe with him, with her hands on her hips. "If you'd ever bother to ask, to talk to me about more than that fucking job of yours, you'd know."

"They'll be here in an hour," he said frigidly. "My boss and his wife will be standing at my door in an hour and what the hell am I supposed to do? Order a fuckin' pizza?"

She picked up her gym bag and brushed past him. "You'll make it work, Lewis. You always do." Trishelle disappeared from the bedroom. A few minutes later, he heard the garage door open and Trishelle peel out of the driveway.

He stood, stunned, that her ass was too selfish to give up a goddamned yoga class for one of the most important nights in his career since moving here.

"Dad!" His twelve-year-old son stood in the doorway of the bedroom. "Did I hear you say we're having pizza?" The boy was grinning from ear to ear.

Lewis had been driving for at least an hour riding the interstate loop around the entire city, blasting an angry and defiant Eminem the whole time. He'd had no choice but to lie.

"Fred," he'd said to his boss on the other end of the phone, trying real hard to sound believable. "I'm afraid we're going to have to take a rain check for dinner tonight." Lewis faked a chuckle. "Yes. Yes, I know it's short notice. Trish is in bed with another one of her migraines." Lewis hated having to lie. He hated that his boss had railroaded him into this impromptu dinner invitation, too, but lying was something he'd just never been good at. "Of course. I'm sure she'll feel better tomorrow. We're definitely looking forward to having you and Lois over. Sure. I'll tell her. Thanks, Fred."

Trish called his cell. Several times, as a matter of fact, but he didn't answer. Lewis needed a drink. He needed to come down off this frustration high fueling him before he exploded.

It wasn't long before he realized that he had to pass by Renee's studio-slash-house on his way to the pub. Lewis couldn't say what compelled him to turn toward her place. All he knew was that he was too pissed to want to sit by himself in a bar, drinking, and sulking and brooding about that mess called his marriage. He needed to take his mind off things, and he needed company. That's all, even if it had to be the decorator's. Shit. It was ten times better than what he had at home.

Renee wore gold wire-framed glasses, balanced on the tip of her nose. Her fro was pulled back off her face, and she wore a white, oversized V-neck man's T-shirt, cut-off shorts, and fuzzy baby blue slippers, holding a half-eaten Oreo in her hand.

She stared at him for a minute before saying anything. "What?"

Lewis shrugged. "It's late."

"It is." For the life of her, Renee couldn't figure out what he was doing standing in her doorway at nine o'clock at night.

Lewis shuffled his weight from one foot, then the other, looking uncomfortable and as perplexed as she was as to what he was doing there. He smiled.

"What do you want, Lewis?"

She was cute, he thought, trying to keep from laughing at her looking like a little girl who'd gotten caught sneaking into the cookie jar. He peered at her, halfway expecting to see a milk mustache across her upper lip. "I came by to pay for the couch. I think I forgot to pay you for that."

"You paid for it already."

"Did I?"

"What are you doing here, Lewis?" she asked, impatiently.

"I just uh . . . well . . ."

"Does Trish know you're here?"

He shook his head. "No. Why should she?"

"I don't know, but you're acting a little suspect to me. Like you're up to something."

"I'm not up to anything," he sighed. "You got anything in there to drink?"

Renee put her hand on her hip and looked him up and down. "I've got plenty to drink. Why you wanna know?"

"Because I'm thirsty," he mimicked her flippant tone. "Or is that it too much to ask for you to just give me something cool to drink?"

Okay, so something was up. She let him in, led him upstairs to her actual living quarters in the two-story house, gave him a beer and sat cross-legged on the sofa next to him. "So, what's up?" she asked, after they'd settled down.

Lewis stared transfixed at the television. "Is that *Desperate Housewives*? I've never seen that show. Is it good?"

Renee flicked off the television. "You wanna tell me what you're really doing here, Lewis? And don't give me that jive about paying for shit because you know how much you owe me better than I know how much you owe me."

"You make me sound cheap." He sipped from his bottle.

"If the shoe fits . . . you know the rest. So, what is it? Is that white woman giving you grief?" Renee smirked.

Lewis looked at her like he couldn't believe she'd said that. "You know, you have a way of overstepping your boundaries in this whole employer-contractor relationship thing we've got going here."

"Oh, *I'm* overstepping *my* boundaries? Tell me, Lewis, *who* came over to *whose* house in the middle of the night—"

He looked at his watch. "It's a little after nine."

"And *who* is sitting on *whose* couch, drinking *whose* beer, pretending he just stopped by to pay an invoice that doesn't exist?"

"Why's it got to be a black-white thing?" he said abruptly. "Why can't it just be a man-woman thing?"

"Because I'm a black woman talking to a black man about his woman who happens to be white. I can't just see a man-woman thing. I have no choice but to see a black man–white woman thing."

"Why is that?"

"Because I'm not a lesbian and I don't have a white man of my own."

"Well, maybe you should get a white man of your own. That way you'd see it's not always about color. Sometimes relationships are just plain shitty for no other reason than it's a relationship."

"Ahhh! So there is trouble in paradise."

"Don't act like you don't already know. Shit, you spend more time with my wife than I do, and I know how you women are. She probably tells you everything about my marriage that's fucked up."

Renee nodded. "Yeah, pretty much."

He looked at her. "So . . . what? You think it's my fault, too?"

"Do I think *what's* your fault?"

"What's wrong with me and Trish. You think I'm the culprit?"

Renee rolled her eyes. "Man, please! Like I give a shit about who's at fault in your marriage with all your problems. Do you think I give a damn?"

"I'm just asking."

"And I'm just saying, the only thing I care about when it comes to you and Trishelle is that lovely house the two of you are living in. Honestly, I think I should be charging both of you more, for therapy sessions. I'm not getting paid enough for all this."

"Oh, you're getting paid for this and plenty more, if you ask me."

Renee laughed. "But I'm worth every dime," she said coyly.

Lewis took another swig of his beer.

"So what happened? You being a self-centered bastard again?"

He nearly choked. "Is that what she said about me?"

"Not in so many words, but—yeah. Basically."

"I'm not selfish," he said, brooding. "Shit, I'm just trying to make the transition. I'm trying to do what I have to do to take care of my family, make a better life for all of us. What's wrong with that?"

Renee shook her head, and looked at him. "And that white woman can't appreciate that. It's a shame, Lewis. A shame, I tell you."

"Cut it out! Shit, women period can't appreciate it. She could be turquoise and wouldn't appreciate it."

"You ever miss it?"

"Miss what?"

"Being able to just be you."

Lewis looked at her. "What do you mean by that? I am me."

"Tell me something, Lewis." Renee scooted over closer to him. "What's it like when you go visit your family, and there's a sea of black faces filling the room, laughing, talking, using words and phrases like 'child, please!' or 'Makes you wanna slap yo' momma!' and the savory scent of smothered pork chops, seasoned, tangy greens, hot buttery cornbread fills the whole house, and nobody, not one single solitary soul, seems to notice that you're even there, because you're just like they are? And you don't have to try and sound white, pretend you like watercress sandwiches and polo."

"Trish's family doesn't eat watercress sandwiches, or play polo," he said, smugly. "Sounds like someone's prejudiced."

Before she knew what was happening, Renee reached over, turned his face to hers, and kissed Lewis, lips to lips, tugging, licking, then she slipped her tongue into his mouth, and welcomed the taste of him in a way she hadn't expected. What surprised her most, was that Lewis kissed back.

She pulled away, breathless, and gazed into his eyes. "Don't you ever miss that?"

Wake up! she wanted to say to him. No, maybe it wasn't about color, but it was about something—shit, she didn't know what. It was about the fact that he was here, he'd come to her, because, she was the only black woman in his Texas world at the moment, and he'd followed the trail leading to her in his time of need. The brotha didn't have a clue, but he missed his people. He had no idea how much. But she did. And she wanted to reach out to him and wrap him in her arms, hold him tight against her bosom, and scream at the top of her lungs, *The wayward son has returned y'all! He was lost, but now he's found. Sistahs rejoice! Another lost sheep has returned to the flock!*

"I need to go," he said nervously. Lewis bolted to his feet, gulped down the last of his beer, and hurried toward the door.

All of a sudden, Renee realized she'd been high on Oreos and soy milk, and scanned her memory for stipulations in the contract that said she could be terminated for coming on to her employer.

"Okay." She chased him down the stairs. "Forget that that ever happened, Lewis! I was wrong, and I'm sorry for doing that, and—oh please don't fire me, man! I'll be finished with the house in a few weeks, and it's going to look good, Lewis! So good! But I really want to finish and I'll never lay another hand on you again for as long as I—"

Lewis stopped abruptly, then turned to her, pulled her to him, and kissed her passionately, backing her up against the wall, and pressing his body hard against hers. Then, just as suddenly, he stopped, swung open the front door, and adjusted the hard on in his pants. "Yeah," he said, out of breath. "Sometimes, I do miss it."

Lewis closed the door behind him, leaving a stunned Renee plastered against the wall, fucking speechless.

Receptionist needed for busy doctor's office.
10-key by touch. Typing 40wpm.
Must have previous experience.

Cashier wanted.
Must be able to start immediately.
Prior retail experience required.

Everybody wanted experience, or someone who could type or who had college degrees. Tess had been searching the want ads all morning, and come up empty. *What in the world have I been doing all these years?* she wondered regrettably. There was a time when it seemed she had the power to rule the world, raising twin boys, maintaining a household, making sure the bills were paid, the house was clean, meals were prepared. Tess felt like she was running around like a chicken without a head most days, running to football games, PTA meetings, tending to her garden, Jesse's needs, the boys' needs, doing everything for everybody, except for herself, and now, she realized she'd neglected herself to the point of ending up helpless and handicapped. She stared disappointedly at the newspaper scattered in front of her, knowing full well there was nothing in it she was qualified to do, except perhaps, to make a damn good soft swirl.

The phone rang. Juanita must've had ESP because it was her calling. "Yes," Tess said, halfheartedly.

"Tess, it's me."

"I know it's you."

"Look, I'm on my way to work—but I was wondering, have you heard anything about George?"

"George?"

"You know who I'm talking about, girl. The man on the motorcycle. I've been worried sick about him ever since it happened."

"Oh, Juanita, I'm sure he's fine."

"But have you heard anything?"

"No. I haven't."

"I just keep thinking about Uncle James, and how he thought he was fine after he fell off that ladder. You remember that?" Juanita sounded a bit panicked.

"That was years ago."

"Yeah, but he lay down and didn't wake up, Tess. It happens all the time. People think they're fine, and it turns out that they're not. I'd never forgive myself if anything happened to that man."

"Well, if I hear anything, I'll be sure to let you know."

"Can you at least get his phone number for me? I'd just like to call and make sure he's okay."

"Juanita," Tess started to protest. Motorcycle Man didn't seem worthy of all this worry Juanita was doling out on his behalf. He'd probably grunted a few choice cuss words intermixed with her name as he sped off on that thing and could've cared less how she felt.

"Please Tess. If you could just ask your daughter-in-law for his number for me? I just need to be sure. Please."

Tess hung up the phone then reluctantly called Keisha. "Hi, Keisha. I'm fine dear, and you? No. No, I'm not calling for Brandon. I need to speak to you. I'm wondering if it would be possible for you to give me your Uncle Gregory's phone number. Yes. I met him at the wedding. Why? Well, sweetheart, as it turns out, your Aunt Juanita and I were in her car. Uh . . . she was driving. Yes. It was her car. And while she was driving, she ran your uncle off the road, and . . . yes. He was on his motorcycle, but, no, she didn't quite hit him. Oh, he fell over, skidded about fifteen feet, and was a little scratched up, but we managed to help him up. I don't know, Keisha. He refused to let us take him to the hospital—baby, I just need his number so—no, he drove off on his motorcycle—Keisha! His number—please."

Tess felt like an idiot standing at that man's door. Keisha insisted that he was "between" jobs right now, and would probably be home. Thank goodness the girl had offered to come along. According to Juanita, over the course of two days, she'd called several times, left messages, and hadn't heard from him all day. She painted a vivid picture to Tess of Uncle Gregory sprawled out on his living room floor with a face, swollen and purple like a plum, and blood oozing from his ears.

"Just go check on him, Tess," Juanita begged. "If he answers the door, you can leave. But if something's wrong—"

"I know," Tess finished her sentence for her. "You'll never forgive yourself."

If he was *between* jobs, maybe he was just out looking for one. That's what he should've been doing, anyway.

He lived in a small house off Jupiter Road, near Lochwood Park. Underneath the carport were his motorcycle, and an old Mustang up on blocks, with the hood up, with a rusty toolbox sitting off to the side. The yard was a mess, with weeds growing wild all around the house, and a tree that looked as if the wind blew too hard, it would blow over and crush that little house to pieces.

Keisha knocked tentatively on the door. "I'm sure he's all right," she said, sounding more like she needed to reassure herself than Tess.

Tess smiled. "I'm sure he is, too."

Gregory eventually answered the door, wearing a do-rag, an old T-shirt she was sure was probably white years ago, and jeans low and loose around his waist. A cigarette dangled from the corner of his mouth as he squinted through the smoke at Keisha and Tess.

Keisha looked so relieved. "Hi, Uncle Greg." The girl flung her arms around his neck and held on for dear life.

Naturally, he looked perplexed. "What's up, Keisha?"

"I'm just glad you're all right."

Tess could hardly keep from rolling her eyes. The child was still young enough to be melodramatic, which meant, she probably had no business being married either, but, that was neither here nor there. She was relieved he was all right, too, and more than perturbed that Juanita had wrecked her nerves about this man over the last two days.

Gregory looked at Tess, seemingly oblivious as to who she was.

Keisha stepped back and reintroduced her. "You remember Miss Tess, from the wedding?"

The look on his face reassured everyone that he didn't.

"My mother-in-law," Keisha reemphasized.

No. He didn't remember. So Tess decided to make it easier for him. "We met again at the scene of the crime the other day?"

"Crime?"

"Yes," she said, clearing her throat to hide her annoyance that this man's memory wasn't any better than this. Hell, if she could make the effort to remember his tired behind, how come he couldn't do the same? "My sister ran you off the road and about killed you on that motorcycle not two days ago." She wanted to ask if he was drunk, but the innocent admiration on Keisha's face, begged her not to. "Don't you remember? Or, maybe, you've got a concussion."

The glint in his eyes recalled the memory, and he smirked. "Yes, I remember. And no. I don't believe I have a concussion."

Uncle Greg was fast turning out to be one of Tess's not so favorite people. Tess sized him up standing in that doorway. Was she the only one that noticed he hadn't bothered to invite them inside? "My sister Juanita called and left several messages to see how you were doing?" she said smugly.

"Did she now?" he asked sarcastically. "When?"

"When—what?" Her frustration was starting to show through, and rain all over Keisha's sweet parade.

"You sure you're all right, Uncle Greg? Did you see a doctor?"

He started to respond, but Tess took the liberty of responding for him. "No. We offered to take him, but he refused."

Greg smiled, wickedly. "That's because I didn't need to see a doctor, but I appreciate yours and your sister—?"

"Juanita."

"Juanita's gracious offer. As you can see"—he spread his arms and took a step back—"I'm alive and kicking. Just the way I was before the two of you ran me off the road."

What the— "Look, we tried to—" Tess was suddenly livid. The audacity of this man to gloat in her face when she had taken the time to come all the way across town to see about him was infuriating.

Keisha tactfully stepped in. "I'm glad you're all right, Uncle Greg. We'll be leaving now." She gently took hold of Tess's arm and led her back toward the car. "Take care!" she called back to him. "Oh, and Brandon says hello."

Uncle Greg stood in the doorway, grinning back at Tess. And then, just before she turned away, the son of a bitch had the nerve to blow her a kiss!

"*You sound strange,*" *Elise* said into the phone.

Jay responded absently. "Do I?"

"What's wrong?"

"Nothing, baby girl," he sighed. "Just tired."

"What time you getting here?" She didn't bother to hide the excitement in her voice.

He didn't answer.

Elise frowned. "Jay?"

"I'm heading west this trip, Elise. So, I'm not coming through this time."

"Oh," she said, disappointed. Well, what about on the way back?"

"Not this trip," was all he'd say.

"All right. Next time, then?" she tried to sound hopeful.

"Yeah. Next time for sure."

"He's not coming?" Daria asked, looking smug. She plopped down on the love seat and crossed her legs in the chair, nibbling on the handful of Lays potato chips she'd gotten out of the kitchen.

"Not this time," Elise said, trying to hide how disappointed she was. "He's got a shipment to take back west."

Daria just looked at her for a minute, and must've decided that it was the perfect opportunity to gloat. "Donny asked me to marry him," she said matter-of-factly. Elise wasn't the least bit surprised. Donny, Daria's latest man of the hour, was madly in love with her, which was evident by all of Daria's footprints on his back from letting her walk all over him. "And I said yes."

"What?" Elise asked, stunned.

Men proposed all the time to Daria. And she usually turned them down. Every once in a while, she'd hedge and say she'd think about it. But in her world, there was always someone better lurking just around the corner that she was waiting on.

She smiled. "Don't look so shocked, girl. I love Donny."

"Since when?"

"Since . . . hell, I don't know. I just do. We're going ring shopping tomorrow. Wanna come help me pick one out?" She winked. "Get some ideas for when your man pops the question."

Her man?

"I didn't think you cared about him like that."

Daria sighed. "I care. And I'm tired of waiting for something better to come along, when the best is always as good as it's going to get at the moment, and besides, he loves me. He wants to marry me. He's good to me. He's not married, or gay, he's got a good job, and he loves me. Did I say that already?"

Daria's words ricocheted around the room, bouncing off the walls and pinging Elise upside the head.

He loves me.

. . . got a good job.

. . . not gay.

. . . not married.

"Get out your best maid-of-honor shoes, girl. You know me. I like to do it big, and I'm going to need all the help I can get." She laughed. "Remember that gown Tara wore at her wedding? The ivory one with the long train? I think I want my shit to wrap around the whole block. And we don't have much time. The wedding's in two months."

Elise was shocked. "Two months! Why so soon?"

Daria shrugged. "I need to walk the aisle before I start showing."

"Showing what?" she asked, dumbfounded.

Daria cocked one eyebrow and glared at her.

Suddenly, Elise understood. "You're pregnant?"

"Hello!" she raised her hand in the air. "Yes. I'm pregnant. A little over a month."

Elise's mouth hung open.

"Oh, don't give me that look," Daria said irritably. "And close your mouth, E, before something flies in it."

"You're marrying him because you're pregnant? What kind of shit is that, D?"

"What do you mean what kind of shit is that? It is what it is." She rolled her eyes. "And besides, he's excited about it."

"But that's not a good reason to get married. You've got to be in love, and—"

"I told you he loves me."

"But you don't love him."

"Elise! We are not in the seventh grade anymore, girl. I love Donny. He's a great guy. Would I have married him if I weren't pregnant?" Daria hesitated before answering. "Maybe not as quickly. But I dig him. I love him," she said, emphatically. "And I'm looking forward to being his wife."

"But—"

"But nothing. Look, why don't you just chill and be happy for me. Stop trying to create problems where there aren't any. He and I are going to do this, and it'll be fine. And when you and what's-his-name get ready to handle your business, I'll return the favor," she shrugged. "I'll be the best damn maid of honor on the planet."

"Matron of honor," Elise corrected her.

"What?"

"You'll be married. So you'll be the matron-of—"

"Well, whatever. But you'd better hurry up. This baby is due in November, so if you don't do it by September, you'll have to wait until after the first of the year."

Daria was a lost cause. She didn't know what it meant to appreciate real love. Too many brothas had filled her head with shallow shit, about how good she looked. And honestly, she'd gotten lost in the whirlpool of all that to the point that she wouldn't know love if it came up and spat in her face.

She'd stayed long enough to give Elise a to-do list as long as her arm. Elise sat up a while longer trying to make sense of the madness of this shotgun wedding, then finally, turned off the light and went to bed.

A million times, she'd come close to telling Daria the truth about Jay. And a million times she'd changed her mind, and stopped short, fearing Daria's snub and bullshit opinions. Jay was married, and that was the problem, a problem she still believed was a test to the depth in her love for him. Elise had always wanted to love and be loved unconditionally. There were moments when she felt she was being tested on just how much she wanted it. There were moments when it was hard loving him, and she loathed herself for going there. Right and wrong waged war inside Elise all the time, condemning and convicting her, and that's usually when he'd show up, looking good and smiling at her in the doorway, with his arms spread wide open, and that twinkle in his eyes.

"Hey, Baby Girl," he'd say. "Damn! I'm glad to see you."

Then he'd grab hold of her and soak her up like he was a sponge.

She was in love entirely too much. Elise knew this. But she never regretted it, and she never would either, no matter what happened.

Daria was playing the game they'd played since they were kids—the One-ups Game. If Elise got a B on the math test, then Daria would shove her paper under Elise's nose and boast, "Well, I got an B-plus." If Daria bragged about her new raise at work, Elise would throw a huge commission back at her, and then go on and on about the benefits and freedom of being self-employed and not having to punch someone else's clock. If Elise said she'd met a nice man at the grocery store, Daria would stick out her C-cup chest, bragging about the slew of men in the accounting department who dropped their pencils when she walked through the aisle wearing her new tangerine cashmere sweater that hugged all her little curves.

Elise had a man, a special man who she'd been bragging about for months to Daria, and everything she had to say about him was perfect, which drove Daria crazy, even though she'd never admit it. So, she came back with the ultimate One-up on Elise this time, and announced her engagement to Donny and her pregnancy.

Elise couldn't help but to laugh. Daria was an idiot sometimes. If Donny didn't know now, he'd know soon enough.

He'd been telling himself all day that it didn't mean anything. And it didn't. The situation just got away from him, and the next thing he knew, he had Renee pinned to the wall, playing tongue hockey with the woman. Lewis found it all quite comical, really. One of those moments that left him feeling surprisingly liberated for a hot minute. It was fun. He'd enjoyed it, but as soon as he got in the car, and made his way home, he'd come to his senses and realized how ridiculous his actions had been and hers, too. Renee was a character. He'd known that from the moment he'd first laid eyes on her with her big hair, tight jeans, and brassy personality. Even if he wasn't already married, she wouldn't have been his type. Nope. Not in a million years could he ever see himself going for a woman like that. The artsy type never did appeal to him. Lewis was the rooted and grounded kind, and it was those same qualities that he found appealing in a woman, too, which was one of the things that attracted him to Trish in the first place. She walked the straight and narrow like he did. They were two peas in pod when it came to their styles and the way they approached life. Every now and then, they failed to see eye to eye, but eventually, they'd both come to realize that they were more alike, too alike, than unalike. Renee—

well, he'd been intrigued. That's all. She'd lured him into a mood, a state of mind, hypnotizing him into stepping outside his nature and tricking him into becoming something else. Not that he could put all the blame on her. Hell, Lewis was a grown man. He let her take him there, willingly, and quite honestly, it was a great ass trip. She kissed good, too. Tasted good, like woman mixed with Oreo. Not a bad combination. Not bad at all.

"Lewis? Lewis—do you have something to add?" Bob Tristan, the COO, was staring right at Lewis, along with a whole boardroom full of executives.

Lewis nervously cleared his throat. "I'm sorry?"

Bob looked confused. "Well, you chuckled, and I was wondering if maybe you didn't have something to add to the slide we were discussing."

"Uh . . . no, Bob—I'm sorry. I had a stitch in the back of my throat, and um . . . excuse me."

"*Do you think I* overreacted?" Trish asked Renee, who was busy hanging the custom drapes in the master bedroom. "I feel like I'm in a constant PMS state when it comes to Lewis and me, bitching from sun up to sun down, about every little thing. Afterwards I feel stupid, until he does something else that pushes my buttons."

"What do you think?" Renee asked, referring to the new curtains. She stepped down off the ladder. "I think they really add the dramatic effect to the room you were hoping for, without being overwhelming, of course."

"They look even better than I imagined they would," Trish

beamed. "And you've done a wonderful job of getting me off the subject."

Renee smiled. "I do my best."

"Are you getting sick of me complaining all the time?" Trish asked apologetically.

Renee shrugged. "Everybody needs to vent from time to time. So, as long as I'm here, you can talk, and I'll just listen."

"If it were up to me, you'd never leave." Trish stared affectionately at Renee. "Like it or not, Renee, you've become one of the very few friends I have here, and I hope that, just because this project ends for you, our friendship doesn't."

Well, what the hell was she supposed to say to that?

Sure, Trish. Oh by the way, I slaughtered your man with some serious tongue action last night after you pissed him off, but, yeah, we can still be friends.

Somehow she managed a sincere smile, followed promptly by a quick and timely departure. Renee drove to her next appointment still trying to make sense in her own mind, where she was coming from last night. It had never dawned on her to get busy with Lewis, but for some strange reason, she managed to get herself worked up in a frenzy over the man, to the point that she'd forgotten that little tidbit.

"I need to get me some," she muttered her thoughts out loud. That's all it was. She'd been without a man so long, she turned into jelly at the first sign of a straight one sitting on the couch in her living room. Hell, it had been so long, that sometimes, even Raymone looked good enough to eat.

It wasn't Lewis per se that she was interested in. And it wasn't like she didn't like Trishelle, white woman or not. Renee wasn't prejudiced, exactly. She just had a deep resentment for brothas who opted to settle down with women outside their race, instead of waiting just a few minutes longer for a colored Mrs. Right to show up and make beautiful little nappy Afro puff–wearing babies with. Trishelle was cool. And the last thing she needed or wanted was to get tied up with a married man. Married men were no–no's and not worth the time of day, and Lewis wasn't even her type, even if he did have a big, stiff hard on that she went to bed thinking about enough to pull out her little battery-operated friend, and work herself up into a foam over.

"Hello?" she asked, answering her cell phone.

"Hello," Lewis responded.

Neither of them said anything for a very long time.

"Look, about last night," he started to say.

"Oh, forget about it," Renee interrupted. "It was nothing. One of those *Oops! My bad!* moments, if you know what I mean?" she laughed. "I think we both got a little carried away, and—let's just forget the whole thing ever happened. Cool?"

Lewis was quiet for a moment, before responding. "I've been trying to forget about it since it happened."

Renee sighed. "Me too. And believe me I'm totally em—" She was about to say *embarrassed*.

"And I can't."

"Can't what?" she asked, taken aback and dreading the next thing that might come out of his mouth, besides *psych!*

"I can't forget about it—or you either, for that matter."

"Sure you can, Lewis. Just remember the neck-swirling ghetto-fabulous sistah you met the first time you saw me, and—"

"Tried that already. Didn't work."

Renee was almost speechless, but then, another brilliant idea came to mind. "Well, what about that funky contract you got stuck with, Lewis? Now that—that shit ought to make you hate my guts."

"Mmmm . . . it should. It should make me want to send a hit man out after your ass. That's a fucked-up contract, Renee, and you know it. How've you been doing business this long with a contract like that?"

"Most people read it before signing it, and there's usually a lot of cutting here, pasting there, until it's actually reasonable. My motto—ask for the stars, and hope you end up with a nice moon or two."

"I want to see you. Bad contract or not."

"Lewis—," she started to protest.

"I'll keep my hands to myself if you will."

"This doesn't make sense."

"No, it doesn't. But oddly enough, that's what I like about it."

Oddly enough, that was what she liked about it, too.

"My place?" she asked reluctantly, regretting it almost immediately.

"Tonight? Trish is going to the movie with Tray."

"Nothing's going to happen, though. We'll just—"

"Talk. We'll just talk and try and figure out why last night happened in the first place."

"I think it's important to know," she agreed, and laughed. "Honestly, my excuse—I'm in heat. But—it's personal, I know."

"Maybe not." It slipped out before he realized it. "I mean, shit—I don't need to go there."

"No, Lewis. You don't."

"Just let me apologize in person. Let me—I think if we talk about it, we'll get it out of our systems."

"Sure. That makes sense."

About as much sense as being desperate enough to kiss a frog hoping he'll turn into a prince. Yeah. Right.

Tess was outside in the yard, gardening when he came home. It was the middle of the week, and Jesse never came home early. The look on his face warned her immediately that something was wrong. He walked out onto the back patio, and sat down in one of the lounge chairs next to the rose bush.

"What's wrong?" she asked. "Jesse?"

It took him a while to speak. Jesse looked like he was searching for something he'd misplaced. "Doc says I gotta come in for a biopsy," he explained, carefully.

"A biopsy? What on earth for?" Tess pulled off her gardening gloves and balanced back on her heels.

He struggled with the words coming from his mouth. With what he'd been told earlier this afternoon from his doctor. Jesse had gone in for a physical a week ago, and he felt fine. But apparently, he wasn't necessarily fine after all. "Said something about PSA levels, and I happened to mention that I'd been having problems going to the bathroom." He stopped.

Instinct took over Tess, and she stood to her feet and came over and sat next to him. She put her hand on his. "Jesse," she said, tenderly. "What did the doctor say? What's wrong?"

Jesse lifted his gaze out over his yard, and tried hard to swallow the words caught in his throat, but there was one that just wouldn't go down. It hung there, like it was caught on something, threatening to choke him. "Cancer, Tess," he said quietly. "He thinks I might have prostate cancer."

Tess had finally drifted off to sleep, only because she thought he had. Jesse lay next to her, wide awake, remembering. He was a kid when his father died. That day at the funeral seemed as clear to him now as it had thirty years ago, and the image of his daddy, big and strong, laying up in that casket like he was sleeping, still sent a shiver up his spine.

"Don't y'all close that top on him!" his momma yelled. Aunt Freida held on to her, arms and legs flailing, tears streaming down her face, her hair wild all over her head. "He ain't leavin' me! He told me he ain't leavin' me!"

"He gone, Marlene! Let him go!" his aunt shouted back. But Momma didn't hear a word she said.

Jesse just sat there, watching the whole thing like it was a movie, staring at the man laying in that box, fully expecting him to bolt upright and yell "Boo!" and scaring everybody in that church half to death. He never did, though, and they put him in the ground and covered him up like he never was.

Years later, his older brother Jimmy was diagnosed with prostate cancer, and that's when Momma finally told them that Daddy had died from the same thing.

"Do you know if it runs in your family?" the doctor asked him that afternoon.

All Jesse could do was nod, but that was enough. The doc didn't seem to need to know anything else.

"I'll schedule you for early next week. The sooner we get it done, the sooner we'll know where we stand, and what course of action we need to take next."

He threw the word *we* around entirely too lightly for Jesse's liking, but it was a silly thing to be pissed off about. So, he just left and came straight home.

Tess lay next to him, sleeping like a baby. And that's what she was, too, despite everything they'd been through, especially lately. She was his baby, and she'd be there for him, just like she'd always been. That's the one thing in this world he knew he could count on. If nothing else, this whole thing had given him a clearer perspective of marriage. Of her. He'd been a selfish man, believing that just because he paid the bills and kept everybody fed and clothed, it gave him the right to do what he pleased and to take his wife for granted. *How many times have I actually thought about leaving this woman?* he asked himself, watching her sleep. And what kind of fool would he have been if he had? Tess was a rock—his rock. She loved him in ways he never deserved, and the whole time, he'd brushed it off like he'd brushed mosquitoes off his arm. He'd fallen in and out of love with her too many times to count through the years, but not Tess. She'd been steadfast in her love for him, until she'd finally run out. Or maybe, she hadn't run out, he thought, running his finger lightly down her soft cheek. He'd hurt her, and she had every right to be angry at him for that. And he'd let her be mad for as long as she needed to be, but that wouldn't stop him from doing his damndest to make all that hurt up to her. He'd been married to this woman for nearly twenty-five years, and Jesse was looking forward to another twenty-five. If it took him that long to make her remember why she fell in love with him in the first place, that was fine, too. But one day, she would remember, and he'd remember, too, why she was the one he chose to marry, over any other woman.

"Hey, Mom," Tess's son Brian said over the phone. "How's Dad?"

Jesse had insisted that no one make a fuss over him the day of his surgery. "I don't want an army of people standing around waiting on me when I come out of surgery," he fussed. "The boys can call when it's over, but that's it."

Since his cancer didn't appear to be aggressive, Jesse's doctor recommended that Jesse forego an actual prostatectomy and felt that an internal radiation treatment was what he needed. The entire procedure took less than two hours, and Jesse was upstairs resting when Brian called. Brandon and Keisha had left a few minutes earlier.

Tess had been up since five A.M., and was exhausted. "He's fine, Brian," she sighed. "Upstairs sleeping."

"Is he going to be all right?"

"Let's hope so." She didn't see the point in feeding the boy a false sense of hope. Jesse was diagnosed with Stage II cancer. If he hadn't gotten treatment when he did, it could've easily spread to other parts of his body, and a much more radical treatment would've been called for.

"Mom?"

"Yes, son."

"Granddad died from this," he said, solemnly, even though he'd never known Jesse's father.

"Yes. He did."

"Uncle Jimmy had it, too."

She could hear in his voice where this was leading, and Tess knew she had to stop it before it started. "Brian, your father's going to be fine."

"But, Ma—"

"And you and your brother will be fine, too," she added, quickly. "When it's time, get your checkups, and don't take your health for granted."

Brian was quiet for a few moments. "It's a good thing he has you there, Ma. I know you two haven't been getting along all that great, but—"

"But, we're married. And sticking together is what married people do. No matter what."

It was an empty statement for Tess, but reassuring to her son as she hung up the phone. Jesse had been going on and on about how he loved her, and how fortunate he was for having her as his wife. It took cancer to make him realize that. For some reason, Tess couldn't find the comfort she needed in that.

Right now, she was too tired to think. The stress of the past week had worn her down, maybe even more than it had worn him down. But that's the way it had always been in their marriage. Tess bore the brunt of worry and concern for all the men in her life, leaving them free to lean heavy on her for the emotional stability they needed in trying times. Up until now, that's just how it was, and she wore her role like a badge of honor. But this time, something nagged tired and deep inside of Tess, pinching her every time she became too comfortable playing the same old part in the same old way for so many years. It was a selfishness that plagued her. Jesse needed her more than he'd ever needed her in his life. She'd stepped up to the plate a hundred times to support him for things less dire than this. She'd forgiven him enough to push aside her anger and sadness to stand by his side and be that woman she prided herself on being for her husband. But something wasn't right. It wasn't coming as easily and she couldn't put her finger on why.

"Tess?" she heard him call from upstairs.

Tess sighed wearily. "Yes, Jesse."

"Baby? Can you bring me some ice water?"

Of course she could. And she would. And she did. But it pissed her off to have to.

Marvin's "Distant Lover" filled Elise's small townhouse. Music like this made it hard for a man to resist the urge to make love to a beautiful woman if she was within twenty feet of him. Elise was much, much closer though, pressed up against the wall of the shower, naked and slippery-soap wet. The water had grown tepid, but Jay didn't give a damn. She was crack. He was an addict. She was a drink of water. He was thirsty. As hard as he'd tried to do the right thing and stay away from her, he just couldn't.

"Get yourself together, man," he'd warned himself. *"Get your marriage back on track and walk away while you still can."* Easier said than done, no doubt.

Her soft breasts begged him to rub and massage them, spreading soap across each nipple with his thumb, feeling it swell hard and erect like he was hard and erect. He grinded against her, trying to figure out a way to put it in, and not bring both of them tumbling down hard into the tub.

Fuck that. He wrapped his arms around her waist, pulled her away from the wall, and pushed her back down flat in the tub. Elise raised her knees in the air, inviting him in. His damn legs were too long, so Jay positioned himself on his knees, pulling her bottom onto his lap. Marvin never stopped singing. He heard his cell phone ring on the nightstand where he'd left it. For a second, the thought crossed his mind to stop and answer it. It might be Sherry, or one of the kids. The second came and went, when he pushed inside Elise and almost passed out on top of her. Nothing in life ever felt so good, and Marvin kept right on singing, like he knew the deal.

"*What took you so* long to get back to me?" she questioned softly in the dark, laying in his arms.

Jay was whipped, and too tired to think, let alone talk. But he did his best. "I told you," he said, groggily. "They've been sending me other places lately. I haven't been able to get here."

She was quiet. Sleeping? He could only hope.

"I get lonely without you, Jay. Too lonely sometimes."

Jay drifted in and out of consciousness. "Mmmm," was the best he could do.

"I think I'm more in love with you than you are with me."

At least, that's what it sounded like she said, or, something like that. "Don't say that," he kissed her head, and squeezed her tight. "Go to sleep, baby."

He gradually gave in to exhaustion and drifted off to sleep.

"Jay?" Elise's voice sounded small and far away, and if he didn't know better, he'd swear he was dreaming.

"Hmmm?"

"I need . . . more," her voice faded in and out of his dreams. "If you love me you'll . . . your wife . . . belong together, and you know it as much as I do."

She was almost asleep when Jay's cell phone rang on the nightstand next to her side of the bed. Elise saw him sleeping, then reached over to turn it off. She pulled the sheet up over her shoulder, then snuggled up behind him.

Let everybody else wait for him this time, she thought smiling. He was with her, and it was her turn to have him, all to herself.

"*Can I get you* something to drink?" Renee offered, motioning to Lewis to take a seat. "Coffee, water, another beer?"

This time he sat down in the leather arm chair across from the sofa. "No, thanks. I'm fine."

Normally, she didn't like navy blue suits, because she felt they were boring and unimaginative. But Lewis had paired his with a crisp white shirt, and a burgundy, pink, and white tie, which looked surprisingly good on him, and turned that suit from dull to—incredible.

Renee sat on the sofa. She'd gotten home in time to shower, and throw on a T-shirt with the words "All About Me" sprawled across the front, along with some baggy gray sweat pants. She decided to downplay her appearance for this discussion, and wished he'd thought enough to do the same, but—

"I love what you're doing to the bedroom," he said, nodding his head, reassuringly. "I have to admit, you certainly have lived up to your reputation as a designer."

Renee smiled. "Yeah, well, I love my job, so it's easy to be good at it."

"I know what you mean. I love my job, too."

They sat quietly for several minutes in awkward silence. "You know, Lewis, about last night—"

He put up his hand to stop her. "It was a mistake."

Renee breathed a sigh of relief. "It really was, and I don't normally take liberties like that with clients, believe me. It's unprofessional and that's just not how I operate."

"And I've never cheated on my wife," he lied. In fact, he'd had an affair with one of his coworkers shortly before moving from Seattle. Lena was her name, and she was married, too. The sex was nice. Lena was nice. And it ended as abruptly and uneventfully as it started. Lena was a black woman, which made him wonder sometimes if maybe his mother hadn't been so far off the mark after all. "Never even thought about it, and just because we're having problems, this is certainly no time to start."

"I agree. If anything, the two of you need to sit down, and talk things through, and make it work."

"We've been together fifteen years. We have to make it work, and I think I can speak for her, when I say, we both want to."

"Oh, I know she does," Renee said emphatically. "She's told me that even though it's been stressful, she's really looking forward to the two of you working through all your problems."

"Well, that's good to know."

"And I like Trishelle. She's a nice woman, and she and I have really hit it off, so the last thing I'd ever want to do is—"

"Precisely. I believe you're a better person than that. And I'm a better man than to—"

"Oh, I know. I can see that. You know. You dig your wife. I can see that."

"I adore her."

"And I can see that."

"I've never cheated on her."

"You said that already."

"Well, I mean it."

"And I believe you."

"Right."

"Right."

Silence passed between them again, and this time, it was Lewis who spoke first. "But I'm struggling here, Renee, and I don't exactly understand why."

"Because, you're under a lot of stress right now," she said, trying to make herself sound reasonable and in control. "New job, new city, issues at home. It's tough."

"It is."

"But, you just have to pull yourself together and do what you know is right," she explained, feeling more like Doctor Phil than an interior designer. "You really don't want another woman, and I don't want to have an affair with a man who's already married. I mean, what could I possibly get out of it except drama I don't need.

"Right," he agreed.

"Besides, it's not me you want. It's affirmation, maybe comfort, reassurance, and just to let off some steam. You came here the other night, and all the pieces just sort of fell into place leading up to that kiss."

"What did you think about that?"

Renee stared at him blankly. "About what?"

"Kissing."

"Kissing? Oh, I love kissing. Kissing's good when you kiss someone who knows how to kiss—well."

"Did you enjoy it?"

Renee stared at him quizzically. "Why would you ask me that, Lewis, when we're supposed to be here trying to make sure it doesn't happen again?"

"I enjoyed it," he said bluntly. "I was just curious if you did."

His statement and demeanor caught her off guard. She'd expected a nervous man to be sitting across from her, a man who'd regretted a moment of weakness shared between the two of them. Instead, Renee watched another man morph into his navy blue suit, one sitting there, daring her, provoking her to come nasty with it and smear it all over his cocky ass. "It was fine," she said unemotionally.

"That's it? Just—fine."

Renee felt herself starting to get defensive. "What are you getting at, Lewis? What are you trying to do here?"

"Nothing," he said, defensively. "I'm just being honest."

"To what end?"

"I want to know what it is that's got me feeling this way. I want to know why right this second, I want to jump on top of you, rip off your clothes, and screw you right there on that couch. I want to know why I'm so attracted to you, and why I can't stop thinking about you."

"I told you why. You're under a lot of stress, moving here, taking on a new job."

"Bullshit, Renee. Yes, I'm under a lot of stress, but I'm thirty-seven years old and I've been under a lot of stress in my life before, believe me. And yes, I'm having problems at home, but I've had problems at home before."

Renee was frustrated. "Well what do you want me to say? That I'm just shit hot and you can't help yourself?"

Lewis's eyes twinkled. "Yes."

Renee couldn't believe she was actually having this conversation with this man, but Lewis was baiting her, and she realized that just maybe, she wanted to be baited. "Do you want me to tell you that you've been too long without black pussy, Lewis," she said seductively. "That you really would like to sample this right here." She gapped her legs open, just a bit.

Lewis leaned forward, and balanced his elbows on his knees. "Yes."

"Why would you want me to say those things?"

He took a deep breath and studied her for a moment. "Because they're true. My palms itch, I want to touch you so bad."

"And what about Trish? What about your wife?"

"I love my wife." He smiled. "I'd never want to hurt my wife."

"Having sex with me would hurt your wife, Lewis."

He extended up one long index finger. "One time," he said in a low, husky voice. "One time, and I'll never ask again."

"And what about me?" Renee asked coolly. "I'm supposed to be cool with you fucking me and leaving me, like it never happened? Do I look like a blow-up doll to you? What do I get out of it?"

Lewis thought for a moment, and then looked at Renee. "You'll get some of the best sex you've ever had in your life. I swear you will. I don't want to fuck you, Renee. I want to make love to you. Just once."

Moral obligation disappeared under the glow of candlelight in her bedroom. Responsibility and reason were overcome by Raheem DeVaughn music and lyrics permeating the room through a Bose speaker. Lewis started at the soles of her feet, kneeling naked at the foot of the bed, rubbing his thumbs firmly into her arches and heels, then he kissed her toes, one at a time, staring at Renee's nakedness, laying prone on the bed. One time, he'd get to do this. One time, and that was it. He'd blink away the moment like it never happened, and go home to his wife. So, this had to mean something for both of them, he concluded. And he had to make it last.

Renee was so much shorter than he was used to. But that doesn't mean there was less of her. Compact. Thick. Smooth and firm, but still soft where it counted. He didn't want to miss any part of her, or to neglect a single inch. Lewis stood up and stared down at Renee, memorizing her curves, her shape, her skin tone, her breasts, lips, and finally her eyes, rich and dark, staring intently back at him. She ran her tongue along her bottom lip, and arched her lower back.

He crawled onto the bed, and kissed a trail from her navel to the space in between her breasts, then slid his tongue along an invisible line to her nipple, licking circles around a dark, rich chocolate areola, her nipple hardening at his touch. Then, he focused his attention on the other breast and wrapped his lips around her nipple, sucking it, and flicking it with his tongue. Renee writhed underneath him, and grabbed hold of the back of his head. Finally, he let himself down on top of her and found her mouth with his. His cock felt like it would explode, and if he put it in now, it would. Renee spread her legs for him. She thrust herself toward him. She rocked her hips up and down, side to side, coaxing him, enticing him, luring him inside her. But Lewis resisted, because this was his fantasy, and he was going to live every last second of it, the way he'd imagined in his mind.

She liked it slow, but Renee was anxious. She hadn't been this close to a man in a long time, and yes, she wanted it. To hell with the superfluous shit, like his wife. *Goddammit Lewis! Just put it in, baby! Let me do the rest!* She wanted to shout, but Lewis had his own agenda, which included teasing her to the point of tears. She reached down to touch him, long, hard, thick, and ready. If he was her man, she might've sucked it for him first. But he wasn't, so she wouldn't. That would've been like eating another woman's pussy and she didn't flow like that.

Lewis kissed her with his eyes open, and she kissed back—with her eyes open. Both of them searching each other's psyche to see just how good it really was, and they each looked high—intoxicated on each other, like junkies getting the best fix of their lives, and willing, wishing, and wanting this event to last an eternity, because absolutely nothing felt this good.

All of a sudden, he sat back up on his knees, grabbed her by the hips, and in one fluid motion, turned her over on her stomach. Renee's heart raced. *From behind? Oh goodness! Is he going to do me from behind? How'd he know? How'd he know I like it best doggy style?*

Lewis hovered over her, turned her head to one side, then

buried his face in the crook of her neck, and nibbled on that . . . that . . . spot . . . that spot . . . that . . . fuckin' spot . . . the one that . . . "Awwwww," she arched her back, her eyes rolled into her head, and Renee held her breath. Lewis squeezed her ass cheeks, kneaded them like dough, then eased a long finger down into the space between her thighs, finding the warm, moist pool, he'd been dreaming of. Her pussy was hot and wet and hungry for him. Renee raised her ass in the air, like a cat in heat, permeating the room with a scent that drove him crazy, as he pumped his finger slowly, in and out of her, preparing it for him. Lewis positioned himself between her legs. Renee attempted to balance herself up on her elbows, but he put his hand between her shoulder blades, forcing her back down on the bed. That delicious, plump ass of hers, smiled wide at him, calling out to him to take it and make it his.

The sound of paper tearing made her feel more at ease, and anxious for him to slide into her. "Hurry," she said, breathless. "Please—hurry, baby."

The sound of latex being snapped into place, made her mouth water for him.

Lewis positioned the tip of his dick at her opening, then gazed at her lovely face, as he pushed himself inside her in one complete motion, as far as he could.

"Ohhhh!" she gasped. Renee grabbed handfuls of the sheets, and balled them up in her fists.

Then, just as smoothly, Lewis pulled all the way out, resting the tip of his dick against her, salivating at the sight of her gyrating hips, and her wet pussy eager to gobble him up. He smiled.

Renee bit down on her bottom lip. "C'mon," she demanded. "Lewis!"

He slid inside her again in a deep, long, thrust, and pulled out again.

"Lewis!" she growled. "Don't!" Renee pounded her fist against the mattress, then looked angrily over her shoulder at him.

He chuckled, then leaned down and kissed her passionately. "I've got to take my time, Renee," he whispered. "This is the one and only time I can have you, and I want it to last."

By the time he finished, Renee's legs felt like cooked noodles. Her hips ached. Lewis finished dressing, and stood over her laying limp in bed. He put on his sports coat, then knelt down next to Renee, smiling, satisfied and spent.

"I'm going to sleep like a baby," she said groggily.

Lewis took her hand in his and kissed it. "Thank you," he said, full of sincerity.

"No. Thank you." Renee raised her lips to his and kissed him softly. "You sure you don't want me to walk you to the door?"

He ran his thumb lightly across her brows. "No," he spoke tenderly. "You get some sleep. I'll lock up."

"We can't ever do this again, Lewis," she reminded him. "This was it. No more."

"No. No more."

"But I'm ashamed to say," Renee continued, "that you were certainly worth it."

"And so were you, lady. Believe that."

Lewis drove home slowly. He glanced at the clock on the dash. It was still early, and he doubted that Trish and Tray would be back from the movies yet. He pulled into his garage, and went right upstairs to shower before Trish made it home. Lewis crawled into bed, and turned on the television, then turned down the volume content to just watch whatever was on, instead of having to hear it.

He'd needed to get her out of his system. That's all. And tonight, he'd done that.

Jesse laughed and flipped ribs cooking on the grill, patted his boys on their backs, told jokes with Keisha's stepdaddy, like all was right with the world and he hadn't been diagnosed with cancer less than a month ago. The doctor said his chances were good that the radiation treatment would work, and he'd go into remission and end up no worse for the wear.

"Am I going to be impotent?" She was there when he asked the question, and Tess saw the fear in his eyes as he waited for the doctor to answer.

"The impotence rate at five years after the procedure is about 25 percent, Jesse," he said, without blinking.

Jesse blinked though.

The doctor smiled. "But you're healthy in all other aspects, so, I don't foresee that as being a problem for you. Be patient, get some rest, and watch your diet. And just be thankful we caught it early."

Tess loathed the Fourth of July. Jesse had been the one to insist they make an appearance at the shindig Keisha's mother insisted on throwing in honor of the kids' announcement. They'd all gathered together in the living room before heading out back to the yard. It was supposed to be a surprise, but Tess could almost smell the news even before anyone opened their mouth to announce it.

"We're going to have a baby," Keisha gushed, squeezing on tight to her little skinny husband, still waiting on his young man body to fill out like his father's. If Tess had been alone with that boy, she'd have probably hit him upside the back of his head, and asked him, *What the hell do you think you're doing?*

"You're going to be a grandmomma, Momma." He laughed and kissed her cheek, then shook his daddy's hand.

Jesse had never looked so proud in his life. Tess did the math in her head. She was forty-one years old. *No! Lord Jesus, please, no!* She wasn't old enough to be a grandmother. She wasn't ready to be a grandmother, and all at once, Tess felt herself get old, and it all seemed so unfair. She had just started to embrace her life, and exploring who she was and who she still had time to be. Tess had devoted a lifetime to children who truly believed it was cool to make her an old woman, and to a husband, who didn't give a damn about her until he was kicked in the ass by cancer, and realized he needed someone to take care of him. The last few weeks had been, *Baby, this . . . baby that. Baby, let's go do . . . Baby, we need to . . . Baby, I don't know how I'd get through this whole thing if it weren't for you.*

Tess choked back a grunt, and swallowed a mouthful of Corona, straight out of the bottle.

"You doing all right?" Keisha's mother Eileen asked Tess. Tess smiled, and raised her glass in a toast, nodding. "Fine. Just fine."

Brandon stood next to his father, looking just like that man, probably acted like him, too, especially now that he was married. Kiesha flitted around the crowd like a honey bee, lighting on everybody with that syrupy smile of hers, glowing, and filling up by the second with enough hormones to make her puke for the next eight months, nonstop. At least, that's what Tess wished on her. She'd spent the afternoon racking her brains over why that girl irritated her so much, with her sweet little self. And eventually, Tess realized the truth. That Keisha was a young Tess, married to the man of her dreams, and looking forward to playing her role as the dutiful wife and mother. She scowled at Brandon, laughing at Jesse's lame jokes, and in an instant, she saw her son, twenty years from now, standing where his father stood, flipping ribs, telling stale ass jokes, trying desperately to rekindle that fire in his lonely and disgusted wife's eyes, which he'd been responsible for putting out in the first place because he'd forgotten she existed until he needed her.

"How many of those have you had, Ma?" Brian asked, sitting down next to his mother. Tess gulped down what was left, then handed the bottle to him. "Get me another one," she said dismally.

God! She felt like she was drowning. Tess was sitting outside in a yard the size of a city block and she truly could not breathe.

The only thing she wanted to do was fly away like a bird and take refuge high in some tree somewhere. Tess was so tired of being anchored by a world she didn't care for anymore. She thought back to her trip to St. Simon's Island, several months ago, and at how she felt as big and wide open as that ocean in front of her. She remembered what it felt like to wake up to the kiss of the breeze, knowing she didn't have a thing in the world to do, but open her eyes, and set her cares free like a kite floating on the wind. Tess was still a young woman back on that island. Young enough to still have dreams and aspirations and to run away and turn back the clock to that eighteen-year-old girl, about to get married, and instead of saying I do, she'd have been smart and turned running as fast as she could've out the door of the courthouse and never looked back.

"Let's get out of here, In-Law," he whispered into her ear.

Tess turned to see who'd spoken into her dreams, and saw the unflinching face of Uncle Gregory, knelt low behind her, like he was the hero, coming to rescue her like an action hero. "Let's get out of here."

Tess stared at him like he was crazy, then looked up and saw that no one seemed to be paying any attention to her or her savior whatsoever, and she almost thought she'd passed out and was imagining this whole thing, until he tapped gently on her arm.

"Let's go for a ride," he smiled, and his eyes twinkled. " 'Cause I don't want to be here any more than you do." She must've looked confused. "They won't even know we're gone. And I'll have you back before you know it."

"What are you talking about?" she whispered. "My husband's right over there."

Gregory glanced over her shoulder at Jesse immersed in a conversation about his days of almost playing pro ball. "He ain't paying attention to you."

Tess stared at him, wondering how in the world he would know something like that.

It was the kind of truth, indicative of the way her life had been for years. Tess felt herself get caught up in this surreal moment, fully expecting herself to be awakened at the sound of the alarm clock. For the life of her, she hadn't even seen this Gregory character come in the house, and now here she was, scurrying off behind him, disappearing into the house, and out the front door to his motorcycle waiting like a chariot to carry her off. Tess stopped dead in her tracks, and tried to shake off the effects of the four Coronas she'd polished off over the course of the afternoon.

Gregory climbed onto his bike and started it up. "Let's go!"

Tess shook her head, folded her arms across her chest and laughed. "You mind telling me what the hell is going on? And what makes you think I'm getting on the back of that thing, with some fool I hardly even know?"

Gregory leaned back on his seat, and balanced the heavy motorcycle between his legs. "I've been inside for ten minutes," he explained, "and I came because Baby Keisha asked me to, and Lord knows, I'd give that sweet girl the world if I could. But the minute I got there, I knew it wasn't someplace I wanted to be, and then I looked at you, Miss Lady, sucking on beer bottles like a baby sucks milk, and I could tell, clear as day, your ass didn't want to be there either."

Tess was stunned. "You could tell just by looking at me?"

"You look like you could use a ride, baby." Something about the way he said it didn't set well with Tess. "I don't think anybody else at that party gave a damn enough to notice you're even missing. Do you? Ever been on the back of one of these?"

She'd never been on one, never wanted to be on one and wasn't about to get on the back of one now.

It was hard to miss the reservation in her eyes. "Well, it's up to you. You can go back inside, and knock off that six pack you were working hard on, or"—he grinned from ear to ear—"you can let me take you on a quick spin around the block."

A quick spin around the—. People were killed on motorcycles. Tess tentatively shook her head, but then—

And it was like an omen from God. "Let's fly, girl," he stretched out his hand to her. "Before they catch us."

She climbed cautiously on the back of his motorcycle. "Don't I need a helmet?" she asked, wrapping both arms tightly around his waist.

"Hold on tight. Relax. Lean when I lean. Enjoy the ride. Let me do the rest."

Gregory rode slowly, around the block, just like he promised, slow enough and long enough for Tess to gather enough courage to stop squeezing the air out of that man, and to open her eyes. It wasn't so bad being on the back of one of these things. In fact, it felt good, letting the wind whip through her hair and pat her face. He was careful, stopping at all the stop signs, slowing down at yellow lights, waiting patiently while pedestrians crossed the street in front of them. Tess heard herself giggle like a teenager, as her courage and confidence sprouted up inside her.

"This isn't so bad," she said loudly in his ear. "I kind of like it."

It was a naughty thing to do, sneaking away from family and friends, sort of like ditching classes to do something so adventurous. It was liberating, and she did feel like she was flying free, even if it was only at thirty miles per hour.

"I had a feeling about you," he shouted back, just before he accelerated to sixty, crossed three lanes of traffic, and dipped down onto the exit heading in to 635.

Tess wanted to scream, but the wind pushed it back down

her throat, and all she could do was hang on for dear life. Have mercy! He was going too fast! Have mercy! They were both going to be killed! Greg weaved in and out of traffic at speeds unnatural to human beings not riding inside the sanctity of four doors, windshields, and air bags. The force of the air threatened to snatch her off the back of that bike, and hurl her into outer space. Tess squeezed her arms as tight as she could around his waist, and her knees pinned him between her thighs. *If I should die, before I wake . . . wake . . . wake the hell up, Tess and get your black ass off this damn thing! Never again, Lord! Never again will I ever walk away from a perfectly good beer, my husband's tired jokes, or my annoying daughter-in-law and her family to do some shit like this! I swear, God! Just—let—me—live!*

Tess didn't say a word when he finally dropped her back off back at the house, half an hour later. She never turned to look at him, or acknowledge he ever existed. It was all she could do to balance herself on her two wobbly legs, and walk back inside to the sanctity of her lounge chair.

"I had a good time," he called out to her sarcastically. "Maybe we can do it again?"

She heard him laugh, just before roaring his engine and pulling away from the curb.

"Son of a bitch," she muttered. Tess managed to slip into the bathroom without anyone seeing the mess he'd made of her, and of her head. She grimaced at her reflection in the mirror, and then used her fingers to comb her hair back in place. She looked a hot mess, that's for sure. But there was no denying that smile creeping across her lips. That fool damn near killed her, and she'd loved every minute.

She eased her way back outside to where everyone was. It

was almost as if nothing had changed. Almost as if she'd never even left. Jesse eventually made his way over to where she was sitting, and kissed the top of her head.

"Hey, baby," he said, smiling. "How was your nap?"

"My nap?" she asked, surprised.

"Keisha said, she thought you'd gone up to take a nap. You feeling all right?"

Tess smiled. "My nap was fine, Jesse. And yes. I feel so much better."

She'd been quiet ever since he'd walked through the door. That's how it was sometimes, though, with Sherry. Sometimes, she'd greet him with a hug after he'd been gone, other times, she met him with an attitude.

"What's wrong?" he'd ask.

"Nothing," is what she'd come back with.

Jasmine had the phone glued to her ear as usual, looked in the pots, sniffed, turned up her nose, then grabbed an apple from the fruit bowl and disappeared in her room. Jayson came home eventually and ate standing at the kitchen counter. Jay ate in the living room, watching the game. He didn't see Sherry eat at all.

It was like night and day between home and Elise's place. He'd left her place feeling high, but the buzz was long gone by the time he walked through the door. Jay finished eating and leaned back watching the basketball game. Or, not watching it. It was on, he was facing it with his eyes open, but he had no idea what was going on. Sort of like his life, he surmised. Half the time, he didn't know what was up with that either. When he was younger, he'd had so many plans and dreams that had all fallen to the ground like dust. Jay wanted to go to college, become an architect or engineer and make a ton of money.

He'd always wanted to work in an office, wear fancy suits, go to meetings, and design some shit that would change the world. Now, all he did was tinker around in the garage, wondering "what if." What if he hadn't gotten married so young, and what if he'd gotten his high school diploma instead of his GED, and what if he'd enrolled in college or gone to the military like he kept saying he would when he was nineteen? What if he hadn't had kids? What if he'd never taken that first job as a truck driver? What if he'd met Elise first? Sherry walked in front of him, on her way upstairs.

Jay rubbed his eyes and sighed. He was just tired. It had been a long trip. He turned off the television and headed upstairs to take a shower. Sherry sat up in bed, reading. Jay walked past her on his way to the bathroom without saying a word. Sherry wanted him to read her mind or something, but Jay wasn't psychic. Fuck her. He stood in the shower until the water turned cold, dried off, and crawled into bed next to her, with every intention of closing his eyes and going to sleep. Too bad it wasn't Elise laying next to him. The thought flashed in his mind. Disappointment followed. Then Sherry's foot, hard, against his lower back, damn near knocked him out of bed.

"What the—" He turned and grimaced at her.

"Who the fuck is she, Jay!" Sherry leapt out of bed, then marched over to his side, breathing fire with her fists curled up. "Who the hell are you fucking?"

Jay attempted to sit up, while Sherry pushed on him and hit him the whole time.

She knows? he thought, looking into her eyes, looking for

confirmation that she'd figured out what he'd been doing for the last year. His thoughts flip-flopped. *No. Yes. Hell no. Aw shit!*

"What the hell's wrong with you?" he shouted, standing to his feet and trying to get out of her way.

Sherry stalked him. "I called you half a dozen times, moth-afucka!" her head bobbed. She pressed her long, thin finger hard in his chest. "I called you and called you and your ass never even bothered to pick up the phone, Jay. Since when don't you pick up when I call, or at least call me back?"

Instinct kicked in, despite the fact that part of him wanted to blurt out the truth. Yes, he was fucking someone else. And the shit was good, all of it, from the food she fed him to the sex she fed him. The truth was on the tip of his tongue, but self preservation held it there.

"The phone was off!" he said, desperate to make her believe him. "I forgot to turn it on, Sherry! I didn't realize it was off until—shit! Until I turned the corner on my way home."

Tears pooled in her eyes. Angry ones, not the other kind. If she was mad enough to cry, then she was pissed enough not to give a damn about his explanation. "You've been tripping." She threw her hands up, and turned and walked away, shaking her head.

"What?" He was genuinely confused and hoped he was convincing enough to convey that. "I've been tripping?"

She turned to him. "A woman knows, Jay!" Sherry choked back tears, but she was losing the battle. He could tell that. "Something's different about you! Something's—"

"Something like what?" he looked perplexed. Jay's heart pounded hard in his chest. He felt like he was being torn in two. Shit! If she knew . . . if she really knew—then what? "What are you talking about? I come in here and you ain't said two words to me all goddamned night! Then all of a sudden you fucking lose your damn mind, and that's *my* fault?"

"When's the last time you made love to me?" she screeched, pointing to herself. "When's the last time we did anything together?"

He shrugged. "We've been working, Sherry! You've been busy. I've been—"

"It's been two months, Jay! That's how long it's been and you haven't even touched me!" She stepped toward him again, until she was toe to toe with him, looking up into his stoic face. "If you're not fucking me, Jay, then who the hell are you fucking? Some bitch you found on one of your routes? Is that it? Some small-town, farm-raised, corn-fed, country heifer you met hauling pigs?"

Jay couldn't help it. And he knew full well it was probably only going to make matters worse, but all of a sudden, he laughed. Sherry looked at him like he was crazy. "I've never hauled pigs, Sherry."

Why'd he say that? Sherry reached up and pinched his nipple—twisting hard between her thumb and forefinger. "Oh, you got jokes!"

"Ouch!" he grimaced.

"You think this shit is funny, Jay? I don't see you laughing now!"

"Let go my titty, woman!"

"The shit ain't funny now! Is it? I don't hear you laughing now, mothafucka!"

Jay wrapped his arms around her waist, hugged her close

enough to him that she had no choice but to let go. He lifted her up off the ground then carried her over to the bed in one quick motion and fell down on top of her, pinning down her arms and legs.

Sherry struggled. "Get off me! Jay! Get the hell up—"

"Say sorry!" he teased.

"What?" Sherry asked, looking at him like he'd lost his ever-loving mind.

"Say sorry, Sherry—or else."

Sherry was beyond livid. "Or else what?"

Jay growled like a bear then chomped on the side of her neck he knew she was ticklish on.

She screamed and laughed uncontrollably, fighting to get away from him. "Stop! Jay! If you don't—stop it! Jay!"

For a minute, they forgot they were grown, with damn-near-grown kids, bills, mortgages, insurance payments, jobs. Sherry wriggled underneath him the way she did when she was nineteen years old, fresh in college, still sleeping in her twin-sized bed in her parents' house. Jay would sneak in while they were gone, wallow in an afternoon of her delight, then revitalized, chased her around the room like they were kids, wrestling and tickling until they were both exhausted and it was time for him to leave.

Exhaustion kicked in a whole lot quicker these days, and eventually, Jay rolled off her, and lay out of breath next to his wife.

"Boy!" She slapped him across the chest. "You almost made me pee on myself."

"Oh, you loved it!" he said smugly.

She chuckled. "I've missed it. Didn't think I ever would, but I have."

"Me too," he sighed.

Both of them lay there for a long time without saying a word. All he knew was that sometimes there were moments that passed between the two of them that left marks on him so deep, he knew they would never go away. And they were all familiar, which was enough to make him glad she was there and happy to be home.

"Are you cheating on me, Jay?" Sherry asked softly, like she was almost afraid to hear the answer.

He was her protector. Always had been, and the thought never crossed his mind to be anything else. So of course, he had no choice but to lie. And he was bound and determined to lie so good, there'd be no room for doubt in her mind. He rolled over on his side, lifted himself up and balanced on his elbow, then gazed long and steady into her beautiful eyes. "I have not, and I never will, Sherry. I swear."

Her eyes clouded up again, and her expression softened. She smiled, and swallowed hard. "I don't want to lose you, baby."

"You won't," he said, convincingly, because damn if he didn't mean it, with every ounce of his soul.

"But I feel like I am losing you, and it scares me."

"I'm right here, sweetheart," he tried to reassure her.

"Not always, Jay. Even when you're in the house sometimes, it seems like you're someplace else."

"I've just been tired, baby. I've been working picking up the slack for fellas who quit just because they feel like they've got it like that. And you've been busy, too. Sometimes when I come home, I get the feeling you just ain't in the mood for a brotha."

She stared intently in his eyes. "Is that how I make you feel? Because I don't mean to do that, Jay. I really don't."

"Well, you're tired, too, honey." He shrugged. "We both are."

"We've been together too long to let something like being tired come between us, Sweetie," she said definitively. "We've built our own little empire here, and we're where we always said we wanted to be. The dumbest thing we could do now is to let it all fall by the wayside because we can't dig a little deeper and pull out something as simple as time for each other."

"You're right," he admitted.

"You're the man of my dreams, babe." She smiled and pressed her hand against the side of his face.

He smiled. "Yeah, well, you're pretty damn dreamy, too, shorty. You wanna go get some ice cream?"

She grinned, then rolled out from under him. "I'll go see if the kids are up."

He grabbed her by the arm, just before she made it to the door. "I asked *you* to go with me for ice cream. I didn't ask the kids."

Sherry leaned down and kissed him softly. "I'll be ready in thirty seconds," she laughed.

Jay watched her disappear inside the bedroom closet to find something to put on. He knew it would take her a hell of a lot longer than thirty seconds to slip into a pair of jeans, T-shirt, and sneakers, so he took his time, slipping into his clothes, then sat patiently on the side of the bed, and waited for his best friend to finish getting dressed.

Elise had memorized the phone number. She'd taken it from his cell phone while he was sleeping.

"Do you love her?" she dared to ask him once about his wife.

He nodded, then hesitated before answering like he really had to search for the answer. "Yeah. I do. But—it's because I've been with her so long. I love my kids, more, though," he explained. "I wouldn't know how to leave my kids. They need me more now then they did when they were small, especially Jayson. He's a young man, and I need to be there to guide him into the next phase of his life."

But he never talked much about Sherry, except to bitch and moan sometimes about the kind of wife she wasn't, the kind he wished she was. All the little things he'd mentioned that Sherry had neglected to do, Elise put twice as much effort into just so that he could see the difference between a woman who loved and appreciated him, and one who took him for granted.

"Seems like all she ever cooks is chicken: fried, baked, smothered, barbecued."

Elise cooked T-bone, pork chops, veal.

"Sex at home is just . . . sex. I roll over on top, we do our thang and that's that."

Elise made sex an event. Kissing and nibbling on his ears while he ate, stroking his chest, sucking on his full lips, orchestrating the whole thing like a chorus, starting low and gradual, then building into a crescendo that shook the rafters.

"She and I don't spend a lot of time together. We don't usually like the same kinds of, movies, music, or restaurants."

Elise made it a point to play good sport, and love what he loved, laugh when he laughed, and to need whatever it was he needed, or to be whatever it was he needed.

Time was the only factor, Elise surmised, turning off the

lamp next to the sofa, and then going to bed. Time would reveal to Jay that he was with the wrong woman, and that Elise was a better fit. Time would make him grow more and more tired of Sherry, and compel him closer to Elise. Time was on her side. All she had to do was wait. And maybe make a few phone calls to help speed up the process.

It had been a week since she'd last been to the Stevens' home and seen Trishelle. The last of the custom furnishings for the formal dining room, and guest bedrooms was arriving today and Renee promised she'd be there to inspect it all. To say she was apprehensive about the visit was an understatement. But Lewis had kept up his part of the bargain, and she'd kept hers, and enough time had passed that she could put on a good game face and act like nothing had ever happened between them.

Renee wore chocolate stiletto pumps, khaki capris, and a white cami underneath a classic jean jacket. Lewis worked some serious magic the night they were together. She made it a point not to let guilt seep in and steal her joy, convincing herself that there really wasn't anything to feel guilty about, for the sake of self-preservation, of course. This assignment would be over with soon, and when it was, she'd move on, and forget these people ever existed, save for before and after photos of their living room on her Web site. Renee sat in her car, coifed her already coifed Afro, and stared at her reflection in her visor mirror. *What if he was home?* she wondered. Would a glance or smile give them away? Would an already unhappy wife see through their façade and make the connection? Could she diss him, like he hadn't been the one to make her come so hard, she couldn't speak? Could he diss her? Of course, she concluded. What else could they do?

Renee saw the reflection of the delivery truck in her rearview mirror pulling up to the front of the house. "Show-time," she muttered.

Trish immediately emerged from the house, smiling and clapping her hands. "It's here! It's here," she said to Renee, as she walked over in her direction. Renee couldn't tell if the hug she got was because Trish was so happy to see her, or if the furniture had worked her up into a frenzy.

"Is Lewis here for the big event?" Renee asked casually, while the deliverymen hauled the heavy custom European dresser up the stairs.

Trish rolled her eyes. "Please. You should know by now, Lewis couldn't care less, for the most part. But when everything's in place and all put away, that's when he'll finally notice and say 'It looks good, baby.' " She mimicked in her best man voice.

Renee breathed a silent sigh of relief.

It wasn't until the Egyptian sheets arrived did the real test begin. Trish and Renee were in the middle of making the bed when he walked in.

Lewis stood in the doorway of the bedroom, still sweating from a game of racquetball, wearing black shorts and a white T-shirt. The women didn't notice him right away. Lewis stared at one, then the other, not really knowing how to feel. He hadn't seen Renee all week, and he'd kept his promise and not called. Seeing her now, however, stirred a few memories in him he thought were gone.

"How long have you been standing there—spying," Trish teased. She looked at Renee and winked.

Renee smiled and kept right on working. "Hey Lewis," she said, casually, "You're just in time to see the finished product."

Trish ran excitedly over to him and kissed him. "All the guest rooms are done, honey, and they look gorgeous. I can't wait for you to see them."

Lewis gave her an affectionate squeeze. "Well, can I at least shower first? I'd hate to get anything dirty."

Trish laughed and turned up her nose. "Yeah, I couldn't agree more. We're going to finish up in here, and by the time you're done, Renee and I will give you the budget tour of the place."

That wasn't so bad, Renee thought victoriously, sliding the pillow into the case. All this time she'd been tripping over nothing, thinking that if they were actually in the same room together, one of them would be foolish enough to confess, *Yes! We did it! We had sex! With each other! Dear God and Trishelle, please forgive us!*

It was just a one-time thing. A really great one-time thing, too. But it started and ended that night, and it was all good. Renee felt a big weight lifted off her shoulders, and roll down her arm all the way to the floor, landing with a big, old, empty thud! Married men just weren't her cup of tea. Being the other woman never had been her thing. She'd needed some service, some quality service, and he'd kindly obliged, and they'd used condoms, played it safe, set some ground rules, and adhered to them like adults should do. Now it was over, and unless he did something stupid like confess, this whole thing was just plain old history.

How come he couldn't get Renee off his mind? Lewis stepped out of the shower, hard as a rock at the sight of that woman. He hadn't called because he'd promised not to. But that didn't mean he didn't want to. That didn't mean he didn't pick up the phone half a dozen times and dialed all but the last digit of her number, before hanging up.

"Ooooh," Trish crooned, as she walked into the bedroom and saw a naked Lewis standing there, drying off his face. She slipped up behind him, wrapped her arms around his narrow waist, and pressed herself against her husband's moist body. "We need a date night," she said softly. "We haven't had one since we moved here."

"No, we haven't." Lewis felt his hard dick start to soften.

"The house is nearly finished." Trish sounded reflective. "Maybe once that's over with, things can start to get back to normal between us?"

Lewis thought for a moment before responding. "What's that, exactly?"

"I thought you might know," she chuckled.

Lewis turned to his wife, wrapped his towel around her waist, and pulled her close. He gazed lovingly into her eyes and sighed. "Maybe we need to create a new kind of normal, Trish. We're not in Kansas anymore, Toto," he teased. "And what worked there might not work so good here."

Trish nodded, seeing sincerity in her husband's eyes. This was the most hopeful conversation they'd had in months, and she felt soothed by it and reassured.

"Trish have you seen—" Renee burst in without even

bothering to knock because Trishelle had left the door open. "Oh, I'm so—" She hurried and left.

Trish laughed, then patted Lewis's bare behind. "I'd better go check on her. From what she's told me, she hasn't seen a man's ass in quite some time, and I doubt she's ever seen one that looks this good." She kissed her husband and went to find Renee.

Renee left soon after, leaving Trish and Lewis to wade through a sea of apologies. It was a reality check, plain and simple. Lewis standing naked in his wife's arms was nothing short of fate smacking Renee in the face to make sure she really was paying attention and that under no circumstances was she ever to make the mistake of thinking her one night with Lewis Stevens was anything more than a damn good booty call—for both of them.

One thing was certain, though. Renee was too damn lonely for her own good. Getting dick was easy. She could walk into any given club on any given night and take home any given fool on two legs if all she wanted was dick. But getting good dick, and good dick that stayed more than one night, that was willing to be patient enough to fall in love with her, and maybe somewhere down the road, really commit and buy a Pomeranian with her, that kind of dick was a little harder to come by. More and more though, that's the kind she wanted. The kind that stayed all night, and that she wanted to stay all night, and the next night, and the night after that, too.

White. Black. It didn't matter. Seeing the two of them standing there like that, holding each other and gazing into each other's eyes, it was as clear as day that they made a really cute couple. Renee's eyes started to tear up and she blinked away tears just in time to see the traffic signal turned from yellow to red. Shit! When was the last time she'd cried over a man? Had to have been back when her father thought he had that heart attack, and had to be rushed to the hospital only for the doctor to determine that the man had eaten too many jalapeños at dinner. Renee had been—what? About twelve back then? Yep. That's the last time she cried over any man, and now, here she was crying over some man she couldn't get, and worse yet, some man she didn't even want. Her period must be coming. She pressed speed dial on her cell phone, dialing Dr. Faye's office. "Hey," she said to the receptionist." This is Renee Turner, and I need to make an appointment to see Dr. Faye. And the sooner the better, 'cause I'm really tripping."

Tess wasn't the least bit surprised when he answered the door in the middle of the day, in the middle of the week. After all, according to his niece, his ass didn't work. She was surprised, however, that she was standing there, with no idea whatsoever of anything she'd planned on saying if he did happen to answer. This was the third time she'd been by his house in a week. The first time, she just drove past it. The second time, she slowed down a bit, and then passed it. But she convinced herself that she was just being silly and immature and that it was imperative for her to make it clear to Keisha's uncle, that he obviously had the wrong idea about her, and that his assumptions were inappropriate and out of line.

He smiled when he saw her. "Well, hello." The man wasn't wearing a shirt. He was lean, and cut, and he wasn't wearing a shirt.

"I uh . . ." How come he couldn't excuse himself long enough to go throw a shirt on?

"In-Law!" he said, feigning excitement. "Come on in."

Tess hadn't planned on going inside. She'd planned on giving him a piece of her mind, laying down some ground rules, all standing there in the doorway, then climbing back into her car and leaving. The whole thing should've taken no longer than five, ten minutes at best. Reluctantly, she stepped inside. Tess didn't have to see him, to know he was standing close behind her.

She quickly spun around, and accidentally elbowed the man in the stomach. "Oh, I—"

"No problem," he said, grimacing. "I was all up in your personal space. Served me right." His tone was condescending enough to make her feel just a little bit pissy.

"I tried to call, but—"

"You leave a message?" he said, brushing past her over to the small open kitchen on the other side of the room.

"Yes. Yes, I did."

"I don't check messages."

Then why the hell do you have an answering machine if you don't check messages? she wanted to ask, then decided she wasn't interested enough in the answer to waste the time.

"What can I do for you, In-Law?"

"Tess," she corrected him, irritated by the fact that he wasn't a decent enough human being to remember her name, for crying out loud. "My name is Tess, not In-Law."

"Uh-huh," he said indifferently. "So, what's up?"

He was a grown man, living and acting like a damn kid, with that flippant attitude and ineptitude for being hospitable. So, if he didn't give a damn, why should she?

Tess cleared her throat, and put on her best I'm-going-to-meet-with-the-teacher attitude, because this man obviously couldn't communicate with a grown woman the way a grown man should've. He hadn't offered her a seat, something to drink, hadn't bothered to remember or even ask her name, and he sure as hell didn't have enough manners to go into his bedroom and throw a shirt over his rippling, firm, sinewy muscles.

"I just came by to talk about the other day," she started to say.

"The other day?" Greg shrugged and looked at her like he didn't know what she was talking about.

It was a game called "Play it Stupid, Stupid." Her sons used to play it all the time when they were kids. It irked her then, and it irked her now. "Yes," she said smugly. "The other day." She waited, and looked at him for some form of recognition, but of course, none came. "That whole motorcycle thing? Fourth of July? You took me—"

All of a sudden, he seemed to shake loose the memory. "Oh, yeah. Yeah." He smiled again. "That was cool. You ride pretty good, too, In-Law. That was your first time?"

"I told you it was," she said, frustrated. Talking to Uncle Gregory was like talking to an adolescent boy.

"Well, you did great. Held on a little tight, though." He rubbed his midsection and grimaced.

"I held on tight because I was scared to death," she said, trying to remain calm. "You told me we'd go for a little spin around the block, next thing I know, we're flying down the highway at a hundred miles per hour. So yes. I thought the moment warranted me holding on tight."

"It wasn't a hundred."

"What?"

"We were only doing seventy-five, eighty tops, but not a hundred."

Did he hear himself talking? And was he really going to argue a twenty-mile per hour difference in speed when the fact was, he was going too fast and she was hanging on for dear life behind him?

"The point is," she decided that was a battle not worth fighting. "I think you might have the wrong impression of me, and seeing as how we're part of the same family now, and we'll be seeing more of each other, I don't want you to—"

"What impression?"

Tess's irritation was obvious. "What?"

He came back into the living room and plopped down on the sofa, leaving Tess standing in the middle of the room, like an actress on a stage. "What impression are you talking about?"

"What do you mean, what impression?"

"No. What do you mean? What impression is it that you feel I have of you?"

"Look, it really doesn't matter, because that's not the point. The point is, you don't know me."

"If it's not the point, In-Law, then why are you here?" Now it was his turn to sound smug.

He wasn't an idiot. Tess could see it in his eyes, the man was playing her, and playing some game he'd dragged her into. Tess felt like an idiot and turned to leave.

Gregory jumped up and raced her to the door, blocking her from leaving. "What impression of you do you think it is I have? It's a simple question, In-Law."

She couldn't answer it. "Hell, how should I know?"

He was close. Too close. Tess took a step back.

"Why are you here, In-Law?"

Because she wanted to clear the air between them. She needed to let him know that she wasn't the kind of woman to sneak out of a party, jump on the back of a strange man's motorcycle, ride around the city of Dallas, and enjoy it.

"Don't you have a job?" she asked, changing the subject.

Now it was his turn to look uncomfortable. Gregory leaned back against the door, and shuffled his weight from one foot, then the other. "I have two jobs."

Tess's gaze drilled into him. "What do you do?"

"What do *you* do?"

"I asked first."

He grinned. "I work construction, when I can find it."

"You working construction now?"

He shook his head. "Can't find it. Competition's tough at the moment, but I'm looking."

"What's your other job?"

"What impression?" he responded, and in an instant the ball was back in her court.

"You think I'm wild and crazy and irresponsible," she blurted out. "You think I'm down for whatever."

"Why would I think that?"

"What kind of married woman would leave her husband at a party, so that she could go ride off with some man she doesn't even know?"

He laughed. "Shit, In-Law! It wasn't like we came back to my place and fucked the day away."

Tess grimaced.

"It was just a ride. And to me, you looked like that's exactly what you needed."

"How would you know what I need?" she said angrily. "You barely even know me, and you never remember my name."

Gregory studied her for a moment. *What the hell was that in her eyes?* he wondered, staring into them. A spark of something, or a seed of disappointment? "I've got X-ray vision, Mrs. . . . In-Law. And sometimes, I just see things other folks might miss. It felt good, though. Didn't it?"

"Well . . ." She wavered, then answered hesitantly. "Scared the hell out of me, but yes. It felt all right."

"It's all good, In-Law," he said reassuringly. "What happens between us, stays between us," he bowed slightly at the waist. "It was just a ride between family."

"Of course that's all it was. I just wanted to make sure you knew that."

"If I didn't know then, I certainly know now." He stepped back and opened the door for her to leave.

She was standing a little too close to resist. Close enough to make him think she wanted him to do it. So, he did. Gregory leaned in slow, grazed his lips lightly against hers, then darted his tongue in and out of her parted lips, quick—like a snake.

Tess drew back, not as quickly as she should've, and slapped his face. "You bastard!"

Gregory laughed, and watched her practically run all the way to her car.

Sparks fly when you least expect it. Gregory wasn't her type. He already knew that. And she wasn't his either. One of those homebody types, probably knitted and baked cookies and shit like that. A prude, too smug for her own good, and hooked on Oprah. He knew the type. But she was a little trickier than that. Most devoted housewives wouldn't have just jumped on that back of his bike like that and lived to tell about it. And that shit about her coming over here to let him know she wasn't that kind of woman—well, that just told him, she just might be that kind of woman.

Nice-looking woman. That old man of hers better watch his shit, though. In-Law was ripe for picking, and right time, right place, right game—she'd play.

"Let the good times roll, baby," Gregory laughed out loud.

So he loved Sherry. But he loved Elise more. How many times had he said he did? Elise couldn't sit in this holding pattern forever, though. And he shouldn't have expected her to. Jay was complacent and content to leave this relationship right where it was, but they'd been together too long for that. Elise needed more, and she suspected that he did, too, but Jay was bound by obligations and maybe even fear of the unknown.

"Hello?" The woman answering the phone sounded half asleep.

Sherry.

Elise's heart beat fast. Her palms sweated. She'd dialed this number on impulse, with no idea as to what she'd say. She'd hoped he'd answered the phone, but no . . . Sherry needed to be the one.

"Hello?" Sherry asked again, more irritated.

It wasn't as if Elise wanted to fuck things up for Jay. She wasn't mad at him, or trying to make things more difficult than they already were, but something needed to be done. The two of them had become like an old married couple, without the benefit of marriage. A routine had set in, and if she didn't make a move, if somebody didn't make a move, then, this is the way it would be for the next twenty years.

"Who is it, baby?" Elise heard his voice in the background, and hung up the phone before Sherry had a chance to.

Panic had set in. Frustration, and impatience. Being the other woman wasn't cool. Being jealous and envious of Jay's wife wasn't cool either, but she was. She always had been, only she'd been careful not to let him know it.

Elise sat up in bed, tempted to call his house again, and say—what? If he found out it was her, he'd be pissed. And then all hell would break loose, and he'd turn on her. Instinctively she knew he would. But if he loved her as much as he said he did, then he would never leave her.

Elise was ready to move forward with this man. He should've been ready to move, too. Sure, he had the kids to think about. The last thing she wanted was for his kids to suffer through all this. But she'd seen no signs of him even trying to get out of his marriage. That's what bothered her.

"I can't keep doing this, Jay," Elise told him. "You can't keep doing it, baby. We need to be together more than just once a week if we're going to do this thing the right way."

"How many times do I have to say it, Elise?" he argued. "I'm doing the best I can, baby. It's not easy to just walk away like that. I have too much at stake."

Of course he did. She knew that.

"Then what am I supposed to do, Jay? How long do you expect me to wait on you?"

The way he looked at her . . . the way he pulled her close to him—persuasive. Very persuasive. "As long as it takes, baby."

Some days, she knew she could wait as long as it took. But other days, Elise knew it would be impossible.

Something had to give. Maybe he needed an ultimatum, but could she live with that? Maybe it was Sherry who needed the push. If she suspected something was going on, if she knew Elise was in the picture, then maybe she'd be the one to make the move he didn't seem to have the courage to make. But she'd have to find out in such a way that Elise would never be suspected of revealing it.

What was it that Dr. Watkins said? Prayer and faith. The secrets to making a marriage successful. She and Jay weren't married, but they might as well have been. And she'd prayed for the two of them to make it from the beginning. Maybe now it was time to put some real faith to work, and to step outside of what was comfortable to make things uncomfortable for both of them. Stepping out on faith was never easy. But the rewards, especially in this case, could be grand.

It's an unnatural obsession bordering on irrationality, Lewis explained to Renee, sitting across from him in a secluded booth at a restaurant uptown called Dragonflys. "And I just can't shake it, Renee. No matter how hard I try." Lewis managed to talk her into having dinner with him on one of Trishelle's yoga nights.

He wondered if she'd even been listening to him the way she had her head buried in that plate of appetizers, like a horse eating from a trough.

"Oh, my God!" she said, rolling her eyes and inhaling a crab cannelloni. "Have you tried this?" Renee patted her chest, and moaned. "I think I've died and gone to heaven."

He was frustrated and it showed. "Should I wait for you to finish before I continue what I was saying?"

All she could do was nod, take a sip of wine, and grunt.

He assumed that meant yes. "What the hell am I even doing here with you?"

"Try the roasted pheasant, Lewis." She filled her fork with a biteful and held it up to his lips. "I'm telling you. You don't know what you're missing."

He hadn't touched his food, but she'd been in heaven ever since the waitress set this Moroccan treasure down in front of her, smacking her lips, and licking the skin off her fingers, like she'd had no home-training whatsoever.

Lewis watched her eat, trying to figure out what it was he ever saw in her in the first place. "You always eat like this?"

Renee nodded. "I haven't eaten all day," she said with her mouth full. "And—" she swallowed hard "—this shit is delicious."

Lewis sat quietly while she finished eating, realizing he'd made a mistake asking to see her. The thrill was gone already, and all he wanted to do was pay the bill and go home.

Renee finished her food, gulped down the last of her drink, then excused herself to go the bathroom. It was the way she walked that did it, ignited him for her all over again. Renee's long skirt, clung possessively to her curves, her ass, bounced just enough to make a few heads turn. A few minutes later, as she walked back to their table, the front side of her made quite an impression as well.

She smiled at him and sighed. "That was heaven on Earth. Good, good food."

"This is one of my favorite restaurants."

"Yours and Trish's?" She leaned forward on her elbows and stared back into his eyes.

Lewis wasn't stupid. He knew what she was doing, what she'd been doing all evening—trying to turn him off and get him to keep his distance.

"By the way." Renee turned and looked around the room. "Is she joining us?"

"No," he said calmly. "But if she were, with the way you inhaled that food, she'd have to get hers to go."

Renee playfully threw her napkin across the table at him. "I told you I was starving. Stop teasing me."

Lewis's expression changed, and he looked serious all of a sudden. "I'm not the one who's the tease here, Renee. Am I?"

Okay, this brotha was tripping, and flipping back into his weird self, and Renee really wasn't going to go there with him. "I saw your naked ass all pressed up against your wife in the bedroom of that huge house of yours the other day, Lewis. I'm not trying to trespass on another woman's boo like that. We had a good romp."

"Very good."

She did her best to ignore him. "So, there was some chemistry here." She motioned between the two of them. "But that's all it was, so why are we having this conversation?"

Lewis's frustration showed through as he leaned away from the table, then forward again to keep his voice from traveling. Renee's ass was hard-headed sometimes. Stubborn and smart-alecky, too damn quick to give him that talk-to-the-hand, neck-twirling routine. "We're having this conversation because I want you," he said firmly.

"Well, you had me—we had each other. End of story. Nuff said. Next."

"Let's go to your place."

Renee looked appalled. "Have you been lobotomized, Lewis?" she shrieked. "I just said—no. No means no." Renee slid out of the booth, grabbed hold of her purse, and hurried toward the door. His ass was scaring her. The last thing she needed was a crazed stalker in her life, one with a wife and a foaming-at-the-mouth-vicious kid hot on his trail. "Lord, please," she said, under her breath. "Not the drama. You know I don't do drama."

Lewis left a hundred-dollar bill on the table then hurried after her. "Renee!"

"Go to hell, Lewis!" she called back over her shoulder. She knew her shit was good, but damn! She'd never had anybody chase after her for it like this. She searched through her purse for her car keys, and almost ran the rest of the way to where she'd parked.

"Renee!" he called out again. "Baby!"

Renee stopped dead in her tracks and turned to Lewis, propping her hand on her hip. *Baby? Baby* was a term reserved for children and significant others, of which she was neither.

The next thing she knew, Lewis stood toe to toe with her, put his hand under her chin, then just like in a fairy tale, leaned his long, tall self down and gave her one of those handsome prince kisses every straight girl dreams about, no matter how hardcore she is. Lewis slipped a muscular arm around her waist and pulled her close enough to him to feel just how much he *really* wanted her.

"Lewis, stop," she said, breathless between tongue wars. "Mmmmm." Damn, that was some good sugar. "Lewis!" she protested. "Stop it. You're making me—"

"What?"

"Shit," Renee averted all her strength to her knees to keep them from giving out on her. "Mmmm. Damn."

"Your house?"

She shook her head no, broke free from his kiss, then hurried into her car. "Be there in five minutes," she commanded.

Lewis ran to his car, and was there waiting on her when she pulled up.

"Jesse?" That was all she had to say. He thought he was over her until he heard her voice.

"Hold on, please." He got up and closed the door to his office, then sat back down behind his desk. "Yes."

Sandra's laugh rolled from the back of her throat, past beautiful full lips he envisioned in his mind. Jesse tried to control his racing heart, taking silent deep breaths, careful not to let her hear the urgency inside him. "I asked how you were."

He leaned back, and searched his thoughts for what he should say. There were so many things he'd wanted to tell her. So many speeches he'd rehearsed if he ever heard from her again. But now, his mind was blank, and the best he could come up with was, "Fine. And you?"

She seemed put off by how cold and indifferent he sounded. "I came across your number, and thought it might be a good time to call. Were you busy? Did I interrupt—"

"No," he said hurriedly. "No, this is as good a time as any, I suppose."

"I was thinking about you," she said hesitantly. "Wanted to see how you were."

"Good. I'm good, Sandra," he lied, but Jesse was relieved knowing that she'd thought about him, just like he'd been thinking about her. And it was so good to hear her say it. "How are things with you?"

"So, so," she said hesitantly. "Some days are better than others. And then, some days are hard, like today. I usually dial your number on those days."

"You've called before? I didn't get the messages," he said, almost too quickly.

"That's because I never left any. In fact, I usually hung up the phone before your voicemail picked up. I wasn't so strong today. I needed to hear you, Jesse. That's all."

"I think about you, too, or rather, I try not to," he explained. "Time has made it easier."

"For me, too." She sounded sad. "But I think today will send me back almost to the beginning again."

"I love you." He said it before he realized he had, but it wasn't something he wanted to take back. She used to love hearing him say it when they were together, and he hoped that hadn't changed.

"I know you do, Jesse. I've always known, but—you just couldn't love me the way I needed you to."

"Don't say that," he begged.

"It's true."

"It's not true," he argued earnestly. "I love you more now than I ever have."

"But not more than Tess. Could you ever possibly love me more than you love your wife?"

"Yes!" he said, too quickly. "I mean—. It's more complicated than that."

"It always was," she said quietly. "And that's the problem. It's never been complicated for me. I love you. It's just that simple.

And no matter how hard I try, I can't seem to get over you. You can't seem to get over the complication."

"Tess and I have been together a long time, Sandra. I can't just throw that time away."

"Does Tess make you happy, Jesse? Have you ever been as happy with her as you've been with me?

He didn't answer.

"I never understood that," she said simply. "I never understood what was so complicated."

The house smelled of fried chicken when he walked in. Tess was sitting in the family room, with her legs tucked beneath her, working a crossword puzzle from one of those books she was always buying at the grocery store check-out display. "How was your day?" she asked, never bothering to look up from her book.

He leaned down and kissed her lightly on the cheek. "Fine. What's for dinner?" He knew the answer to that question before he'd even asked.

"Chicken, mashed potatoes, gravy, and string beans. Want me to make you a plate?" she offered.

Jesse headed into the kitchen. "No. Don't get up. I got it." For over twenty years he'd come home to evenings like this. Did he really want to come home to them for twenty more years?

He showered, then crawled into bed early, and flicked through the channels until he came to his favorite cop show. Jesse's thoughts were on the call from Sandra. Hearing from her seemed to change the course of his thinking. Or at least, of the kinds of things he should be thinking about. Jesse had seeds in his body, pumping radiation through him on a constant basis to hold back the cancer that had taken his father's life and his brother's. His chances were good that he'd come through this thing just fine, and when he did, then what? He and Tess hadn't made love in months. And honestly, neither of them even seemed interested in each other to want to have sex. Tess had a chip on her shoulder, she tried not to let him see, but he knew it was there, and he knew he was a tolerance to his wife, more than anything right about now. She was still angry about the affair—hell, she was angry about a lot of affairs. But how long would he let her anger be his responsibility? How much longer would he be allowed to walk this Earth, and how much longer could he deny himself the chance to be with someone who made him happy?

She eventually made it up to bed. Tess slipped out of her robe, then crawled into bed next to her husband, kissed him flatly on the cheek, then turned over on her side, her back to him. "Good night," she muttered.

A few minutes later, he turned off the television, rolled over on his side, with his back facing her, and drifted off to sleep, recalling the softness in Sandra's voice.

"*It's cold as shit* out here," Jay complained, tightening the collar of his jacket around his neck. He shoved his hands deep into his pockets, and welcomed the warmth of Elise pressed against him, her arm looped around his. "Maybe coming out here was a bad idea," he joked.

Elise smiled but didn't say anything.

He'd waited at the coffee shop across the street from her office, after pulling into town, until she got off work. Jay knew right away she had something on her mind, but when he asked, she smiled, shrugged, and wrapped her arm around his.

"You hungry?"

She shook her head. "No. I had a late lunch."

He was starving because he hadn't eaten since breakfast. But it was cool. He could wait a while longer.

It was his idea to walk through the park. Elise seemed to be doing everything in her power not to talk to him for some reason, and he needed to know why. "So, you wanna tell me what's up?"

"What do you mean?" she asked nonchalantly.

"You're mighty quiet this evening." He looked down at her and smiled. "You sick or something?"

Elise managed to laugh and roll her eyes. "You trying to tell me I talk too much?"

He shrugged, and she playfully hit him on the arm. "You wanna tell me what's on your mind?"

Elise stared reflectively up ahead in the distance and sighed. "You're on my mind, Jay," she said ruefully, "You're always on my mind."

"I would be flattered, but something tells me, I shouldn't be. What did I do?" Lately, he'd been busy loving his wife. Maybe Elise knew. He and Sherry had been spending more time together, and he missed her when she was gone. Letting go wasn't an easy thought when she was close to him. He knew good and damn well, though, that after he spent the night and made reluctant, but satisfying love to this woman, that he'd climb back into his rig, head down the road a bit, and come to his senses. That's when he'd tell himself that he needed the woman at home more than he needed this one, and that he was a fool for risking everything he ever wanted in life, for something that he should've never messed with in the first place. Right now, though, she smelled good, and the sound of her voice was like a sweet song in his ears, she was beautiful candy to his eyes, and his dick was getting hard. But leading her on wasn't cool. In fact, it was just mean.

"I need to know where this is going, Jay? *This* meaning you and me. We've been together a year now."

"And I've enjoyed every minute of it."

"So have I, but . . . where do we go from here?"

Jay looked at her, and he saw that opportunity he'd been looking for. Without knowing it, Elise had just opened the door wide open and all he had to do was step through it, and take his ass back home.

"Face it. You're not ever going to leave Sherry," Elise said, disappointed. "And there's no way I can ever compete with her." Her eyes glistened with tears, but Elise blinked them away before they fell. "I think we need to stop seeing each other, and you need to go home." She let go of his arm, and turned and walked quickly back toward the car.

It was automatic. Jay could've just let her walk away. He could've accepted that it was over and left her alone, then pulled that truck of his back out onto the highway, breathed a sigh of relief, and rested in the fact that he no longer had to worry about splitting himself between two women anymore. He could be happy with the one he had, the one he loved and was married to, the mother of his children. But a pang stabbed him in his chest so strong, it overrode logic and replaced it with desperation. Just one more night.

"Elise!" he shouted, then ran after her. He reached out and grabbed her by the arm. "You know I can't just let you walk away like that," he said.

Elise jerked away from him. "I can't do this, Jay! I love you too much, and I can't spend the rest of my life sharing you with somebody else!"

Jay gathered her up and pulled her close to him. He wrapped his arms around her and pressed her to his chest. He couldn't breathe, all of a sudden, and she was the oxygen he needed. It didn't make any sense to him, but he held on tight, because he needed to, and she needed him to.

Elise stopped struggling and held on to him. "You're messing me up, Jay! I know you're going to—"

"Not on purpose, baby," he said desperately.

He was sprung like a mothafucka. Jay drove down the highway, spent, and disgusted with himself for being weak. For cheating on the woman he loved and for loving the woman he cheated on her with. The bottom line was, he didn't deserve either one. He knew it, and if he didn't straighten up, both of them would know it, too, and they'd both be kicking him to the curb.

No, this was the last time, he vowed to himself. He needed to leave Elise alone, for all their sakes. It was a bomb waiting to go off, and Jay was the one who would set it off if he wasn't careful. The last thing he wanted to do was to hurt Elise. But like she'd said, there was no way around it. He'd have to hurt her, to save her. And he'd hurt himself in the process. But he deserved it. She didn't.

"Hurry up!" Daria demanded irritably, standing in front of the full-length mirror with her hands propped on her hips. Her poor cousin was behind her, bent over at the waist, trying to get Daria zipped into her wedding dress.

Elise walked into the madhouse, shaking her head. Daria was fussing, her mother was fussing, her sisters were arguing, and her cousin was stuck in a fixed position at Daria's backside, trying to zip up a dress that was entirely too small.

Elise walked over to Daria, and nudged her cousin out of the way. "A size twelve would've fit."

"This one fits," Daria grunted.

Elise pulled the two sides of the dress together as tight as she could, and gradually inched the zipper up Daria's back until she finally got it all the way up. She looked at Daria in the mirror, who looked like she was about to explode. "You all right?"

"How long do I have to be in this thing?" she said, taking short breaths.

"Fifteen . . . twenty minutes—tops," Elise assured her.

Daria nodded. "Go tell the minister I can't do no more than ten."

It was a good-size wedding considering they'd put it together in less than two months. Daria was doing her best not to look four months pregnant and Donny tried his best not to look like he was making the biggest mistake of his life. A match made in heaven, Elise thought, watching the two standing side by side at the altar. The only thing missing was the shotgun, but knowing Daria, she had one up underneath that dress of hers.

All eyes were on Daria and Donny, smiling, nodding, dabbing away tears from their eyes, or rolling their eyes. Daria's mother smiled and winked at Elise. She'd taken on the role of mother to Elise ever since her own mother moved to Florida. Daria's cousin—what's her face—stuck her tongue out at Elise, then snickered to herself. Her mother drilled her elbow into her until she stopped, then muttered something under her breath, making the girl's face turn to stone.

Daria's life would be completely changed in the next ten minutes. Elise looked at her friend, her eyes bulging, sweat beading around the bridge of her nose and forehead, her apprehensive smile, and realized, if that preacher didn't hurry, Daria would pass out cold in a minute.

"You may kiss the bride," Elise heard the minister say.

It happened so fast. One minute, there was just Daria and now there was Daria and her baby and her baby daddy.

Elise and Daria stood huddled in the corner of the room at the reception. Daria had changed into something that fit and could now breathe like regular people.

"Girl, you lying!" Daria blurted out.

"Shhhh!" Elise tried to quiet her down. "I don't want the whole world to know, D!" she tried to whisper.

"Are you sure?"

Elise nodded.

"Positive?"

She nodded again. "I'm a month late. I took the test this morning and it came back positive."

The two stood without talking for several minutes. "You gonna keep it?" Daria finally asked.

Elise stared at her blankly. She hadn't thought about it. Not enough time had passed to think that far ahead. Keep it? She shrugged. "I don't know."

"You want it?" Daria asked cautiously.

Elise thought for a minute. She was carrying Jay's baby. She was carrying their baby. It was a part of something in her life that she'd come to treasure, but it would be a constant reminder, too, of something she could never have.

"He's married, D," Elise blurted out.

Daria stared at her. "Who?" Elise didn't answer. But then, she didn't need to. Daria's eyes lit up. "Jay?" she said in a loud whisper. "Girl, you lying! Why didn't you tell me?"

Elise felt flushed. "I wanted to. No. No I didn't. I didn't want to, D. Because he was all that, and he was cool, and it was just supposed to be this thing . . . this thing that wasn't supposed to last this long, and I wasn't supposed to fall in love . . . and I was horny, D. I just wanted to do the deed and move on, but he's so perfect, and right and he's everything I ever told you he was . . ."

"Except you never told me he had a wife."

"Because I couldn't! Because you'd think I was crazy and you'd tell me I needed to leave him alone!"

"And I'd have been right! And you know it! Now look at you! I know you're not keeping it, E. Tell me you're not keeping this man's baby."

"Hey, baby." Donny slipped up behind Daria, and wrapped his arms around her waist. "Come dance with your husband?"

Daria wanted to shoo him away. She glared at Elise the whole time Donny led her to the dance floor, shaking her head, and promising with a look that this conversation was not over.

Elise slipped out of the reception unnoticed before Daria could find her and cuss her out. Before Daria could talk her into having an abortion she wasn't sure she wanted. She needed time to herself to process everything that had happened since peeing on that plastic stick this morning. Elise pulled her wrap tight around her, and slowly walked to her car. She hadn't even told Jay yet. She stopped and stood still, wondering what his reaction might be. Instinctively, she knew it wouldn't be good. But maybe, she'd be surprised. She started walking again. He had a way of doing that sometimes. Jay had a way of coming through for her when she least expected in ways she least expected, because he was just kind like that. And he cared for her. She knew he loved her. He could love this baby, too.

She realized she was getting ahead of herself and Elise drew back her most ambitious thoughts. She needed to pull herself together. Was she ready for a baby? Did she even want one right now? The idea of being a single mother never appealed to her and she always believed she'd have a husband when she had kids—her own, not someone else's.

She leaned up against the side of her car, then let her hand slip tentatively down to her stomach. There was a child growing inside her and the confusion, fear, and apprehension she felt couldn't help but be overpowered by the joy in the center of them all. Jay was like water, and he could slip through her fingers at any moment. But this baby . . . Elise felt herself smile. This baby was hers. Even if she never told him, or if he never wanted it, it belonged to her, and it was a creation bigger than the two of them put together.

Elise climbed into her car and started the engine. Tonight, she knew that she wanted this baby, and that she wanted to have this baby. Tomorrow—was never promised.

renee

"*Married men are only* after one thing, Renee."

"Well, then I should be a married man because that's all I'm after, too, Doc."

"What about his wife? I thought she was your friend?"

"I wouldn't do this with my friend's man, Dr. Faye. So what does that tell you?"

"I find your attitude appalling."

"Lighten up. It's just sex. Seeing Lewis is sort of like babysitting your niece and nephews, spoiling them rotten, and then sending them home to their real mommas. It's like playing with a puppy without having to bother with housebreaking. It's a good time, Doc. Quick and easy."

"Is that what you really believe?"

"Look. It happened. It wasn't planned, or even all that well thought out. We did what we did, and his wife will never have to be the wiser. Not unless he tells her, but she'll never hear it from me. It's not even all that serious. I'm not trying to take her man from her. Hell, half the time I don't even like her man."

"Then why would you do something like this?"

"Why do I get the feeling you're taking this way too personally, Doc? It's not like he's the Reverend."

"But he could be. That's the point I'm trying to get across, Renee. There's a woman out there putting all her faith and trust into her husband, and she has no idea that he's laying up with a woman like—"

"Like me? That's what you wanted to say, right? You know, Lewis isn't the first married man I've slept with. I hadn't planned on doing him either. Married men have very little to offer except sex."

"And that's enough for you?"

"For the time being—yes."

"Then I feel sorry for you."

"Women like you put way too much stock into that lame idea of the sanctity of marriage, Dr. Faye. Men cheat. It's the nature of the beast and it's been that way since the dawn of time."

"But who would they cheat with if we weren't there to accommodate them, Renee?"

She shrugged. "Shit. Each other. Down low, Doc. It's all the rage. Or haven't you heard?"

"I'm disappointed in you. I thought you were stronger than this. I thought you put more stock in yourself, Renee."

Disappointment and anger snuck up on Renee, glistening in her eyes like tears. "I didn't tell you this so that you could judge me," she said resentfully.

"Then why did you tell me?"

"You're my counselor," she said resolutely. "This is where I should be able to come to talk, to vent. I needed someone to talk to. Someone to listen without passing judgment."

"I'm also a Christian."

"Yeah, Doc. Like I don't already know that."

"*You could at least* pretend to show a little enthusiasm, Lewis," Trishelle said, helping him to adjust his tie. She'd been looking forward to hosting their first dinner party ever since the fantastic results of Renee's designs had started to take shape. And Trish had been making more of an effort to make herself feel at home in this strange land. She'd start a new teaching job next fall at one of the local high schools, and she'd even made a few friends here and there. Lewis, on the other hand, was as distant and brooding as ever, it seemed. There were moments when the tension wasn't so thick between them, but they were fleeting moments. Tonight he was getting her to do what he'd been wanting her to do since they first moved here, to be the socialite wife, the gracious hostess. But he'd wanted her to do it in a monster of a house, with its bare walls and hollow rooms, at the drop of a hat, and he knew her well enough to know that she'd never been that spontaneous.

"I am enthusiastic," he said dryly. "Or haven't you noticed?"

"You should feel relieved, Lewis. You've been begging me to do this for months."

"And you made sure to shut me down every time. But this is your party, baby." He kissed her forehead and headed toward the bedroom door. "And I'm going to be the good husband and support you tonight with your little shindig." Before she could respond, the doorbell rang. He smiled. "I'll get it."

In a matter of weeks, Trishelle had managed to pull together a guest list of a hundred people, hire one of the best caterers in the city, and throw one hell of an event. Lewis' coworkers were there, patting him on the back and filling him up with kudos on his lovely wife and home.

Renee finally arrived fashionably-colored-people's-time late, wearing a black, form-fitting crepe dress, silver stiletto sandals, and a faux fur super short jacket that just barely covered her arms. Her full head of hair was pulled back off her face and into a puff at the nape of her neck. A hush seemed to come over the whole room when she entered. She looked gorgeous. Earlier that day, she'd left him a curt message at his office.

"I tried to get out of it, but Trish wouldn't take no for an answer. I'll be there, but I'm not staying long."

Lewis glanced around the room, and noticed other men with their wives, trying hard not to stare, too.

Trish breezed through the crowd over to Renee, and gave her air kisses. "Renee! I'm so glad you could join us."

"Oh, you know I wouldn't have missed this for anything in the world," Renee lied.

Trish addressed the guests. "Everyone. I'd like you all to pay homage to my fantastic decorator and friend, Renee Turner!"

Renee felt herself blush as the crowd gave polite applause.

"If it weren't for this woman, well, Lewis and I would still be living in what amounted to not much more than an expensive box," Trish joked.

Lewis feigned a weak smile, and lifted his glass in a feeble toast to his wife. For a brief moment, he and Renee locked eyes, but both quickly broke the connection.

He had to admit, his wife did look lovely tonight. Trish wore white like nobody's business, and with that long, lean frame of hers, the sea of color never seemed to end. She looked like she floated over to him, instead of walked, fluid and loose, and gliding across the room like an apparition. She smiled at her husband, took his glass from his hand, and sipped.

"Am I making it up to you yet?" she asked playfully.

Lewis couldn't help but smile back. He nodded. "Yes. I have to admit, you are making it up to me pretty good."

"Your boss is having a good time. He and the missus drink like fish and eat like piranhas, but they seem to be enjoying themselves."

"Well, at least now we know."

"I love our home, Lewis," Trishelle said sincerely. "I really do."

"I'd hoped you would." He ran his hand lightly up her arm. "I've only ever done any of this for us, Trish. Not just me. I know you don't believe that, but—"

"Sometimes, I do believe it, when I let myself. We've had hard times. That's all."

"Yeah, well—" Lewis spotted Renee over Trish's shoulder, talking to one of his neighbors, and felt pinched by jealousy.

"All I ask is that we keep the lines of communication open between us, baby," she explained. "Don't shut me out, Lewis. And don't forget that I have needs, too."

Renee laughed at something the neighbor said, or at least she pretended to. Lewis could tell she was faking. The neighbor managed to slip his hand on her back, leading her to a couple a few feet away, introducing her, but he was obviously in no hurry to take his hands off her.

"I'll try to do better, Trish," Lewis responded, then turned his attention back to his wife. "I promise."

Trish kissed him softly. "Then I promise I'll try and do better, too."

Renee excused herself to the restroom. Trish was busy in the kitchen with the caterers. Lewis waited until Renee disappeared down the hallway, then changed her course and headed to one of the bathrooms upstairs because the two downstairs were occupied.

Making his way through the crowd, he smiled and acknowledged his guests like the perfect host. He accepted their compliments and well wishes on his new assignment, and assured them that he and his wife looked forward to making appearances at dinner parties, Christmas parties, Bar Mitzvahs. He ascended the stairs, following her trail to the large bathroom down the long corridor heading toward the guest bedrooms. Lewis caught up just in time to see Renee disappear into one of the rooms. Each one had private baths.

Renee closed the door to the bathroom, not realizing he was behind her. Lewis quietly closed the door to the guest room, and crept over to the bathroom door. He listened as she peed, flushed the toilet, and finally washed her hands. Then Lewis slowly turned the knob and let himself in before she had time to protest.

"What the—"

Lewis hurried and scooped her up in his arms, then covered her mouth with his. Renee hardly knew what hit her.

"Lewis!" she whispered loudly, pushing him off her. "Are you crazy?" She looked closer. "Are you drunk?"

The wild look in his eyes was alarming, and Renee quickly assessed the situation, wondering how in the world she was going to get past Lewis to the door, down the stairs, and out of this house.

Lewis backed her up against the wall, pinning her in place.

Renee struggled to get free. "Your wife is downstairs, man! What the hell do you think you're doing? Do you want to get caught?"

"Don't fight me, Renee," he said calmly. "I just want to talk, baby."

"In the bathroom?"

"What's wrong with the bathroom?"

"Anybody could walk in here at any minute."

He reached over and locked the door. "There. Now, no one's going to walk in. Just calm down and give me a few minutes. That's all I'm asking."

Renee stopped struggling, and Lewis eased up off her, and leaned back against the sink.

"We don't have anything to talk about, Lewis," Renee said, frustrated. "Why do you keep pushing this?"

"Because you turn me on," he said simply.

"That's your problem, because I'm done, Lewis. It was short. It was fun. It was sweet. The end."

Lewis couldn't help but laugh. "You have such a unique way of putting things."

"I'm putting it as forthright as I know how to. Pay attention."

Lewis ran his finger across her lips. "I am paying attention. Or haven't you noticed?"

"Now see—shit like that is going to get me into trouble. Watch your mouth!"

"No." Lewis pulled her close. "I'd much rather watch yours."

Lewis put the lid down on the toilet, and pulled Renee onto his lap. He moved her thong over to the side, unzipped his pants, and pulled out his penis that was hard and waiting for her. Renee, caught up in kisses, handed him a condom she had in her purse. A girl's always got to be prepared. It took no more than a few minutes, but it was a rich few minutes of deep erotic lovemaking that brought her to climax first, and his, shortly thereafter. They washed up next to each other in silence. Lewis wrapped the used condom up in a tissue, and then balled it up in his fist to throw away in the garbage outside.

She came downstairs first, flitting around the crowd like a butterfly, graciously accepting accolades and business offers. Lewis appeared a few minutes later, and commandeered a glass of champagne from a waiter walking by. A few minutes later, Renee said her good-byes to Trish and her husband before excusing herself for the evening.

tess

She left a voice mail for Faye's receptionist. "This is Tess Martin. I'm going to have to cancel my appointment for today with Dr. Watkins. Something's come up."

Where she ever found the courage to even ask was beyond her. "I know this is going to sound crazy, coming from me." She cleared her throat nervously, knowing he probably thought she was a lunatic. "But—do you think, I mean, if you're not too busy—I was wondering . . . I really enjoyed myself and I've been fascinated by that thing ever since—"

Gregory finished the request for her. "You wanna ride."

Tess squeezed her eyes shut tight, feeling like a fool for even calling this man. But she was a fool. Had been her whole life. "Yes," she said. "Would you mind?"

"Naw, In-Law." He sounded smug, and she hated him for it. "It would be my pleasure."

They discussed a time and place to meet. He wanted to just swing by the house and pick her up, but that was out of the question. "I'll need a helmet," she told him before hanging up. "Otherwise—well, it's just not safe."

"You can use mine."

He drove like he had some sense this time, taking a more leisurely route through the city until they finally stopped at White Rock Lake. Riding on the back of that motorcycle, Tess let go of all her worries, regrets, anger. Gregory never said a word, even when they met up at the grocery store across town from where she lived. Why she was being so secretive surprised her. They weren't doing anything wrong, and thanks to the bonds of matrimony, he was practically family. But discretion was a by-product of being married to a man who sometimes forgot how to be.

They walked out to the edge of a dock, sat down, and let their feet dangle over the edge. Today, for whatever reason, Gregory was surprisingly well-behaved, even polite. She couldn't help but ask.

"So what's gotten into you?"

He didn't answer her right away, and Tess almost thought he wouldn't. "I need a damn job," he said bitterly.

She gazed longingly out across the water. "Yep. You sure do."

He shook his head, frustrated. "Yeah. Just be glad I don't have one, or else your ass would be sitting at home darning socks or some shit like that."

"I don't darn socks," she said, appalled, but strangely relieved to see the real Gregory show up. The smart-assed one who wasn't about shit.

"What do you do?" he asked flippantly.

Tess glared at him. "I do plenty. More than you."

Neither of them spoke for several minutes. Tess finally broke the silence.

"You ever been married?"

"Why? You wanna be my girlfriend?"

She rolled her eyes. "Hell no."

"Then what do you care?"

"How come you can't just hold up your end of a decent

conversation," she snapped. "Why does everything have to be a joke or smart-aleck remark?"

He chuckled.

"You make me sick," she muttered.

"Then why the hell you want to be with me?"

"What makes you think I want to be with you?"

He looked at her like she was crazy. The expression on his face spoke volumes, and all of a sudden Tess was embarrassed.

"I called because I wanted a ride," she said with attitude. "And that's it."

"Sure it is," he mumbled. "It's all good, boo."

"Don't call me that," she grunted.

"Why? Remind you too much of your old man?"

Tess didn't answer. Obviously, she'd lost her mind somewhere on her pillow this morning when she got up. What other reason would she have to be out here with this fool? There were times when she didn't know what she wanted anymore. Tess was so lost these days, everything she ever thought she wanted got on her nerves, and whenever she tried to figure out what it was she did want, her mind just went blank.

"He ain't taking care of business?" He didn't wait for an answer. "Hmph. Must not be."

"My personal life is none of your business."

"Well, you all up in my Kool-Aid all the damn time. Seems to me you could share some, too."

Tess stared at him for a moment, and then surprised them both by laughing. "That's the dumbest, most ghetto comment I've ever heard."

He looked offended. "Oh! Oh now my ass is ghetto?"

"Yeah," she laughed harder. "Very ghetto."

Shit. It was funny. And hell yeah, he was ghetto. Had been his whole life and he'd go to his grave ghetto as hell. "What the fuck ever, Tess," he said laughing.

Tess composed herself and looked at him. "You remember my name?"

"What the hell's that supposed to mean? Of course I know your name."

"You never say it. Always calling me In-Law."

"That's what you are."

"No," she said adamantly. "I'm Tess. Tess Martin." She held out her hand for him to shake.

Gregory reached out his. " 'Sup," he teased.

"You're a mess." She snatched her hand away.

"So when you gonna tell me why you're out with me?"

"I'm not out with you." She picked up a small rock and threw it into the lake. "I just wanted a ride."

He smirked.

"What?" she asked suspiciously. "I like your bike, Gregory. All I wanted to do was ride."

"Just my bike?" he asked smugly.

Tess stared back at him, appalled. "You need to take me home." She started to get up to leave, but he grabbed hold of her arm and held her in place.

"I'm digging you, too, Tess. Ain't nothing wrong with that."

"There is something wrong with it," she snapped. "I'm not digging you and I've got a husband."

"If you gave a damn about your husband, you wouldn't have called me up."

She jerked from him, and bolted to her feet.

He took his time following after her. Unlike his date,

though, Gregory wasn't in denial. She dug him the way he dug her. Otherwise, she'd have gone out and bought her own motorcycle.

"What are we doing here?" she asked nervously, as he pulled up to his house.

He let her climb off the bike, then turned off the engine and climbed off, too. "I need to get something," he said, heading inside.

Tess waited outside in the driveway for at least ten minutes before finally going inside. "I really need you to take me home, Greg."

He'd taken off his gloves, unbuttoned his shirt, and slowly made his way over to where she was standing.

Her heart raced. Tess wanted to turn and run away screaming—or did she? Calloused hands cradled her face. Soft lips caressed hers. An untamed tongue wrestled with hers.

"You are driving me up the fucking wall," he said, pressing her back against the door. "Let's do this, baby. C'mon now."

It was all a blur to Tess. She ended up bent over the back of the couch, her face buried in the cushions. He'd pulled down her jeans, then his, bit the cheeks of her ass, then . . . *Slap!*

"Oh!" she yelled. It stung, but she wanted him to do it again.

"You like that?" he asked, rubbing the sore spot. "Tell me you like it, baby."

Did she like it? Did Tess want him to hit her again?

He didn't wait for her to answer. *Slap*! *Slap*!

"Yessss!" she screamed. "I like it." Her voice was muffled by the pillows.

"You like that shit?"

She was hotter than she'd ever been. Juices pooled between her legs, moistening her thighs.

Gregory inhaled deeply, then stuck a long finger between the folds of her pussy, then put it in his mouth. "Mmmmmm . . . sugah!" He leaned down close to her, pressing his body down on top of hers and whispered in her ear. "Don't let a man tell you your pussy ain't sweet, baby." Gregory flicked his tongue against her lips, then forced it into her mouth.

She felt his hand between her and him, fumbling with his zipper, freeing his cock, then rubbing the head against her, easing himself in, slowly.

"Please!" She wanted him to stop? to hurry? to fuck her the way she'd never been fucked before? the way Jesse never thought she deserved?

"You want this dick, girl," he teased, darting it in and out, enticing her. This was ecstacy. And it was torture.

"Put it in," Tess whispered. She stared ahead, feeling high and like she was lost in a dream.

"Now, baby?"

She rose up on her toes. "Now—god damn it!" she growled. "Put it in!"

The whole room smelled of sex. Half-empty food containers and soda and beer bottles littered the coffee table. The couch was old and musty smelling. But Tess might as well have been in heaven, because that's how good he felt. She'd never had a real orgasm before. Not one from a man. Hers had always been manufactured by her hand, or a plastic device. Tears streamed down her cheeks. He was hurting her in the best way. Gregory pounded her flesh unmercifully. Tess wanted to scream, but couldn't. She wanted to take a breath, but she couldn't. Her legs felt numb. Her pussy burned. And moments later, she came so hard, that she sank down to the floor on her knees at his feet, and he had to pick her up and carry her to the chair.

He cradled her half-naked body in his arms, and kissed her tenderly on the eyes and nose. She felt small, weak, helpless, and spent. She felt better than she had in her whole life. If this is what it felt like to give in to impulse, then no wonder Jesse fell prey to it.

"Beautiful women shouldn't have to go without some good loving," he whispered. "You like that roughneck fucking." He brushed her hair back off her face. "Don't you, baby? You like it nasty?"

Tess couldn't move. She couldn't say a word.

"That wasn't nothing," he assured her. "But damn if I ain't got some shit in store for you."

Jesse came home and kissed her cheek. "What's for dinner?" he asked like he always did.

"Pork chops," she answered. "Want me to make you a plate?"

"No," he said, heading into the kitchen, the way he always did. "I got it."

elise

"You disappointed in me?" Elise sounded like a child, waiting nervously for Dr. Faye's response.

"I just wonder why you would do something like this, Elise. And why bring a baby into this situation."

Elise could barely bring herself to look the woman in the eyes. "I can't have an abortion," she said meekly. "I won't do that, Dr. Faye."

"Have you told him?"

She shook her head no. "Not yet."

"How do you think he'll react when you do?"

Elise thought for a moment, but she didn't have an answer. "I don't know."

"If he doesn't want the baby, Elise? Then what?"

Elise toyed with the bracelet on her arm.

"Bottom line, Elise, there's a child to think about now. And that child comes before you and it comes before Jay, and even before Jay's wife."

She nodded. "I know."

"Then you have to be prepared for that, and you have to do whatever it takes to be there for this baby."

"I feel like such an idiot."

"Did you get pregnant on purpose?"

Elise looked at her.

"Well?"

"I wasn't as careful as I could've been," she admitted. "I think that's a yes, Dr. Faye."

"Hoping he'll decide to leave his wife for you?"

"Yes," she said softly.

"Why, Elise? Why would he leave her for you over this baby, when he has two kids with her, that he won't leave? Did you even think about that? Did it dawn on you that you've been so desperate to get this man, you haven't had a rational thought since you met him?"

Elise started to cry.

"The very thing you want from him is the very thing you're trying to take away from his own family, and that's just plain selfish!"

"If she were doing what she was supposed to be doing, then he wouldn't be with me!" she sobbed.

"It's none of your business what that woman is or isn't doing! Because all you know is what he tells you! And if he's low down enough to cheat on her, then what in the world makes you think he's being honest with you?"

Elise snatched up her purse, and headed for the door.

"Elise!"

Elise stopped dead in her tracks.

"You have made a fool of yourself!" Faye was crying, too. "You have let yourself be used and disrespected and you have put an entire family in jeopardy!"

"And what about him? I didn't make this baby all by myself!" She turned to Faye. "He's to blame, too!"

"Of course he is. But he's not in this room, baby."

Elise never looked back and quietly left the room.

"Hey," Elise said to Jay over the phone. "Are you coming down this week? I really need to see you?"

"This week's not good," he said slowly. "They've got me heading down to Florida," he lied.

"Oh, I see," she said disappointedly.

"I know, love. And I'm sorry, baby." Lately he'd been coming to the realization that it was time to cut ties with Elise. He had everything he wanted at home, and trying to have more than his share would get him in trouble if he wasn't careful.

"No, Jay," she said desperately. "I really do need to see you. It's important."

"I'll be up next week, honey," he relinquished. If he was going to end this relationship, the least he could do was to be man enough to do it in person.

"I'll be waiting for you at home." She sounded relieved.

Who knew the ocean could look and smell so good? Jay sat on the porch of the Cabana nestled on a hill above the beach, with his long legs stretched out in front of him. Tonight was their last night here, but they'd promised each other that it wouldn't be their last visit. The Bahamas was a good place to start over and renew what they'd let fall by the wayside in their marriage. It was a short trip, four days and three nights, but he'd loved every minute of it. The sea air cleared his mind of all the cobwebs in it and brought him back to reality.

"I'm ready," she said, standing in the doorway behind him. Jay stood up to the sound of her voice, and turned and saw how lovely she looked, wearing a pink-and-white dress with white sandals.

"You look beautiful, baby," he said, smiling and reaching out his hand to take hers.

She closed the door behind her, and followed him down the steps. "I'm starving," she said to him, squeezing his hand tight.

"Me too." He glanced back at her, and licked his lips. "And some dinner would be nice, too."

Sherry giggled.

They ate slowly, savoring every bite of dinner, gazing into each other's eyes. He enjoyed the mahi mahi baked in butter, rum, and onions. Sherry had lobster simmered in curry, butter, onions, milk, and lemon juice. Jay washed his meal down with a couple of bottles of Kalik Beer, and Sherry did her best not to get drunk on that Bahama Mama she was drinking, but Jay knew she was fighting in a war she had no chance of winning.

She ate one last bite, then sat back in her seat, sighed, and fanned herself. "Whew!" She smiled at him. "I think I'm done."

"You sure you don't want to try and finish up that Bahama Mama . . . Mama?" He winked.

"I'm drunk already, babe. What more do you want?"

"Good. Just don't pass out on me later on."

She leaned forward and ran her finger across his lips.

"I don't have any intentions of passing out," she said seductively. "But you better finish what's left on your plate and save your strength. You're gonna need it for what I have in store for you tonight."

With that, she slowly got up from her seat, picked up her purse and wrap, and sashayed out the door, turning to look at him one last time over her shoulder.

Jay pulled way too much money from his wallet, left it on the table to pay the check, and quickly followed behind her.

They made love to the rhythm of the ocean waves. The breeze drifted in through the open windows, and God bless anybody within a square-mile radius because they certainly got an earful that night.

Smothered pork chops, homemade mashed potatoes, fried cabbage, and sweetened lemon iced tea . . . she'd spent all afternoon cooking for him, knowing how Jay liked to eat, and fully expecting his mouth to start watering before he even stepped through the door. She quickly showered, and slipped into a slinky black satin gown, and matching kimono robe, then dabbed scented oil behind her ears, between her breasts, and on the insides of her thighs.

She stared at her reflection in the mirror, and applied clear lip gloss and some blush to her face. Elise tousled her hair and tried to blink away reservation from her eyes. He wasn't going to be happy about what she had to tell him. She knew better than to think he would be. Elise wasn't even sure she was happy about it. But the alternative just wasn't happening. She'd thought about it, forcing herself to think rationally and reasonably about the situation, but rationality and reason were nowhere to be found. It didn't make sense to have Jay's baby, but, it didn't make sense to do anything else either. She swallowed hard, running her hand across her stomach. She had a doctor's appointment tomorrow. She'd promised herself that she'd at least ask about an abortion. But Elise knew she wouldn't. She was old enough to know that life happens sometimes, and it's during those times that instinct kicks in, and a person just ends up running on automatic, until they finally land where they were meant to end up all along. This baby might as well have been crying in the other room for all she cared. It was just that real and she was dealing with that. Now, it was his turn to deal with it, too.

The doorbell rang. Whatever happened tonight, she'd just have to live with it.

"Hey," he said, kissing her on her cheek.

Elise's nerves gained new life and fluttered in her stomach. Jay looked gorgeous with a fresh haircut, and trimmed goatee. He was dressed simply, like always, wearing a white undershirt, jeans, and the black boots he wore when driving.

"Mmmm." Jay took a deep breath. "Something smells good, baby." He looked at her, and started to say something. Jay brushed passed her into the kitchen. "Damn! Is that fried cabbage? I haven't had fried cabbage in a grip!"

He was moving too fast for her. Elise couldn't quite put her finger on it, but for a second, it almost seemed as if he knew. Or like he was avoiding her for some reason. She watched him dip his finger in the mashed potatoes and put it in his mouth. "Mmmmm," he moaned.

He was just hungry, she concluded, feeling relieved. Of course he was. Jay'd been on the road for hours, and knowing he was coming over, and that she'd cook, of course he wouldn't stop and eat.

"Let me make you a plate," she laughed.

Jay sat down at the table, while Elise piled plenty of everything on his plate, poured him a glass of tea, then sat down next to him to watch him eat.

"Ain't you eating, baby?"

She shook her head. "I'm not really hungry. But you go ahead."

Jay started digging in, hardly looking up long enough to notice her sitting there. Elise's feelings were hurt. He'd stopped short of the compliments he normally showered her with.

She hadn't seen him in weeks, and watching him eat, she couldn't help but wonder if he'd missed her at all. "How was the drive down?" she asked, trying to make conversation.

Jay shrugged, and kept on eating. "This is good," he said with a mouthful of food.

He'd barely touched her when he walked in. Elise was on fire for Jay's touch, so she reached across the table and ran her finger lightly up and down his forearm. "I've missed you," she told him. Just a touch was all she needed to grow warm inside, and anxious for him to hurry up and finish his food.

Jay kept eating like he hadn't heard her. Like he didn't appreciate her advances, but Elise knew him better than that. Whatever game this was he was playing, for whatever reason, it was intriguing and Elise found herself feeling the need to rise to the challenge. Most of the time, it was him coming after her. Maybe it was time she needed to flip the script for a change, and to show him just how much she missed him, instead of feeding him or telling him.

Elise slowly stood up from the table, coaxed Jay's fork from his hand, and pushed back his plate and drink. He was such an easy man to figure out, she thought confidently. The look in his eyes at the sight of her coming toward him told her that. She stepped around to stand behind him, and slowly ran both hands down his shoulders, to his torso, and his groin, growing hard in his lap.

Jay forced down the food that was still stored in his cheek, almost choking on it. "Baby," he said, clearing his throat. "You gonna let me finish eating?"

Elise unbuttoned his belt buckle, then his jeans, and slid her hand down into his pants between Jay and his underwear, grabbing hold of that big piece of meat that couldn't hide the fact that he was happy to see her.

She lightly licked and bit down on his sensitive earlobe. "You are finished," she whispered. Elise's large breasts pressed up against the back of his neck. Somehow, she managed to free herself from her robe. Jay's chest heaved up and down, and he sat rigid at that table, like he was afraid to move. Elise couldn't help but smile. She liked this game. She liked being the one to take charge and manipulate this man in such a way that his body couldn't help but betray him. She leaned his head back, and pressed her lips to his, tasting the remnants of potatoes inside his mouth.

"You taste good, baby boy," she whispered. "Come see what Mama tastes like."

He was like a dog on a leash. Elise led him over to the sofa, lifted up his arms, and pulled off his shirt. She pushed him back on the couch, then straddled him, and bent down to take one of his nipples into her mouth, then the other.

Jay's head fell back limp. "Awww, baby," he said, almost inaudibly, grabbing and holding on to the back of her head.

Elise sat up and looked at him, then took one of his hands, put it in between her legs, and pushed a finger inside her. "See how wet you get me, baby? You got me all hot and bothered, Jay."

She freed him from his pants, then climbed onto him, slowly easing his thick dick into her. That's all it took. Whatever reservations he had when he walked through that door, whatever reservations she had when he walked through that door, all melted away on that sofa in the heat of making love.

Elise waited until he came, and then, when he was spent and empty, she whispered in his ear. "I'm pregnant, Jay." She pulled away and looked at him.

Jay's head rolled back and he laughed. "Damn! Already?"

The look in his eyes told her that he hadn't grasped the reality of what she'd just told him. Elise swallowed hard, and spoke slowly. "We're going to have a baby—baby."

All expression left his face, and this time she knew he got it. "Don't tell me that, Elise," he said sternly, pushing her off him. "Don't play."

"Do I look like I'm playing?"

He sat there, staring into her eyes.

Elise pressed her hand against his cheek. "Jay," she said, concerned. "It's not that bad. Really," she reasoned. "Jay, please—say something. Don't just sit there, like . . . like—"

"Like my whole fucking world has been turned upside down?" he blurted out, glaring at her like somehow she'd managed to get pregnant on her own and without his help.

"So has mine! It wasn't like I planned this."

Jay bolted up and stomped across the room, shaking his head. "Fuck! Fuck! Fuck!" he grunted over and over again.

She knew he wouldn't be happy about it, but Elise still hadn't prepared herself for his reaction. She hadn't wanted to think about what it could be. "We can work through this," she said calmly, hoping her rationale would rub off on him. "We just need to talk about it, and—"

Jay turned abruptly. "Talk about—what? Dammit, Elise! The only thing we have to talk about is a damn abortion because you're not having it!" He opened up his wallet, peeled off some hundred-dollar bills and threw them on the coffee table. "That's the solution to this whole mess, right there!" he said coolly.

Mess?

Elise couldn't believe he was treating her like this. Like she was some cheap-ass ho he'd been fucking and a couple of hundred dollars would make her and his so-called *mess* disappear. She stood up and picked up his money. He was angry. Probably scared and unprepared. She could accept all those things, because the Jay she knew didn't act like this. She knew him better than he knew himself, and the man she loved, loved her enough to act like he had some goddamned sense.

"Jay." She choked back tears. "I know this is difficult for you to hear right now." Elise looked at him through the tears clouding her eyes. "This isn't cool for either one of us. I knew you'd be upset because of the situation. And believe me," she said, ignoring the anger on his face, "it's not cool for me either."

"Then you know what you need to do," he snapped.

"But—I don't want to do it!"

"Well, what the hell do you plan on doing then?"

"I plan on keeping it. That's what I plan on doing!"

"Aw, hell no! Ain't no way, Elise! No way! I've got a wife and kids and I ain't messing that up! Not over some shit like this! Hell no!"

His words cut her so deep, Elise felt like she could barely stand up. "Some shit like . . . what?" she said, exasperated. "Like me? Like the relationship we've been having all this time? Is that the shit you're talking about?"

"What the hell did you think this was?" The chill from him cooled the room, and Elise shivered.

"I thought you loved me," she said weakly. "You told me that a hundred times, Jay! So, what? What—was it a lie? Was all that shit you said to me a lie?"

Jay looked at her, and that told her all she needed to know. Elise leaped at him with her fists, landing blows on his chest, on his face. "Mothafucka! You mothafuckin' asshole!"

Jay grabbed her by the wrists, and pushed her back toward the couch. He held her down, and looked into her eyes. "Take care of it, Elise. Call me when you do. And we'll act like none of this ever happened."

"But it has happened," she said, clinching her teeth. "And you and I have to deal with it!"

"Then take my money and deal with it," he growled.

Jay buttoned up his pants, turned to look at her one last time, then slammed the door shut behind him.

You have made a fool of yourself! Faye had told her. *You have let yourself be used and disrespected . . .*

She'd been right.

"Did she tell you I called, Teddy?" I hated him. "I found the bitch's number and I called!"

He pushed past me at the front door and headed upstairs to the bedroom, as if I weren't even there. But I'd be damned if he was going to ignore me. I followed him, step for step, pushing him hard in the back.

"You fuckin' lied to me!" I screamed. "I trusted you! I believed you, Teddy! How the hell could you lie to me like that?"

He started taking his clothes out of the closet and placing them on the bed. "I called that ho! Were you there? Is that where you've been all afternoon? Because you sure as hell weren't at the church, Teddy! I called there, too, and I know for a fact your ass wasn't there. Were you in bed fucking that skank when I called?"

He went over to the dresser and started taking out his socks, underwear, and T-shirts.

"Answer me!" I hit him hard across his back. "Goddammit, Teddy! Say something!"

He turned and for the first time since he'd walked through the front door, he looked at me.

"I can't do it," he said, frustrated. "I'm tired, Faye, and—I can't do this no more."

No! He was so right. He couldn't keep doing this to me. Not to me!

I had loved him, even worshipped him, and he could not do this to me again!

"I deserve better than this, Teddy!" I cried. "I've been there for you, long before all of—this!" Before the big house, fancy cars. Before he'd become head of one of the fastest-growing churches in Texas. I'd been there for him, supporting and encouraging him every step of the way. "I don't deserve to be treated this way! How could you do this to me? Teddy?"

"I know, Faylene," he said solemnly. Teddy turned his back to me, and started packing his things.

"What?" I gawked at him. "What are you doing?" I grabbed his arm, and he jerked away from me.

"I'm leaving."

"You're—" Oh, dear God! "No!" I said in disbelief. Who the hell did he think he was to believe that he could be the one to decide to leave? "No! Teddy!"

"I'm through." He pulled away from me again.

Sobs swelled in my throat. Teddy blurred behind tears. To have him betray me, lie to me, and then, walk out on me, too? It was too much. Lord, have mercy! It was too much! "You don't walk out on me! I'm the one, Teddy! I'm the one who tells you to leave! You don't leave me! Not for her! Not for—"

I scratched his face, then grabbed a handful of his shirt, and pulled. Pulling him to what end, I don't know. "Get off me, Faye!" he growled.

"Mothafucka! No! You don't leave me! I'll tell you when to go! I'll tell—"

He pushed me so hard, I stumbled back into the dresser and fell to the floor.

"It's over, dammit!" Teddy closed his suitcase, picked it up, and headed out the bedroom door. "I'm sorry, Faye," he said, looking down at me just before he left. "I—I did the best I could."

I have no idea how long I sat on the edge of the bed. I remember feeling nothing. Not pain or disappointment. Not even sadness. I wasn't the woman I always believed I was. All of a sudden my life wasn't my life anymore. I sat there, slowly unraveling.

Looking back, I could see that I'd been coming apart all along. Only, I'd been so busy looking and pointing fingers at other people, I hadn't noticed what was happening in me. I'd changed in the way I looked at other people and spoke to them, in the way I'd slowly withdrawn into the madness of my thoughts and obsession with this other woman. Without realizing it, I looked for her all the time, even in some of the women I counseled at the church, looking for clues of what this woman must be like. Was she careless and flippant like Renee Turner, just out for a good time, to hell with how she was destroying another woman? Or was she pliable and desperate like Elise Clayton, living off the fuel of fantasy and false hopes, wanting a man, anybody's man, so badly, she was willing to sacrifice herself in the process? I searched for myself in Tess Martin. She and I shared the same kind of pain, and in her, I felt determined to fill her with the hope and promise of a happy ending.

Just hang in there, Tess. *I encouraged her all the time, but she was bright enough to see through the bullshit. And I hated her for giving up so easily.*

But none of them were quite like me, in my denial. Not one of them was as together as me, or as insightful, stable, content. Bless them, Father! *I prayed.* Because these women are all fools.

As I sat there, watching the sun come up and reeling in the fact that Teddy had indeed left me for another woman, I had to face the fact that I had more in common in those women, more than I ever thought possible.

god's gonna
trouble
the water

Lewis came out of Renee's bathroom wearing absolutely nothing, and fell full length across her bed. "You play a mean game of racquetball, girl," he said, exasperated. "I don't know when I've ever had such a fierce and relentless opponent in all the years I've been playing."

Renee hit him with a pillow. "Shut up," she laughed. "I told you I'd never played before."

"Yeah, but you could've fooled me," he said, teasing. "If I didn't know better, I'd think you let me win."

Trishelle was at an all-day orientation for new teachers, and Tray was on a camping trip with one of his friend's families, so Lewis had the whole day to himself and decided to spend it with Renee, if she was willing. And she was—reluctant, but willing. He'd picked her up bright and early and talked her into playing a game of racquetball with him, then they stopped off for breakfast at Sonics (at her insistence) for huge breakfast sandwiches and coffee, and finally, ended up back at her place, freshly showered, exhausted and full, and it wasn't even noon yet.

"So," Renee stretched her legs across Lewis's torso. "What do you want to do the rest of the day?"

He looked at her, surprised. "You're giving me the rest of the day? Damn!"

She rolled her eyes. "Well, I'm *kinda* enjoying your company, maybe."

Lewis grinned. "Oh yeah?"

"Yeah. It's not all about the dick, you know?" she winked. "And besides, having you around is almost like having a real boyfriend."

He scooted up underneath her legs, and ended up on the pillow next to her. "I'll take the compliment and leave it at that."

"Good," she sighed. " 'Cause I'd hate for you to ruin the moment."

Lewis liked to cuddle. Renee didn't realize how much she'd missed cuddling until he cuddled with her. He liked to tickle. Renee hated being tickled. He liked to tell dumb jokes that weren't funny, to kiss, to talk about his son, life as an Army brat, his new job and how he got there, and about how he'd always wanted to run his own company someday.

He discovered some fascinating things about her, too. As it turned out, Renee was the daughter of someone famous.

"Oh damn!" he exclaimed. "Cleo Turner is your mother? *The* Cleo Turner?" Lewis had been holding her close most of the day, and they hadn't left her room once since they'd gotten there.

"Yep," she said proudly. "She's my mom."

"She's phenomenal," he said, impressed. "I saw her years ago in Seattle at a concert, and that woman is phenomenal. Incredible voice." He looked at Renee. "Can you sing?"

"Not a lick. I inherited my dad's tone deafness, and Mom's sense of panache and style," she joked.

"So who's Dad? Herbie Hancock?"

"No. Dad's a podiatrist, believe it or not. Mom met him

when she was having problems with a bunion and fell head over heels in love."

"Mom's a famous jazz singer, and dad's a foot doctor," Lewis pondered. "Hmmm . . . interesting combination. So, they live in L.A.?"

"Mom moved back east to New York, and Dad lives here."

"You moved here to be closer to him?"

"I moved here because it was easier than living in airports and nightclubs and trying to keep up with Mom. I was sixteen and exhausted. Life with a podiatrist was more relaxing."

"So they're divorced?"

She shook her head. "Just living in separate houses," she said like it was no big deal. "Neither one of them ever wanted a divorce, and they don't want anybody else either. So, about four to five times a year, they hook up. Dad loads up on the Viagra and they have at it."

"That's weird."

She shrugged. "That's love."

As they lulled the day away, Renee taught him to step dance, which he insisted on calling the hustle. And for lunch, Renee made chicken salad sandwiches. Lewis chased his down with a beer, and she hers with iced tea.

"I'm not married because I never wanted to get married," Renee explained. "I think it's archaic."

"Sometimes."

"I mean, who's to say people are meant to be with one person for a lifetime? Forty, fifty years with the same person? Impossible."

"No it's not. My folks have been together for over forty years, and still going strong."

"They live in separate cities like mine?"

"Nope. Same city. Same house, and it still works."

"I'll never walk down the aisle," she said emphatically.

"One day you will. A fine woman like you—you'll make a perfect little wife for some brave, determined, deserving man."

She punched him hard in the arm.

"Quite frankly, I can't figure out how you've been left to roam around free for this long."

"I run fast. But you know, there have been plenty of men who came and went in my life, who don't quite see what it is you see. But then, you see me through a miserable married man's eyes," she smiled mischievously. "So to you, I must look like a million bucks."

Lewis looked disappointed. "I see you through a man's eyes, Renee. Period. And yes, sweetheart. You do look like a million bucks."

They spent the afternoon in bed, kissing, snuggling, stroking, suckling, licking.

Lewis lay on top of her, careful not to put all of his weight on her, and gazed intently into her bright eyes. "If I didn't know any better," he said quietly, "I'd almost think I was in love with you."

Renee started to protest, but he pressed his finger to her lips to hush her, and smiled.

"Don't ruin it, baby. It's romantic. That's all. Let me just hold on to it. Is that all right with you?"

"Yeah, whatever's clever, brotha."

"Excuse me," Tess said nervously, as she approached the woman at the checkout counter.

"Yes," the woman smiled. "May I help you?"

"I saw an ad in the paper that your store was hiring." Tess squeezed her hands tight to keep them from shaking. "I was wondering if I could possibly speak to—"

The woman cut her off. "Human resources is on the fourth floor. At the top of the escalator, turn left, and follow the signs."

Tess had spent the morning practicing answers to questions she felt she might be asked, and had searched long and hard for just the right outfit, a dark blue pantsuit, low-heeled pumps, and light blue, tailored blouse underneath. The last time she'd filled out a job application other than one for volunteering, was back in high school.

No Experience Necessary. Will Train. Words that were music to her eyes stood out in this particular ad, and Tess was sure she was at least trainable. She finished filling in her application and turned it in to the clerk sitting behind the desk. The young lady quickly scanned through it, then looked up at Tess and smiled.

"Thank you very much," she said politely. "I'll give your application to the manager, and we'll be in touch."

Tess tried not to let her enthusiasm wane. "That's it?"

The young lady nodded. "That's it for now. Someone will call you."

Well, shoot! Tess rode down the escalator with her hand on her hip, and an attitude. She'd gotten up at the crack of dawn for nothing. She'd rehearsed her little speech about her go-getted-ness and her willingness to learn and all that mess for Happy Sally to sit up behind that desk and take her application just to tell her, "Someone will be in touch"? Tess was fuming, and she wondered just how much that little heifer got paid to put people off.

Tess wandered through the store, sorely disappointed that this whole job hunt thing wasn't going well at all. She'd spent thousands of dollars in stores like this through the years, and all she wanted to do was stand behind the counter, and ask someone, "Are you ready to check out now?" It wasn't like she wanted to rule the world anymore. Just the accessories department, and make minimum wage in the process just to see her name on her own paycheck for once.

According to Dr. Phil, she was going through the empty-nester syndrome, basically trying to find a purpose for her life now that it wasn't consumed by raising kids anymore—he'd put a title on what she'd been going through, which gave her some comfort. At least she wasn't crazy—which sometimes crossed her mind—or trapped, lost, useless, restless, or even old. She and Jesse had settled down into a routine that included just the two of them and it was boring as hell. But neither of them liked each other enough anymore to want to engage the other in something new. It was a fact of married life, though, that after the kids grew up and left the house, and all that was were two people who were virtual strangers to each other, that the two of you just settled down into that emptiness and grew old in it.

Tess passed by a rack of wrap dresses. She'd heard that these things could make anybody look good, but Tess wasn't so convinced. Material like this showed all the potholes on a woman's body, and the last thing she needed was for someone to walk by pointing and laughing at her potholes and gullies.

"Aren't these cute?" a saleswoman about Keisha's age came over and said to Tess.

Tess smiled. "Before the twins," she nodded. "Yes. But now—"

"Oh please," the girl said. "You have a great figure and you'd look great in one of these." She started flipping through the rack. "You look to be about a sixteen?"

Tess was offended. "Fourteen," she corrected the girl, but she didn't seem to notice.

"Here's a nice black one," she looked at the tag. "Size fourteen," she handed it to Tess. "Just try it on. I think you'll be amazed at how good it looks. My mom has one and she loves it."

Tess's palms itched to slap that girl.

Ten minutes later, she walked out of that store, sixty dollars poorer, with a new addition to her wardrobe. Damn! She did look good in that dress. Tess skipped all the way to her car, wondering where she'd ever get the opportunity to don her new outfit.

Driving home, she thought of trying to talk Jesse into taking her out dancing. But Jesse didn't dance. At least, he hadn't danced with her in years. Maybe she could get him to take her to a nice dinner, to that nice French restaurant he took her to a few years ago on their anniversary? No, she thought disappointedly. Tess wasn't in the mood to sit up in some stuffy restaurant forcing herself to make conversation with Jesse who didn't have a thing to talk about but the boys or that new grandbaby on the way. Tess rolled her eyes. She'd love it when it got here, but for now, she resented the hell out of that kid, catapulting her from the ranks of momma to granny, just like that.

But then, there was the Oasis. Gregory worked there as a bouncer. Back when it first opened, Bev raved about the great time she'd had there.

She felt nervous walking into a club alone. But the fact that she knew he'd be inside set her at ease a bit.

"Hello," a man standing outside said to her as she passed by him and his friends.

She smiled shyly. "Hello."

Her confidence grew gradually with each step she took, as men in all shapes and sizes nodded in her direction, and gawked at her in her new black dress. Either men hadn't spent too much time checking her out before, or she'd just never paid attention. Either way, she was paying attention now, and loved every minute of it.

The club was packed. She searched the room for Gregory, but didn't see him. Tess made her way through the crowd to the bar, and waited patiently for the bartender's attention. She was starting to have second thoughts about coming, especially since she couldn't find Gregory. Of course, she should've called him first to make sure he was actually working tonight. She decided that if she didn't see him by the time she finished her drink, she'd just head home and call it a night.

"Hello," someone said to her.

She turned to a man standing behind her.

"Can I buy you a drink?"

Her first instinct was to say no, but then, her second instinct came quickly on the heels of the first, and she decided tonight was not the time to let the magic of this little black dress go to waste.

"Sure," she smiled.

His name was Paul. He was nice-looking, well dressed, and worked in sales. He drank Grand Marnier on ice, and she had Grey Goose and tonic with a twist of lime. It was all coming so easily to her, and no one was more surprised then Tess. She'd lied to her husband tonight, without batting an eye, and told him she was going out to dinner with Bev. She was sitting here laughing and drinking with a man she didn't even know, acting like a woman she didn't know. And she'd come here under the pretense of meeting her lover.

She and Paul danced so much, they were sweating. "I'd like to get your number." He leaned in and tried to ask over the sound of the music.

Tess pretended she couldn't hear him, and just smiled.

It was late, but she didn't care, and she was in no hurry to get home.

Back at the bar, Paul put on the charm, big time. "You're a beautiful woman," he told her. "But I'm sure you're used to hearing that."

Tess was flattered, and said no. She wasn't as used to hearing that as she would've liked to have been. She was about to say thank you, when someone whispered in her ear.

"You through playing?"

It was Gregory, standing behind her, and staring down poor Paul until he excused himself and left.

"I've been looking for you," she said, glad to see him. "Are you just getting here?"

"I saw you when you came in," he said indifferently. "Been checking you out."

Tess looked confused. "How come you didn't say anything to me?"

He looked irritated. "I'm saying something now, boo."

She hated it when he called her that, and no matter how many times she asked him not to, he kept right on doing it.

"Are you working?" She had to admit, he looked nicer than she'd seen him look since she met him. Wearing a rich black blazer, slacks, and pristine white v-neck sweater underneath, he looked downright fine. Tess felt herself starting to get worked up. Since she'd been seeing him, Gregory had enlightened her to the joy of sex, literally. He'd done things to her Jesse had probably never even thought of doing.

"I'm working," he said simply.

"You look good," she finally admitted.

He glanced at her dress and grinned. "So do you."

Before she knew what was happening, he'd taken her by the elbow, and practically lifted her up off her seat. "C'mon."

"What is it?" she protested.

Gregory led her through the crowd on the dance floor, down a narrow corridor past the restrooms, and finally shoved her into a room, no bigger than a broom closet, and locked the door behind them.

"What are we doing in here?" she asked, fighting back panic. He wasn't acting right, and she really didn't feel being shoved in a broom closet in a crowded club was normal. "Gregory?"

Without hesitating, he lifted up her dress, smiled when he realized she wasn't wearing panties, and fingered her.

Shocked, she stared horrified at him, and struggled to push his hand away. "Stop it!" she demanded. "Not here!"

He shut her up with heated kisses, while finger-fucking her.

Her heart raced, as she pushed against him as hard as she could and struggled to get him off her. With his finger inside her, he began massaging her clit with his thumb. It was the whole package that made her succumb to this act. Tess rolled her hips against his hand.

"Mmmmm," she moaned, holding his head in her hands, licking and sucking his full lips. "Gregory," she whispered, over and over again.

Gregory expertly worked his magic, feeling her clit swell and pulsate under his thumb. Tess's juices pooled in his hand and dripped through his fingers. She came hard, like he knew she would. Like she always did whenever he so much as breathed on her, and when it was over, she stood against the wall, shuddering, and wondering what the hell had just happened. Gregory pulled a white handkerchief from inside his breast pocket, dried his hand off, then her, and threw it into an old mop bucket.

"Now," he said sternly, "time for you to take your ass home."

He left her standing alone in that closet where she stayed until she could compose herself. When she came out, he was nowhere to be found, and Tess hurried out the door as fast as she could.

Jay clutched the steering wheel of his truck tight with both hands, staring out into the dark road ahead of him, wondering how in the world he'd been dumb enough to let pussy get in the way of reason. The knot in his stomach had settled in permanently from what he could tell, and all he could see was his life unraveling right in front of his eyes, taking everything he wanted with it.

"How the hell she call herself keeping the mothafuckin' baby," he mumbled out loud.

But see . . . it was his own damn fault. Jay recounted every instance when he knew he should've stopped long enough to put on a condom, but didn't. He remembered seeing her pop birth control pills—every now and then, but not every time.

"I'm not even sure I want kids," she'd told him. "At least, not until I'm married."

She'd played him, he thought angrily. She knew what the fuck she was doing, and played him like a goddamned fiddle, knowing all along this was how this bullshit would turn out. She probably thought he'd leave his wife if she told him she was pregnant.

"I ain't going no-fuckin'-where!" he muttered again.

Hell, the bitch probably wasn't even really pregnant. It was like a lightbulb coming on over his head. How the hell did he know if she was pregnant or not, and even if she was, how in the hell did he know it was his? Shit, he saw Elise two, maybe three times a month. That left a lot of time in between for her to be fucking somebody else, and maybe it was some other dumb mothafucka's kid she was carrying.

Whatever the case, he was through. It served his ass right to be hit upside the head with some bullshit like this. But maybe it's what he needed to start thinking with the head on top of his shoulders instead of the one in his pants. Even tonight he'd been an idiot. She'd fed him a good meal and a good piece of ass, and he'd forgotten all about the real reason he'd stopped by. It was over before he even knocked on her door this evening. In Jay's mind, he'd already left Elise for the woman he truly loved. The only woman in the world that mattered was Sherry. And he'd be damned if Elise or any other woman would mess that up. He'd done his part. He'd left her more than enough money to terminate that shit, or go out and buy herself some fuckin' shoes if that's what she wanted. But as far as Jay was concerned, that was the end of it. He'd lose her number, and change his if he had to. He was through.

"Oh no, he didn't!" Daria handed Elise a cup of chamomile tea and sat down next to her on the sofa. Elise couldn't stop crying. The money Jay'd left lay crumpled on the table. Elise couldn't even bring herself to touch it. "That son of a bitch needs his ass whipped for some shit like that! He didn't

have no problem laying up in it, but as soon as it gets real, he runs off like some scared little bitch? What the hell did you ever see in him, Elise?"

Elise sipped on her tea. "I saw what he wanted me to see," she said somberly.

"He's a married man. That's what they do, and they do it better than any other kind of man on the planet."

"The things he said, and the way he said them . . . the way I felt when he was here . . . I should've seen through all that bullshit," Elise sobbed. "I should've known better, and I shouldn't have given him one minute of my time."

"You gonna have the baby?"

Elise shrugged. She didn't know what she was going to do. Having an abortion made sense. Getting rid of this baby meant getting rid of the residue of Jay, and maybe one day, she could put this ugly scene behind her and act like it never happened. But Elise knew instinctively that she'd always regret Jay, and she'd regret whatever happened with this baby, whether she kept it or not.

"If you decide to get an abortion, E, just let me know, and I'll be there with you," Daria said sincerely. "But if you decide to have it, girl . . . I'll help you file child support papers on his ass, and that mothafucka will pay for your kid from day care to Harvard."

Elise tried to smile.

"I ain't playing," Daria said, seriously. "Don't let him get off scot-free. He doesn't deserve it."

After Daria left, Elise sat in the dark in the living room.

"Hello?" Sherry answered the phone. Elise had called the

house, knowing that Jay wouldn't be there. She called to hear Sherry's voice and maybe to tell her who she was, and what she'd been to Jay.

"Hello?" Sherry asked again, sounding irritated this time.

My name is Elise, and I've been seeing your husband. No. No. I've been sleeping with . . . no . . . fucking your husband and now I'm pregnant.

"Who is this?"

The words were in her head, but she couldn't say them.

He was here earlier. He's been coming here for almost a year, telling me how much he loves me. And like an idiot, I believed him when he said could hardly wait to get back to me, and how he wished you were more like me.

Sherry slammed down the receiver in Elise's ear, but Elise didn't hang up right away.

I'm pregnant. I just wanted you to know.

Tears streamed down her face.

"If you'd like to make a call, please hang up and dial again.

"If you'd like to make a call, please hang up and dial again."

I should've left your man alone. He should've left me alone.

"*I did not abandon* my son, Trish! The man said they wouldn't be back until six!"

"He said they'd be back *by* six, Lewis! But then, if it doesn't pertain to you directly, you don't hear a thing! Do you?"

"You know, I'm getting sick and tired of being accused of being selfish all the goddamned time. That's my son! Why the hell wouldn't I pick him up, if I knew he was back?"

"I called your cell phone, Lewis, two, maybe three times, at least!"

"I didn't have it on me! I told you I was playing racquetball all morning."

"I called in the afternoon." Trish's gaze was like a knife cutting right through him. "Where the hell were you this afternoon?"

Lewis searched for an excuse. "I left my phone in my gym bag," he said calmly. "I didn't realize it was there until I got home and saw that you'd called."

"That doesn't answer my question. I asked where you were. And I don't think you were in your gym bag."

"What the hell is that supposed to mean," he said defensively. "What are you accusing me of?"

Trish swallowed hard. "I'm not accusing you of anything.

All I know is that lately, you haven't been where you say you are. You've been spending a lot more time away from home."

"Working, Trish. I'm usually at the office. Call my secretary, if you don't believe me."

"I want to believe you." Her voice cracked. "But something's not right between us. Something's not right with you, Lewis. I can't explain it. But I feel it."

She'd all but accused him of messing around. Lewis didn't know what or how she'd figured it out, or thought she'd figured it out. But he couldn't afford to give her any more ammunition than she already had.

"You want to know what's wrong with me, Trish? I'm tired. I'm tired of working like a slave then coming home and getting kicked in the fucking gut by you when I mess up. He's my son, too, and if I'd known they'd gotten back early, I'd have busted my ass to get to him. You know that. But I made a mistake, at my kid's expense. I made a mistake and for that I am more than sorry."

"Is there someone else? Just tell me! Are you seeing someone?"

"Where the hell is this coming from?"

"You haven't touched me in weeks! And every time I reach out to you, you kiss me on the hand, pat me on the backside, and send me off to bed like I'm a fucking six-year-old, Lewis! If you're not fucking me, then who the hell is she?"

Lewis slumped down on the side of the bed, and rubbed his head in frustration. He didn't know what was harder. Making up lies on the spot, or breaking down the truth once and for all.

"You've been absent in this marriage for too long, and I want to know why. I want to know who she is, Lewis."

Lewis stood up slowly and walked toward his wife. "My bitch is an eighty-hour workweek, bent over a fucking desk all day, trying to clean up messes for a company who'd just as soon throw my ass out the window if I don't come through to make this shit work. That's my bitch, Trish. All I ever asked for, all I ever wanted, was to come home to my wife, and have her tell me to hang in there, man. It's going to be all right, and you can do this. But ever since I took this job, all I get from you is grief and bullshit, and complaints that I'm not paying enough attention to your needs. I've got needs, too, Trish. I've got plenty."

Lewis brushed past her on his way to the bathroom to shower.

He'd left his wife standing speechless in the bedroom, buried in a mixture of truth or consequences. He hadn't lied. Lewis told her how he felt, and he meant every word. And he'd managed to sidestep the truth, too, the whole truth, that there was someone else out there, whose company he sometimes preferred over hers.

They lay in bed next to each other in the dark, not touching, or sleeping. "What's going to happen to us, Lewis?" Trish whispered. "What if we can't ever get back to where we were?"

Lewis could tell she was crying. Hell, he felt like crying, too. "I don't know," was all he could say.

"Do you even want to fix it? Do you want our marriage to work?"

Yes. Maybe.

He turned his back to her. "I honestly don't know what to do about us, Trish." Lewis was tangled in a web. That's all he knew.

Jesse stood in the doorway of the kitchen watching Tess put away the dishes.

"There's something different about you," he said quietly, startling her.

She quickly glanced at him. "What do you mean?"

Tess felt flushed. Transparent and guilty. The way he watched her lately made her uncomfortable, especially since he was spending more time at home now with nothing better to do than pay attention to her. A long time ago, she'd have sold her soul for his attention. Now, he got on her nerves.

"I can't put my finger on it," he said introspectively. "You change your hair again?"

"No." She struggled to maintain her composure.

"Lose weight?" he probed.

"I wish," she laughed quietly.

"Gain weight?" he teased.

Tess propped her hand on her hip and glared at him.

"Okay. Okay." He retreated. "All I'm saying is that whatever it is, it looks good on you."

Jesse smiled, then retreated back into the living room, and Tess felt like a criminal.

"Flowers?" Sherry beamed as Jay handed her a dozen long-stemmed red roses as soon he met her at the door. She stood up on her toes to kiss him. "What's the occasion, honey?"

Jay took her by the hand and led her into the kitchen. "Since when do I need an occasion to give my wife flowers?"

She took a deep breath when they walked into the kitchen. "You made dinner, too?" Sherry went over to the stove, and lifted the lid from one of the pots still simmering. "Mmmm . . . the usual?"

He shrugged. "You know all I know how to make is spaghetti."

She turned to him and put her arm around his waist. "Some damn good spaghetti."

"You're only saying that because I gave you those roses."

"Yep," she chuckled.

Jay sat at the head of the table with his family at dinner. It was hard not to feel proud, and so he didn't even bother to try. Pride washed over him and he let it soak into his pores and down to his bones, realizing how fortunate he was. Jayson was the spitting image of him, only that boy was growing like a weed, and would soon be taller than Jay one day. Basketball—that boy lived and breathed basketball, but Jay knew he needed to get on him about those grades he'd been bringing home lately. Later on, he'd take Jayson out for some one-on-one and stress to him the importance of good grades, especially if he wanted to get into college, and eventually go pro.

Jasmine spent most of her time rolling her eyes, and picking at her food. She was a beautiful little girl, though, and Jay imagined himself having to ward off knuckleheads that would soon be finding their way to the front door of his house looking for his baby girl. Like it or not, he was daddy, and any little fool who decided to court her would have to court him first.

To think he'd ever had ideas of ever leaving them behind. Jay didn't have much of a family growing up. His mother raised him alone, and his father felt like ten dollars here, or twenty dollars there could make up for the fact that he was never around. He'd promised himself he'd be a better dad than that if he ever had any kids; he'd be a better man altogether. A moment of weakness almost made him forget that promise. Without realizing it or even trying, Elise had been the one to bring him back to his senses. If she hadn't told him she was pregnant, he'd have probably still been creeping back to her, unable to cut the ties like he knew he should, because deep down, Jay knew he did care about her. He could even go as far as to say he loved her, but not enough. Not nearly enough to let go of home.

She'd called. He never answered, though, and he never returned her calls either. Elise might not know it now, but it was better this way, better just to cut the ties all at once, and hurt her now for a little while, than to drag this whole thing out, and hurt her even more later on.

Jay lay in bed, watching the weather report on the evening

news when the phone rang. It was late, and the first thing he thought was that it was one of Jasmine's little friends. No phone calls after eight-thirty on weeknights. That was the rule and he was prepared to tell some little gossipy girl this when he answered.

"Hello?"

The person on the other end of the line didn't say anything.

"Hello?" he asked, agitated, then hung up. Yeah, it had to have been one of her friends. Tomorrow, he'd make a point to remind Jasmine to tell all of them not to call his house after a certain time, or he'd take the phone out of her room altogether.

"Who was it?" Sherry asked, coming from the bathroom, rubbing lotion on her arms.

He shrugged. "Don't know. Probably one of Jaz's friends."

"They didn't say anything?" Sherry crawled into bed next to him.

He shook his head.

"That's been happening a lot lately."

"Well, I'll talk to her tomorrow. Tell her to tell them not to call so late."

"I don't think it's anybody she knows. I think the calls are coming from someplace called Middleton or something like that," she said absently. "The first time it happened, it showed up on caller ID. After that, it showed up as blocked."

Jay's heart skipped a beat, and he looked at her. "Middleton?"

Sherry nodded. "Well, I got a call a couple of weeks ago from Middleton kind of late, but nobody said anything. I didn't think much of it. Maybe a crank or some kids playing around." The room seemed to close in on him. "A couple of nights later, I got another call, and nobody said anything then either. So, I tried to star sixty-nine to get the number, but it was blocked, because I was not in the mood and had every intention of calling whoever it was back, and cussing them out." She laughed.

Jay felt sick all of a sudden. It was Elise calling his house. But . . . how'd she get the number? He'd only ever given her his cell phone . . .

Sherry curled up next to him. "I wonder if you can block a blocked call," she joked. "I might have to call the phone company and find out. You think it's a bill collector?"

Jay held her close and kissed the top of her head. "I'll call the phone company tomorrow," he said, hoping his tone didn't give him away. "Probably just some telemarketer or kids messing around."

"Good night, baby," she said groggily. "Can you turn the television down some?"

Jay did as he was told, then spent the next hour staring at the television, with no sound coming from it.

"That's it?" Elise asked excitedly, staring at the monitor on the ultrasound machine in the doctor's office.

"That's it." The doctor pressed the probe down against Elise's stomach, then pointed at the monitor. "There's the head . . . an arm . . . legs . . . and this." She adjusted the monitor so that Elise could see it better. "This is the heart."

Elise was overwhelmed with emotions she hadn't expected. She'd come in to confirm her pregnancy.

"You're about six weeks along," her doctor told her.

She'd come in to ask about the abortion procedure, but

before she could, the doctor had turned on the ultrasound machine, squeezed clear goop from a tube and smeared it across Elise's belly with the probe.

"You want a picture?" she asked, smiling.

Elise nodded. "Can you tell what it is?"

The doctor studied the monitor closely. "Well . . . whatever it is, it appears to be shy. The little legs are closed and drawn up, so I can't see the goodies."

Elise laughed. "You can print me a picture?"

"I sure can. In color, even."

Back at the office, Elise stared at the photograph of the fetus growing inside her. This baby was real. Not just the plus sign on a plastic stick or something she talked about. It was a real little person, with arms and legs and a heart, moving around inside her, growing and busy becoming somebody. It was a child, her child—and Jay's, too. Looking at the photograph, she realized how impossible it was for her not to love it already, and she wondered how he could ever think to deny it so easily.

"My baby," she mouthed, running her fingers across the picture.

What in the world ever made her think she could abort her baby and not be affected by it? And what kind of man was he, to suggest it? Jay might spend the rest of his life denying Elise. That's something she would have to live with. But who the hell did he think he was to deny this baby? It was as much his kid as the two he had living in the house with him, and Elise would be damned if he was going to walk away from it, and pretend it didn't exist.

She picked up the phone and dialed information.

What city? the automated voice asked.

"Dallas," she said, definitively.

What listing?

"Jay Vincent, spelled J-A-Y," Elise responded.

Please wait and an operator will be available to assist you shortly.

"I'm sorry, but I'm not showing a listing under that name . . . oh wait . . . but I do have a J period Vincent listed at 8793 Albrook Drive. Do you want the number?"

The operator confirmed the number Elise already had.

The last time she called, he'd answered, and Elise lost her nerve, thinking that he was right all along, and the best thing was for her to have an abortion. But seeing her baby today for the first time gave her the strength she needed to stand up to him and to remind him that she was not about to disappear and fade away like smoke.

Renee hadn't seen Trishelle in weeks, not since the dinner party that night at her house. Trishelle just showed up on her doorstep this particular evening bearing wine, two glasses, and a big grin.

"I'll bet you thought you'd gotten rid of me," she practically sang, coming inside.

"Well—sort of," Renee responded, bemused.

Trish laughed, kicked off her shoes, tugged hard on the cork, then filled both glasses to the rim. "Well, I missed you. And I thought I'd take advantage of your good nature and stop by to have a drink with my friend."

Friend. That word coming from Trishelle made Renee's skin crawl. Or maybe it was her guilty conscience making her skin crawl. Honestly, Trish was a lovely woman, and if things were different, she could very well see the two of them being friends. But now, Renee just felt backed into a corner by both Trish and her husband, and something inside warned her that she was probably going to have to come out kicking and screaming before it was all said and done. She needed her head examined, or she just needed to stop seeing Lewis, which was much more logical.

Trish talked nonstop about all the raves she'd been getting on the house, how comfortable and at home she felt in it. She went on and on about her family coming down to spend a week with them, and about how the neighbors kept making up excuses to come by and take a peek inside.

Trishelle was excited about going back to work. "As much as I love my house, I'm growing morbidly obese and bored sitting around all day watching talk shows and reruns. I refuse to go anywhere near a soap opera," she quipped.

"Bored—yes. Obese, I don't think so." Renee wished she'd leave. But Trish had obviously dug in for the long haul, and Renee did her best to entertain her, searching for a way out of an uncomfortable situation.

Trish pinched a layer of skin just below her naval. "No, really." She squeezed about an inch of fat between her fingers. "I'm gaining weight as we sit here."

"You look fine to me." Renee sipped from her glass.

"To you, maybe." Trish studied Renee sitting across from her. "A full figure works on you better than it does on me." She gulped down what was left in her glass, then filled it again, ignoring the annoyed and astonished look on Renee's face. "But then, black women don't have an issue with body image the way us poor white women do." She smirked.

Full figure? Who the hell was she calling full-figured?

"What's that supposed to mean?" Renee asked indignantly.

This time, Trish noticed she'd hit a nerve. "Oh, don't get your panties all wadded up. You know what I mean."

"No, what do you mean?"

Trish had a mischievous gleam in her eyes. "Oh my." She

leaned forward balancing her elbows on her thighs. "I think I've ruffled your feathers a bit, Miss Cool, Calm, and Collected."

"No," Renee said calmly. "I'm still cool, calm, and collected."

"I meant it as a compliment."

"You meant what as a compliment, Trish?"

"That full-figure thing. At least I didn't call you fat."

Renee looked appalled. "Because I'm not fat."

"Exactly, Renee. You're not fat. And you're not skinny. And you have enough love for yourself to be perfectly fine living in your own skin, being a beautiful black woman, no matter what anybody else says."

Okay, Trish was obviously drunk, and talking a whole lot of nonsense about absolutely nothing.

"Why'd you come here, Trish?" Renee asked bluntly. "What's up?"

"I told you, Renee. I wanted to come by and see how you were doing."

"No. For real."

"I'm being for real," Trish insisted.

Renee stared at her until she finally had a meltdown.

All the life seemed to drain from Trish's eyes, and her rosy complexion suddenly lost all color. "I think Lewis is fucking around on me." She swallowed a whole glass of wine, then filled it again, and drank half of that.

A chill ran up Renee's spine. *Oh shit!* Trishelle knew. "What would make you think something like that?" Renee asked, guarded, prepared to leap up out of that chair and swing it at Long Tall Sally if she had to.

Trish stared straight ahead, lost in her own thoughts. "You

know how you hear other women say things like they just knew their man was being unfaithful?" Her eyes darted back at Renee, then back across the room. "It's just a feeling. Instinct, maybe, from being with someone who is so interchangeable with you, you're almost the same person," she explained quietly.

Renee swallowed hard and tried not to breathe too loud. She'd never had a fistfight in her life, but if she had to, she'd fight to the death to defend herself.

"It's just a feeling," Trish sighed, and let her head fall back on the sofa. "He hasn't made love to me in ages, Renee. Isn't that a sign?"

Gradually, Renee began to realize that Trish really didn't have a clue that she was sleeping with Lewis. Trish was guessing, speculating, and giving way to that instinctive feeling all women have that alerts them to the fact that their man has been creeping.

Trish looked at Renee. "And it's not just that. He acts different. He says he's just tired, or that work is getting to him, but I know he's lying. I can just tell." Her clear eyes started to water. "I feel like I'm losing my husband, and I don't know what to do about it. If there is someone else, then—she's got a stronger hold over him now than I do, and that scares the hell out of me."

Renee sat motionless, watching this woman fall to pieces over what was really nothing more than a tryst. For a moment, she was caught up in the pain and despair Trishelle found herself wallowing in. And then she remembered the role she was playing in all this, and decided that the smart thing to do would be to keep her mouth shut.

The phone rang, startling both women. "Excuse me," Renee said, getting up to answer the phone. "Hello?"

"Hey, baby," Lewis said from the other end. "Trish is out with friends and I wanted to stop by and see you for a few minutes. You gonna be home?"

"Sure," she said, smiling weakly at Trishelle. Renee's heart beat like a million loud bongos and she knew that that woman had to be drunk off her ass not to hear them. "But I'm afraid I have company, so now's not a good time."

Lewis hesitated for a moment, trying to make sense of her tone. "Well, who's there?"

Renee tried hard not to stammer or sound unnatural. "A friend of mine. We're just hanging out—girl talk." This was too much. Too fuckin' much. She had the married lover on the line, and his drunk suspicious wife sitting ten feet away from her, on the couch. Renee felt beads of sweat form on the back of her neck.

"Is everything cool?" he asked warily.

"It's cool. Look, I really have to go. I'll call you later." Renee hung up before he had time to respond.

"Look, Trish," she said nervously. "I don't mean to be rude, but I have an early meeting in the morning and—"

"Oh." Trishelle slowly stood to her feet, and finished her last glass of wine. "I'm sorry, sweetie. It was rude of me to just barge in anyway and burden you with all my hokey marital problems." She picked up her purse and headed for the door.

"Maybe you shouldn't drive. Let me call you a cab," Renee offered.

"Nope. Because by the time they get here, I'll be halfway

home." Trish walked out the door and down the sidewalk to where her car was parked.

Renee plopped back down on the sofa, and closed her eyes, looking for what should've been her brain floating around in there somewhere. It wasn't there. Was she that hard up for a man, that she'd lower herself to the point of sharing someone else's? Goddamn! That was pitiful. And for what? Some company. Some time. A few compliments?

"Renee, Renee, Renee," she muttered. "You done gone crazy, gal! Plum crazy!"

Shit like this could get a woman shot. It could get her hair pulled out, and her faced scratched up, and her feelings hurt. But not if she did what she knew to be the right thing. This whole deal with Lewis had to end, and she had to be the one to end it because he was too ravenous to end it. He was gorging himself on two women, and if it were up to him, he probably wouldn't let either one of them go. Renee wasn't about to leave it up to him, though. She had herself to look out for, and Lewis and Trishelle could fend for themselves.

The knock on the door came about half an hour after Trish left. Renee went to the door, thinking the woman had come back because she was too drunk to figure out how to put the key in the ignition or something. But it was Lewis standing at her door, not his wife.

"What's up?" he said, pushing past her through the doorway.

"What are you doing here?"

Lewis ignored her and headed up the stairs to her apartment.

"Lewis!" Renee hurried after him. "I asked you a question! What are you doing here?"

"I just thought I'd stop by for minute." Lewis went directly into the bedroom and looked around.

"What are you looking for?" Renee pushed him out of the way, and stood defiantly in his path.

"Nothing," he answered too quickly.

It took her a minute, but Renee finally figured out what he was doing and it pissed her off even more. "Get the fuck out of here!" she blasted him. "I can't believe—"

"What?"

"You trying to see who's upin' here like you got it like that!"

Lewis looked stupid. "No. That's not true. When I called earlier, you sounded as if—"

This whole evening was starting to get a little too damn creepy to her, and Renee stormed past Lewis back downstairs. "Get the hell out of my house, Lewis!"

"We need to talk," he said, trailing behind her. "Renee!"

She held the door wide open for him, hoping he'd find his drunk wife over on the side of the road somewhere passed out. "Get out!"

Lewis pulled the door from her, and slammed it shut. "Not until we talk!"

"We don't have shit to talk about!"

"Who was here earlier?"

"None of your goddamned business!"

"Was it another man? You fucking somebody else? Because if you are—"

"Even If I was, Lewis, it's none of your damn business!"

She was livid. "As long as you have a goddamned wife sitting in that big ass house of yours waiting on you every night, I can do whatever the hell I please, and you ain't got shit to say about it!"

Lewis deflated. After all, she was right. Wasn't she? He'd practically flown his Lexus here after she'd hung up on him. Racing to get to her before some other man had a chance. Hoping to convince her that she didn't need to be with anybody else, because she had him. "I don't want you seeing anybody else, Renee," he said quietly. "I know it's selfish of me, but—"

"Lewis—" She started to say, *Just go away and leave me alone.*

"I love you," he whispered. Lewis reached out to her, but she jerked away. It didn't matter, though, and he pulled her close to him.

"You must be high." Renee struggled to get free.

He sat down on the back of the sofa, and gazed into her eyes. "I believe I do, Renee. And I know what it means to say that."

"Do you want to know who was here tonight?" she finally said.

"Someone was?"

"Trishelle was here, Lewis."

His eyes glazed over.

"She wanted to talk because she thinks you're cheating on her."

"She knows—"

"She doesn't know about us. But see, that's some shit I can't get into, Lewis. I had your wife sitting here on my couch when you called, and it messed me up. And that's not the kind of scene I want to be a part of, because it's embarrassing and belittling and humiliating. This is a joke, Lewis. It's a big-ass bomb, waiting to go off. You know it, and so do I."

Lewis slowly backed away.

"You don't love me," she said emphatically. "Because you're too smart for that."

He didn't know what to say.

"Go home," Renee said, suddenly exhausted. "Handle your business."

Tess went to all his appointments with him. Jesse held her hand in his lap as the doctor scanned through his latest test results. Nearly ten months had passed since he'd had the implants and so far, the procedure seemed to be working.

"Your last PSA numbers look amazing, Jesse," his doctor said reassuringly. "By all indications, the cancer appears to be in remission."

Tess squeezed his hand and kissed his cheek. "I told you everything would be fine," she whispered to him. And she had, too. All along Tess promised he'd beat this thing.

"Let's go celebrate," he told her.

"Where are we going?"

Jesse drove through Fort Worth near the neighborhood where Tess grew up, and found Lipton's Ice Cream shop, still in business. He pulled up alongside the curb and parked. Then gallantly he strutted over to her side of the car, and held the door open for her.

"Miss Lady," he said, bowing low at the waist.

Tess giggled like a schoolgirl. "I can't believe you brought me here. Oh, my goodness! I didn't even know they were still open."

This was where they'd had their first date. Tess was seventeen (almost eighteen) and so in love with this young, handsome man, she hardly remembered her own name when he came around.

"He's too old for you," her daddy fussed.

"Oh, he's fine. A fine young man, too," her mother recounted. "At least he come up to the door to see about her, and don't go sneaking her off someplace."

"He a grown man." Daddy was entirely too overprotective.

"Grown enough to knock on that girl's door and ask her daddy if he can take her out for ice cream. That ought to be the kind of man you want courting your baby girl."

They ordered their ice cream, then walked across the street to the park where he first laid eyes on pretty young Tess. Jesse even laid out his sport coat for her to sit on.

"I never told you." He lay sprawled out on the ground next to her. "But the first time I saw you was at Ronnie Johnson's cookout a week before I saw you and Rhonda sitting here."

"You did not! Really?"

"I certainly did. In fact, I knew you were going to be here that Saturday."

"Ronnie tell you?"

"He said that Rhonda came out here every Saturday afternoon to manhunt, and chances were you'd be with her."

Tess laughed. "She wasn't manhunting. She was . . ." Tess thought for a moment, then realized: "Manhunting."

"Well, I was hunting you."

She blushed. "Why me? Why not Rhonda?"

"You had a nicer behind." Jesse made a half circle in the air with his hand. "Nice and round. Rhonda's was flat as a board."

Tess playfully slapped him on the arm. "Stop it, Jesse. You're so crazy."

"I'll be damned if she ain't. Flat as a board."

Conversation flowed easy between them, easier than it had in ages. Jesse felt good again, hopeful and confident that he would live a productive long life. Long enough to enjoy his grandchildren, and maybe even to see their children. He and Tess lay flat on their backs, looking up through the leaves lush on the tree, just starting to slip into their fall colors.

How come it couldn't have always been like this? she wondered. How come time couldn't have just stopped way back then, before the children and job promotions and houses and affairs? And just left them there in that very spot, on hallowed ground underneath that tree? They'd have lived on ice cream, kept warm with the leaves that fell from the branches, and they would've been as happy now, as they had been back then.

"Ten months ago, I was scared to death that I wouldn't be here," he spoke quietly, more to himself than to Tess. She lay next to him, listening and being happy for him. "Life has a funny way of getting your attention. When you're hardheaded like me," he looked at his wife, and chuckled, "sometimes the lessons ain't so easy. I really thought I was going to die, Tess," Jesse choked back tears. Tess could see the relief in his eyes. "And I was scared. I was so scared, baby."

She pressed her hand to his face, and then rolled over and lifted herself up on her elbow. Tess gazed deeply into his eyes, and softly kissed his lips.

"I never doubted for a second that you would make it through this, Jesse," she smiled. "A little thing like cancer wasn't going to get the best of you."

She spoke from her heart, and from memories brought to the surface by Lipton's ice cream, and this big old shade tree she'd practically grown up under, and by the glimmer of the handsome young man who'd been brave enough to stand up to her daddy, and court her properly.

I can't leave." Jesse stared at Sandra's back, her shoulders bouncing up and down in the tears he knew she cried. "As much as I love you, Sandra, I can't just walk away from twenty-five years."

"Half of which have made you miserable," she spat back. "So miserable they drove you to me, Jesse!"

Jesse couldn't stand to see the pain he'd caused her again. Lord, why'd it have to be this way? Why'd it have to be so hard? He was a man who would lose, no matter which way he decided to go. Sandra was his heart's desire. But Tess—she had watched him grow up, helped him to grow up, and grown up with him. She'd been there through thick and thin, the hard times and the good, and proven herself to him, over and over again, that she would never leave him or walk away and abandon him, just because things got rough. They'd had babies together, and were about to have grandbabies, and honestly, he didn't want to share those things with any other woman but Tess.

"I'm sorry," was all he could say, and Jesse knew it wasn't nearly enough. But he'd been given a second chance, and instead of starting over, Jesse made the choice to go back and make amends, and start fresh with his wife.

"Go, Jesse." Sandra was through. He knew, he'd never see her again. "Just—go."

"*You loaded up and* ready to roll, J!" Jay's dispatcher threw the keys to his rig at him, and Jay caught them in mid air.

Jay climbed into his truck, turned it on and eased it out onto the road. This would be a short trip to Middleton and back. But after dropping off his cargo, Jay had one more stop to make before heading home.

"*It would've been easier* to just call you, but I thought you at least deserved better than that," Jay said, standing in Elise's doorway. She stepped aside and let him in. "You've been calling the house," he stated, as if she didn't already know that.

Elise stared him in the eyes and admitted, "Yes."

"You need to stop." The expression in her eyes gave away the pain she felt from the way he spoke to her, but Jay didn't see any other way to get through to her. "What happened between us is over, Elise," he continued. "I'm not going to stand here and say I'm not to blame, because I know I am. I led you on, told you things I shouldn't have, and I let it go way too far." Jay ignored the tears pooling in her eyes. He had to finish what he'd started and no amount of tears was going to change that.

"The last thing I ever wanted to do was hurt you. But that's exactly what I did, and for that, I am sorry."

"So, I should just let it go? Just like that?"

He shrugged. "What else can you do? What else can either one of us do? I'm not leaving my wife for you."

"I wouldn't want you to leave your wife for me! I don't want you anymore—period!"

Jay fought to stay calm. "Then stop calling my house. Leave my wife and family out of this."

"I'm not the one who dragged them into it!" she spat. "You did that the first time you laid up in here with me!"

Jay wasn't about to stand here arguing semantics. "The fact is, it's over, and you and I need to accept that and move on."

"Seems to me like you've already accepted it and moved on."

"What the hell is calling my house going to do? Do you think it's going to make me walk out on Sherry? Do you think it's going to fix things between you and me?"

Elise shook her head in disbelief. "You are so fuckin' vain. Since when is it all about you, and what you want, Jay?" she asked venomously.

Jay stared back, looking smug. "Just stop calling my fuckin' house, Elise."

Elise took a step toward him, and glared up into his face. "Sherry has no idea of the kind of man she's really married to," she said in a low voice. "I don't think she realizes how much of a cold-hearted son of a bitch you are, Jay, and maybe I think she might deserve to know the truth about you."

Jay bowed up and pointed his finger in Elise's face. "Don't fuck with what I got at home, Elise," he threatened. "You fuck with my home—" Jay swallowed hard, but he'd never been more serious about anything in his entire life.

Elise blinked back in disbelief that he'd talk to her that way. "I'm keeping this baby, Jay," she vowed. "I'm keeping it, and I'm having it, and there's not a fuckin' thing you can do about it."

Jay pushed past her and opened the door to leave. "Then you can have it by your damn self! Just stay the fuck away from me!" he said before walking out.

"*Ray, walk to the* park with me." Raymone was always the first person she called when she needed to talk.

"Renee, girl—you know I don't do nature," he complained.

"Then can I come over?"

"What's wrong?"

"I've been showing my ass."

It was seven in the evening. Renee had been home all day long in her pajamas, not bothering to answer the phone or the door. She'd had a fitful sleep after Lewis left, and Renee just needed a shoulder to lean on for a few minutes until she could regain her emotional balance. Raymone had strong shoulders.

"Come on," he sighed. "And stop and get some Marnier on your way over."

"You got the Sprite?"

"Yes, honey, I've got plenty of Sprite."

Renee laid in bed next to Raymone, with the covers pulled up, peeking out over the top like a kid scared of the boogeyman.

He laid next to her, wearing a T-shirt, plaid cotton boxers, and a citrus colored floral scarf tied around his head. Between the two of them, they'd consumed a large vegetarian pizza with extra cheese, and a couple of Grand Marnier and Sprite cocktails.

Erykah Badu was Raymone's favorite artist and the only woman on the planet he'd ever consider doing, given the chance. She crooned from the stereo, filtering softly through his bedroom.

"People like that ain't nothing but freaks anyway, chil'," he said, making sure his head scarf was tied tight.

"I'm as much of a freak as they are, Ray. I mean, I've been knee deep in this from the beginning."

"Yeah, but you're my friend, and I love you. I don't love them, Nay, so to me, they're the freaks. You're just confused and dumb as all hell."

"Thanks Raymone," she said disgustedly.

"I mean, he's fine and everything, but ain't enough fine in the world to put your peace of mind at risk. What were you thinking?" he fussed.

"That's just it, Ray. I wasn't thinking. I was just going with it. You know? It was all primal, just instinct and passion. It felt good."

"Oooh, stop it, girl. You're giving me a hard-on. Gonna make me have to put you on the couch and call somebody."

"I'd think about his wife for a second, just long enough to warn myself that I should feel bad, and then he'd kiss me or touch something, and poof! She'd disappear in a puff of smoke."

"I told you to get you some. I'll bet if you'd done somebody before he came along, you'd have looked at that fool like he'd lost his damn mind if he'd come at you like that."

"It's not like I haven't been trying to get me some, Ray."

"You need a man of your own, honey. A woman like you

needs a whole man, all to herself. You too much woman to have to share."

"I don't know what I want. Sometimes I want a relationship, and sometimes I'm cool without one. Yes, I get lonely, but then again, I love my privacy. There are times when I'd love to share my life, but then again, men are like babies, and I just don't have time."

"No wonder you're still single," Ray said, turning off the lights. "How's a man supposed to know how to come at you, when you don't even know what you want?"

"I never said I made sense. I just have a tendency to change my mind a lot."

"Come here." Raymone wrapped his arms around her and held her close. "Anytime you need a hug, or to snuggle baby, you just call Raymone and I'll hook you up. How's that?"

Renee lay snug in his arms and sighed. "You give great snuggle, Ray. But I can't flip you over and ride you like the Lone Ranger rode Silver when I get horny."

"Don't make me hit you."

Tess lay on that musty sofa of his, with her head in his lap, wearing one of his shirts. "What exactly is it that you see in me?" she asked Gregory.

He bit into an apple. "Probably everything he doesn't," he said matter-of-factly. "The point is," he chewed a couple of times, swallowed and finished what he started to say, "I see you. Chances are, he never has."

Sometimes Gregory was just deep, thoughtful, and insightful. He dropped a small piece of apple on her cheek, then picked it up and put it in his mouth. "My bad, boo."

Other times, he was just a moron. Tess wiped apple juice from her face and sat up and moved to the opposite end of the couch.

He returned the question. "What do you see in me?"

Tess studied him, and obviously didn't answer him fast enough.

"Damn!" He sounded wounded. "Why is it taking you so long to come up something?"

She laughed. "Because you're so charming, I don't know where to start."

He held his apple between his teeth, grabbed her by one of her ankles, and started tickling the bottom of her foot.

Tess kicked and fought until he let go.

"I was about to tell you what I see in you—crazy!" she fussed.

"I'm listening."

"Actually, it's probably easier to list all the qualities I don't like about you."

Gregory glared at her.

"You're a slob," she starting counting on her fingers. "When was the last time you cleaned this place up?"

He flipped her off. "It's the maid's day off," he retorted.

"You're rude, and mean."

"Mean?" He was offended. "Woman, I changed the oil in your car for free. How you gonna sit here and call me mean?"

"You can't keep a job."

"Now, that's not my fault."

"Skinny."

"Then feed a brotha and fatten me up like you did ol' boy," he laughed, patting his stomach.

"And you're a smart aleck."

Gregory pondered her list, and then asked the obvious question. "So, why the hell are you sitting here then?"

Tess smiled affectionately at him, then scooted over closer, and kissed his cheek. "Because you see me."

"I thought you were going to say because my sex was off the chain."

"Oh, it's off the chain, all right."

"Damn good."

"Freak," she teased.

"Takes a freak to know a freak, baby."

"Your momma's a freak."

"I wouldn't doubt it."

Too much stress isn't good for the baby.

What now?

"Daria?" Elise whispered into the phone.

Daria was half asleep. "Who is it?" she asked, irritably.

Elise's hands shook.

She stared at the clock on the nightstand but couldn't make out the numbers.

"Daria?" she said again. It was the only thing she could say. Everything else was meaningless.

"Elise? Girl? What? What is it?"

Elise sat on the toilet, her blood-stained panties lay crumpled on the floor at her feet. She'd gone to bed early.

"I was so tired," she said, her voice quivering.

She'd gone to bed early and slept better than she had in weeks.

"Elise? What's wrong?" Daria sounded panicked.

Elise wasn't panicking, though. She knew better than to panic because it was all over and there was nothing more she could do. But she was sad, and hurt too deeply to comprehend.

"I lost it, Daria."

She stared out at her bed, covered in blood, and the trail of bloody footprints leading to where she was now. There was no pain, like she'd seen in movies. Nothing but blood, and then she peed.

"E? What are you saying, girl? Talk to me."

Elise quietly hung up the phone. There was nothing left to say.

Lewis spent half the night sitting in a bar and the other half, driving around and around and around the city until it made him too tired to see anymore. Six months ago, he knew who he was and what he wanted. He knew where he was going in his career, in life. Seemed like the minute he stepped off that plane, and put his foot down in Dallas, he'd left his old self behind and become a stranger even to himself. Change. He thought he could handle it. He thought he had handled it. Change was a part of life, his life, all his life. But this time had been different. He'd changed at some point between now and then, thinking it was everything and everyone around him who was different. Lewis was different, and he'd seen that different side of himself in his new position, this new city, a new woman. He was a man he didn't know, and whom he wasn't even sure he liked anymore.

He didn't hear her come downstairs. Lewis rested on the sofa with his head back and his eyes closed, opening them just in time to see Trishelle standing over him.

"It must be some good pussy to keep you out all night," she said coolly. "Don't bother denying it, Lewis. Don't waste the time."

Trish crossed the room and sat down on the chaise across

from him. It was obvious that she hadn't slept. She looked pale and disheveled, old and tired. "Is it someone from the office?" she probed too calmly. "Did you meet her at a bar, or maybe at the gym?" She waited for a response, but none ever came. "I don't care who she is, Lewis. I don't care what you see in her, or that somehow, you might even blame me."

Lewis chose to ignore the silent alarm going off inside him.

"I'm going back to Seattle, and I'm taking Tray with me."

He slowly opened his eyes and fixed them on the ceiling.

"You can keep your fucking empire. I'm going home."

Trish left the room and went upstairs.

Lewis didn't budge. Why should he? Unless he had some insatiable urge to fight this early in the morning, going upstairs after her would be a moot point. Besides, he'd been fighting with Trishelle ever since they moved down here, and the thought of her leaving—going back to Seattle—was a relief. Losing his family had never been a part of his plan, but lately, all his plans had gone to shit anyway. There was nothing left between the two of them. It felt empty every time they were together, trying to fill in the blanks with the good old days. The bottom line was, their marriage had come up too short too many times, and Trishelle in Seattle was becoming a more appealing image by the second.

She came back downstairs. It was obvious she'd been crying. Trish stared tragically at him, broken by the fact that he hadn't chased after her, begging her not to leave him.

"Who is she, Lewis?" she hiccupped pitifully through tears. "If you can't be anything else to me—at least be honest."

"What difference does it make?" he asked wearily.

"A big one," she whispered. Trishelle sniffed, then begged

the one question she never thought would ever cross her lips. "Is she black?"

He stared back at her, surprised she'd even go there, and Lewis couldn't help but to laugh. He laughed long and loud at the irony, and at his mother's old-world predictions, and even at Renee's insightfulness on the subject of interracial relationships. And finally, he laughed at his beautiful wife, looking wounded and beaten, who truly believed that one answer to this question could ultimately make a difference. In this moment, Lewis felt downright mean.

"Very," he said definitively.

Trish's eyes glazed over, almost as if she'd just had an epiphany. "Do I know her?"

Lewis didn't say a word. He didn't have to.

"Come on, big head." Renee playfully smacked Raymone on the behind. The man's alarm clock had gone off three times, she'd woken him up at least four and his lazy ass was still in bed. "Get up, Ray. I want you to walk me home."

He grunted, then pulled the covers up over his head. "Walk your own self home, dammit. You're a big girl."

"I thought you wanted breakfast?"

"I do, but not until lunch time."

Desperate times called for desperate measures, so Renee stood at the foot of the bed, gathered up Ray's sheets and blankets in her hands and pulled them completely off his little skinny self.

"Renee!" He bolted up, reaching and grabbing for his bedding. "Girl! Give me back my covers before I have to put my foot up your ass."

"Ooooh! I'm so scared of Raymone. Please, whatever you do, Lord, don't let him put that big ol' foot up my ass."

She finally got him riled up enough to get out of bed, shower, brush his teeth, and walk back to her place with her. "We should've drove," he complained, walking down the sidewalk, with her arm looped through his.

Renee sucked her teeth. "We live less than five blocks away from each other, Ray. You should be ashamed of yourself."

"I'm walking, ain't I?" he said with attitude. "Don't you see me walking?"

"Then hush."

And he did, too, for a minute. "You give me a ride home?"

Renee conceded. "Of course."

Neither of them heard the woman getting out of the car. They never saw the fire in her eyes, or realized she was headed straight for them.

"You bitch!" Trishelle screamed at the top of her lungs, standing in the middle of the street, clad in a pink velour jogging suit and in her bare feet.

Renee and Raymone turned in time to see Lewis's car screeching up behind Trishelle's, and Lewis jumping out of the car and catching his wife in midair at the moment she lunged at Renee.

"Oh my God!" Raymone shrieked. "What the hell is your problem, bitch?"

"You were my friend!" Trishelle screamed. "You were my fucking friend! How could you?" She broke down crying in

Lewis's arms. "How the hell could you do this . . ." Her voice trailed off.

"It's all right, baby." Lewis held her tight in his arms.

"You told her?" Renee blurted out. "Why would you do that, Lewis?"

Raymone held Renee back from the street. "Get back, girl! Don't be stupid."

Lewis stared expressionless at Renee, still struggling to contain his wife.

In an instant, Trishelle seemed to get her second wind, kicked Lewis hard in the groin, and broke free of his grasp. She charged at Renee like a bull, elbowing Raymone in the stomach, doubling him over and sending him crumbling down to his knees. Renee tripped over a stone behind her as she backed away, and Trish fell on top of her, slapping and punching Renee hard in the face, neck, chest.

"You—were—my—friend! You—were—my—"

Renee tried to fight back, but Trish's long arms beat her to the next punch every time, her long legs pinning Renee to the ground. Trishelle spat in her face, pulled her hair, and slammed her head down hard on the ground.

"How could you do this? Why? Why?" she wailed.

Finally, some relief. Lewis gathered up enough strength to pull his wife off Renee, and dragged Trishelle back into the street. "That's enough! Trish! That's enough, baby! Come on!" he said, trying to calm her.

Raymone came to Renee, and helped her to sit up. Renee saw Lewis cradle that long, white woman in his arms.

"Get that crazy ass bitch out of here, man!" Ray shouted to

Lewis. "Did anybody call the police?" Ray looked at the crowd gathered around. "If it was the other way around y'all would've sho' nuff called." He helped Renee to her feet.

"It's all right baby," Lewis told Trishelle over and over again. "Let's go home. We're going home, Trish. She's not worth it, baby. She's not worth it."

Lewis poured his wife into his car and sped away.

Raymone told her she was crazy for not pressing charges, but Renee figured they were all square now. Tit for tat, and eye for a swollen eye, that sort of thing. She stared out the window of the plane, anticipating the sandy beaches waiting for her in Bermuda. A whole other kind of world waited for her there and she couldn't wait to get to it, even if it was only for a week. Ray wanted to come, but not this time. Renee needed time to gather her strength, her spirit, and her dignity.

"I can't believe you let a white girl beat you up," Raymone teased.

Shit! White or black, it didn't matter. Mess with a woman's man, it wouldn't matter if she was a blind midget with one leg, she could beat the hell out of another woman over some shit like that.

Lewis's punk ass was who'd surprised her the most. He'd almost had Renee convinced that he really cared. He'd almost convinced her that she was crazy for warding off the love jones over him. He was hard to resist sometimes. Hard to dismiss. Hard not to imagine what it might be like to be his woman. But not anymore.

The flight attendant interrupted her thoughts. "Miss? Would you like another cognac?"

Renee handed the woman her glass. "Yes, please. And keep 'em coming."

Jesse called the house just before eleven, intending on asking Tess to come down and have lunch with him at noon. Hmmm. No answer. He was going to call her cell phone, but then decided against it, and to surprise her instead, by bringing lunch to her. He'd stop and pick up her favorite, barbequed pork sandwich and coleslaw from Jabos, her favorite soul food restaurant, and afterwards, he might just take an extended lunch with his wife, and make love to her. He laughed out loud at the idea.

Jesse saw her at the intersection near the house, and honked, but Tess pulled off before she noticed it was him. He decided to make a game out of it, and follow her to the store, or Juanita's or wherever she was going, then jumping out of the car, and sneaking up behind her, surprising her. She'd like that. He knew she'd get a kick out of that.

He was curious about where she was going. Jesse knew just about all of Tess's stomping grounds, and this was new to him. As far as he could remember, none of her friends lived this far north. There were no stores she frequented this way either, unless she'd found something new. An odd feeling grew in his stomach, and slowly, his appetite began to diminish. Stop being silly, man! He laughed at himself for daring to think such devious thoughts about his wife. *Tess is better than that, Jesse. She's better than you.*

She stopped in front of a small house on the corner. Jesse stopped a block away and watched her get out of the car, and walk up to the house. A man was standing in the carport. He held some kind of tool in his hand, his T-shirt hung from his back pocket and he stood half dressed in front of Tess. Jesse could see them talking, but he was too far away to hear what they were saying. Tess stepped closer to him. He slipped his arm around her waist, pulled her into his arms, and kissed her. Moments later, they went inside the house.

You want this?" he asked, breathless, pushing her down on the bed, then yanking off her jeans. "You want this dick, bitch?"

"Yes!" she could hardly say the word. "You know I do!"

He threw her jeans and panties across the room, unhooked her bra, and engulfed one of her breasts, sucking hard enough to hurt, and make her nipples swell.

"Turn over," he commanded.

Tess did as she was told, and raised herself up on the bed, on her hands and knees.

"Come on, baby!" she begged. "Don't tease me, Gregory."

He pushed it in hard.

This was the kind of sex she'd come to crave. There were no sweet words, tender touches, soft kisses. He fucked her hard from behind, hurting her, drilling into her, smacking her ass when he felt like it, and she relished it, every thrust, slap, dig. Gregory grabbed a handful of her hair, and pulled her head back, then sucked viciously on the side of her neck.

Tess's bare breasts bounced heavy back and forth, slapping against her chest, as he pushed and pulled inside her, until she burned and throbbed, and pulsated around his erect shaft. Tess regretted nothing about coming here. He knew what she wanted better than she did and he gave it to her, full force and without wavering.

"That's some good ass, baby girl!" he grunted. "That's the kind of hot ass I like! And you knew I'd like it! Didn't you?"

He yanked her head back again, until she responded. "Yes!" she gasped. "Yes, baby!"

Jesse sat in the car, unable to move. He was frozen in the one thing he never once given thought to—that someone else would want her. That she'd want someone else. But how could this happen? Why? He'd started over, fresh, and committed to her. He'd given up everything—everything—Sandra! Fuck! Jesse gripped the steering wheel so tight his hands throbbed. No! He'd told himself that Tess loved him more, better, longer. She was his soul mate, his rock, his partner for life. Sandra wasn't shit.

He willed his arm to move to open the car door. He willed his legs to move one step at a time, slowly making his way up the block to that house. The bitch made too much noise.

"Yes!" he heard her say through an open window. "Harder! Harder!"

Jesse walked to the front door, prepared to kick it in, only to discover it was unlocked. He turned the knob and let himself in. The smell of sex wafted from the back of the house, leading him to the bedroom. The skinny mothafucka stood naked at the foot of the bed, pumping in and out of Tess hard, while she begged him over and over again not to stop.

"I'm coming!" she said, breathless. "Oh, my—I'm coming!"

"What the—" Jesse wrapped his large hands around Gregory's skinny-ass neck, and squeezed, lifted him up off the floor, and threw him across the room, into the wall, where he landed with a thud, eyes wide as dinner plates, and shocked as hell.

"Jesse!" she screamed, scurrying to cover her naked ass, pulling sheets around her to cover herself.

He yanked them away, then backhanded her hard across the face. "Fuckin' slut!" he growled, pointing his finger in her face.

"If it ain't big daddy," Gregory said sarcastically as he managed to get to his feet. Jesse had size on him, but Gregory moved too fast, ducking and dodging, swinging his fists, which landed in Jesse's face. Jesse wavered, out of breath. He couldn't catch Gregory, so he turned his anger back on Tess.

"You—"

Tess crawled off the bed, and backed against the wall. Tears streamed down her face. "Jesse, please," she whispered, attempting to guard herself with her hands. "I'm sorry. I'm so sor—"

He spat in her face. "You mothafuckin' bitch! How the hell you gonna pull this shit on me, Tess?"

Gregory had slipped on his jeans, and was just about to bust his nose, when Tess surprised them both and slapped the hell out of Jesse. He reacted quickly and hit her hard enough to send her crashing to the floor. Gregory jumped on his back, but Jesse was too strong for him and flipped him off.

He was lost and a madman crazy with rage. Jesse put one hand around her neck, then lifted her off the ground, pressed against the wall, slowly choking the life out of her. And the whole time, the only thing that kept coming back to him was Sandra.

"I could've had her," he growled, while Tess struggled to breathe. "I could've had her!"

Gregory kicked Jesse in his back with all the force he had. He let go of Tess, then stumbled forward, landing head first into the wall. Gregory was just about to put his foot in Jesse's face when Tess stepped between the two men, glaring down at Jesse.

"I'm not the mothafucka, Jesse," she said, coughing, and trying to catch her breath. "I'm not the mothafucka!" she screamed.

"Shut up!" He clutched his throbbing head.

Gregory bounced on the balls of his feet behind his boo.

Tess didn't want to cry, but she couldn't help herself. "You did this! It was you, Jesse! I'm here because of you! Because you didn't want me! Because I needed somebody, too!"

Jesse struggled to breathe. "You up in here, fuckin' this nigga and that's *my* fault?" he asked, appalled.

"I wanted to fuck my nigga!" she told him. "You! My husband! But you were too busy fuckin' every other woman in town *but* me! You didn't want me, Jesse, and now I don't want your sorry ass!"

Jesse cried, too. "How come you can't let that shit go, Tess? It's over! It's been over! How come you can't let it go?"

Tess wiped her face with the back of her hands. She stared down at him, knowing that the last twenty-three years of her life had just come to an end. She never hated Jesse. If anything, she'd loved him too much, more then he'd ever deserved. But not enough anymore.

"I think I have," she said sadly.

Tess brushed past Gregory, and picked up her clothes laying on the floor. She went into the bathroom to get dressed. Jesse slowly rose to his feet, feeling every one of his forty-five years. He never even looked at Gregory on his way out of the house.

The boys naturally took sides with Jesse, if there was such a thing as sides.

Brandon was humiliated and embarrassed. "How could you do this to me, Mom? How do you think that makes me look to Keisha's family?

"I don't care what they think, Brandon," she said indifferently. "Or you either, for that matter."

"Then—to hell with you, too, Mom." He slammed the phone down in her ear. He might never speak to her again, she surmised. And if that ended up being the case, then all she could do was accept it and go on with her life.

Brian sang a different song. "Dad's been good to you, Ma. He's been a good provider, a great dad."

"A lousy husband." She finished his sentence for him.

"Like you've been such a great wife? That shit wasn't cool, Ma. And now, look at what you've done to this family. I used to brag to all my friends about how my parents were the only parents I knew who weren't divorced."

"We should've been divorced years ago, Brian."

"No. No. I don't think you knew how good you had it, Ma. He's a good man."

"Stop telling me how good a man he is, and open your eyes, dammit! You and Brandon have no idea what kind of marriage we had because you never saw it! I wouldn't let you see it! It wasn't always so good, and he wasn't always so grand, Brian! So, don't tell me what I should be doing!"

In their eyes, he walked on water. But that was her fault. She'd helped to make him their hero, because he'd always been hers. And Jesse's faults were minor in comparison to his greatness.

Tess had no clue as to what her next move would be. Jesse had moved out of the house that held too many memories for her to want to grow old in. It was ironic, though. Brian and Brandon hated her. Jesse couldn't stand the sight of her. And for most of her life, she'd sacrificed her own happiness for theirs.

It's going to be all right, sweetie," Daria said reassuringly to Elise. "You need to eat, E." She put a spoonful of soup to Elise's lips, but Elise wouldn't take it. There was no reason to eat or to sleep or to think or to remember. Everything that meant anything to her was gone, and Elise was numb.

Daria stayed as long as she could, but then she had to leave. Elise vaguely remembered hearing her say good-bye. "I'll call you in the morning to see how you're doing," she said before leaving.

"Miscarriages are common in first pregnancies," her doctor told her. "It's not your fault, Elise. There's nothing you could've done to prevent it."

People needed to just hush. They needed to keep their mouths shut and hush, because sometimes words didn't mean enough.

She sat up in bed all night. If she slept, Elise didn't know it. The sun chose to rise anyway, despite her efforts to pray that it wouldn't. And to add insult to injury a goddamned bird started singing at dawn right outside her window.

She needed to see him. She needed to make sure he didn't forget her, and she needed to make sure he wasn't happy either.

Teddy wanted me to let him go, without argument or protest. Just quietly sign the divorce papers when they came, and leave him alone. He was asking too much from me. I knew better than to think he'd ever want me back. And I knew that deep down inside, I really didn't want him back either. He'd hurt my pride and taken the love and esteem I held for him for granted, and there was no forgiveness in me for that.

I sat in my car outside of the apartment building I'd followed him to. It's where he came to everyday after leaving the church. It's where he parked his car at night. She was there. I didn't have to be a genius to know it. And it panged my heart knowing it.

I couldn't rest without knowing what had happened between him and me. Teddy never told me why he fell out of love with me, or why he insisted on pretending that he still did, after she came into his life. Sitting alone in that house without him, I'd convinced myself of so many reasons, that by my conclusions, I was the worst woman in the world.

My cell phone rang, startling me. It was my receptionist. "Sorry to bother you Dr. Watkins, but Elise Clayton has been calling for days asking to see you. I wouldn't be calling except, well, she says it's urgent." Elise could wait. "What should I—"

I cut her short. "I'm going to have to call you back, Tina. Tell her to call back tomorrow."

I got out of the car, and slowly made my way toward the complex. It was huge and I had no idea which apartment she lived in. But I was determined to find it, searching floor by floor, if I had to. I needed to see this woman. I needed to hear from her own mouth, the reason she'd come after my husband. I needed to see him with her. And then, I'd leave quietly. I'd walk away and he'd never have to see or hear from me again. I had no idea if I could actually pull the trigger. Sometimes, I was angry enough to believe I could. But I knew for certain that I could wave it around in their faces and make them think I would. Maybe that would be enough for me. Or maybe, I'd pull the trigger and kill someone.

Lord Jesus, I'd prayed. Help me to do what's right. Help me to get through this. Help me to understand.

Had I gotten too old for him? Had I grown indifferent to his needs? Or was this just his pattern? Was he predestined and wired to cheat on his wives and leave them for his mistresses? After all, he'd left his first wife for me. It was different between us, though. She never loved him the way I did. She didn't treat him the way he deserved to be treated. She ignored him, and took his dreams for granted. I paid attention. I listened. I supported his goals. I stood by him when times were tough. He fell in love with my strength. The strength she didn't have. That's what he told me. He fell in love with my devotion to the vision that he'd had since he was a boy. He fell in love with the way I sucked his dick.

"After you did that, Faylene," he used to tease me, "she never had a chance." So, what was he telling this one? Lynette. What were her special talents he found irresistible enough to walk out on me for? That remained to be seen.

I'd made it to the second floor when the unmistakable sound of his voice carried down the hall. I followed it to apartment 2C.

"No . . . no, Lynn. Please . . ."

"You want too much, Ted. I can't ever seem to—"

"Fine! Fine! Just don't do this! Baby I can't—I can't—"

"Don't even say it. You know I—Ted?"

"I'm not letting you do this, baby."

"It's not up to you. Don't trip. Ted! I've made up my mind, and that's all there is to it. I'm sorry."

"Lynette. I can't let you."

"Ted? What's that? What? No!"

"You don't understand."

"Don't do—"

The sound sent a shockwave through the building. I stood still, unable to move, expecting someone to come running out of that apartment at any moment. But neither one of them did.

"What was that?" A lady in the apartment next door asked, peeking her head out into the hallway. "Did you hear that?" she asked me.

I nodded. "I think—I think it was a gun."

She hadn't seen him in over a month. Lewis looked thinner, maybe a little older. "Can I come in?" he asked politely, standing outside her door with his hands deep in his pockets.

"No. You can say anything you've got to say to me right there from where you're standing," Renee said smugly.

Lewis looked disappointed. "I called."

"I know."

"Quite a few times, as a matter of fact." He let his sarcasm shine through.

"What do you want?"

"To apologize."

Renee raised an eyebrow, as if to beg the question, "Oh really?" She didn't bother trying to hide her repugnance. "And just what do you think you could possibly say to me that would convince me to accept an apology from you, Lewis?"

He frowned. "From the tone of your voice and the look on your face, I guess—nothing."

"Then why are you standing here wasting my time?"

"I just wanted to say I'm sorry, Renee," he sighed. "Just let me say it even if you don't accept it."

"You know, Lewis"—she had been rehearsing this little

speech ever since she got back from her trip, and her mouth had been watering for the opportunity to say it—"I'm not going to stand here and play the victim. I had a part in all this too. We both should've known better, Lewis. You didn't drag me kicking and screaming into your life. I walked in on my own, and that's something I'm still trying to resolve, so yeah, maybe I did deserve to get my ass kicked." She stared arrogantly at him. "But you're not worth losing my self-respect over. And you're certainly not worth a second ass whooping from that tall glass of water you call your wife."

"That's not why I came, Renee. I know it's over between us."

"Hell yeah, it's over!" she said angrily. "And if you ever bring your ass to my door again, I'll sic my Rotweiller on you."

He looked confused. "You don't have a Rotweiller."

"For you, Lewis," she put her hand on her hip, "I'll get one." Renee ended the conversation by slamming the door in his face.

He stood outside her door pondering the course of events that had changed his life. Trishelle and Tray were back in Seattle. She didn't have too much to say to him either these days. Lewis was in the process of trying to find another job. He really didn't care if he found one here, or back in Washington. He just needed to get out from under a situation he'd never really fit into comfortably anyway. He'd put the house on the market a few days ago. Despite how cool Renee had made the place look, it never did feel like home to him.

"Can I call you sometime?" he yelled loud enough for her to hear him through the door.

Moments later, Renee answered. "Call me and I'll rip out your damn larynx with my teeth!"

Lewis chuckled quietly to himself. That woman was definitely a piece of work. But if he did decide to stick around, with a little patience, some perserverance, just maybe she'd come around.

Of course, the silence between them was deafening. Jesse and Tess sat across the table from each other waiting on their lawyers to join them. It was the first time they'd seen each other since he found her with Gregory.

"Never thought we'd end up like this," she said, trying to make conversation.

He just grunted and half nodded.

She'd gotten beyond being angry with him. Obviously he hadn't gotten past it where she was concerned. "How are the boys?" she asked, knowing that at least they spoke to him. She'd fallen off the radar in their lives, and it hurt, but damn if they weren't some selfish bastards.

"Fine," he said curtly. Jesse still wouldn't look at her. He tapped nervously on the table, bouncing his knee the way he did when he felt impatient.

"How've you been feeling, lately? Have you been back to the doctor? Is everything—"

"Tess," he interrupted her. "Please. We don't have anything to say to each other. So let's just sit here and wait quietly until we can get this over with."

"Of course we have something to say, Jesse," she said softly.

"We've been together for too long not to have anything to talk about."

Jesse sighed, frustrated.

"I think you should get custody of the twins, since they're not speaking to me," she said, trying to lighten the vibe.

He glared at her.

"I'm kidding."

"This is a joke to you?" he said bluntly. "You find being here like this funny?"

"No. I don't find it funny at all. But we don't have to hate each other, Jesse."

"Why the hell not?" he snapped. "I caught you with somebody else, Contessa. You don't think I should hate you for that?"

"I never hated you," she said simply.

He shifted uncomfortably in his chair. "Yeah, well—you never caught me in the act," he said gruffly.

"Sure I did, Jesse. I caught you all the time—in lies, smelling like perfume, phone numbers in your pocket, a Viagra prescription that I know you didn't use on me."

"How many times do I have to apologize for all that, Tess? How long are you going to hold that shit over my head?"

"I don't have any reason to hold it over your head anymore, Jesse. I'm just saying that now you know how I felt all those years. Now you know how much it hurt me to know what you were doing."

He didn't say anything right away. In his mind, he'd made amends for his mistakes. Or at least he'd tried. "I wanted it to work with us, Tess," he said, trying to hold back his anger. "I was really trying to make it work."

"And what about all the times *I* tried to make it work?"

"So you want to play the blame game? Who did who bad? Is that what this is? I made mistakes. I did wrong. I know I did. But so did you."

"Of course, Jesse. And looking at that, looking back at the last twenty-some odd years, what does that tell you? That we were a happily married couple?"

"Maybe not for all twenty years," he argued.

"How about half of them?" she asked. "I can tell you for a fact, that I wasn't even happy for half of those years, Jesse. And if you're really honest with yourself, you weren't happy with me either, because if you were, I'd have been the only woman you needed."

"So—what are you saying? That we wasted twenty-three years of marriage?"

"I'm saying that maybe we should've gone our separate ways a long time ago."

The two sat quietly for a few minutes, thinking through this conversation. "You might not believe that I ever loved you, Contessa," he said sincerely, "but I did." he looked at her for the first time since they'd been in that room, and almost smiled.

"I know, Jesse."

He shrugged. "I guess it just wasn't the right way," he admitted.

Tess was proud of him. "You did the best you could. But no, baby"—she smiled back at him—"it wasn't the right way."

He hesitated before asking the question, uncertain as to whether or not he really wanted to know. But he decided to ask it anyway. "Does he love you the right way?"

She was surprised by the question. "If it ever gets that far, Jesse, I'll be sure to let you know."

Jay's blood ran cold when he pulled up to his house and saw Elise standing in his front yard talking to Sherry. Both of them watched him park the car, waited as he turned off the engine and got out of the car. Elise smiled at him. Sherry didn't.

"Hi," they both said in unison.

Elise wore a business suit; her long hair was pulled back away from her face and pinned up in the back. Sherry still had on her hospital scrubs from having just gotten off work.

He looked nervously at Sherry, trying to gauge what was happening here, avoiding Elise's gaze altogether. "What's going on?"

"Elise Clayton," she held out her hand for him to shake. Jay took it and stared at her, confused.

"Baby," Sherry started to say, "She's a realtor talking to people in the neighborhood about what's it's like living out here."

Elise nodded, and spoke between them both. "I'm new to the area, and have some clients interested in possibly buying out here and I wanted to be able to provide them with some feedback and options," she spoke professionally.

"Like how the schools are," Sherry chimed in, "shopping, that sort of thing."

He stared suspiciously at Elise, wondering what kind of game this was she was playing.

"Jay." Sherry lovingly touched his arm. "Could you please tell her what you can?" She smiled at Elise apologetically. "I'm sorry, but I just got off a double shift and I can hardly keep my eyes open. I don't mean to be rude."

"That's quite all right," Elise said politely. "I understand."

"My husband will tell you everything you need to know."

Sherry went inside the house, leaving Jay staring stunned at Elise.

"How the hell did you find out where I lived?" he said in a hushed voice.

"You're listed. It wasn't hard," she said indifferently.

"Why are you here, Elise?" He grabbed her by the elbow and led her away from the door, and out of earshot of the windows.

She unassumingly pulled away from him. "To show you something, Jay. To teach you a lesson."

"What?" he asked, dismayed. "What the hell is that supposed to mean?"

"It means that you've got an angel on your shoulder."

He looked more confused than he was when he first saw her there. "You trying to get me back? What? You want money?"

Elise laughed. "Dammit, man. Don't you get it, Jay? Or are you just that stupid?"

She'd hit a nerve and he looked offended.

"If I were a different kind of woman, I'd have your poor wife in tears by now. I'd have told her about you and me. I'd have told her everything."

Suddenly Jay looked afraid that she would. "Elise—"

"As easily as I found you, some other woman could've just

have easily done the same thing. But God is watching out for you, Jay, because if your lying ass had to hook up with somebody, you got lucky and hooked up with me."

"What are you saying?"

"I'm saying that you don't deserve a woman like me." Hot tears burned her eyes. "Or that nice woman in there." She pointed toward the house. "That hard-working woman deserves better than the likes of you."

As much as he wanted to, Jay couldn't argue.

"I've been to hell and back these last few months over you." She choked back tears, refusing to give him the satisfaction of seeing even one of them fall. "I lost my baby, the man I thought I loved, and almost myself because of you."

Jay felt humbled. "Elise—," he started to say.

"Shut up and let me finish!" Elise's lips quivered. This wasn't about Jay. Not anymore. This was about her. "You'll let me finish this, Jay. Because you owe me that much. You owe me at least that much."

He nodded apprehensively.

"You were selfish, Jay. You wanted what you wanted, to hell with everybody else. And I damn near lost my mind over you. And when I miscarried—" she took a deep breath "—I thought God had turned his back on me. I thought I was being punished for being with you. I thought I didn't deserve that baby."

Jay hated himself for what he was feeling, relief that Elise wasn't pregnant anymore. He really was a son of a bitch.

"It took time for me to see that losing that baby was a blessing, not a curse. Because if I'd had it, I would've had to live with the reminder everyday of how little you valued me. And who knows? Maybe I'd have taken my resentment of you out on that kid. I don't know, but God knows. And He knows that I'm too good for you, Jay. He knows that the time you spent with me was a privilege that should've best been left to someone who deserved me and who'd sacrificed for me, because I am all that."

"You are," he interjected, taking in the full impact of what she was saying.

"I don't need you to tell me that. I know that, Jay, because I had to pick myself back up from nothing to get to that realization and I will never let another man steal that from me again!"

She stepped back and composed herself, and took another deep breath to calm herself down. Elise had come through the fire and out onto the other side, strong enough to finally let him go in her heart, and carry on without him.

"I've done the right thing for me, Jay," she continued. Elise looked him in the eyes and dared him to turn away. "You have a lovely wife, and some sweet kids. Now, you be the man and stand up and do the right thing for them. Stop fucking around, or else the next time, you might not be as lucky as to get another Elise Clayton."

She left him standing on that curb, never looking back as she pulled away.

Jay came into the house and followed Sherry's trail up to the bedroom, where she lay sprawled across the bed, napping. He lay down next to her, and tenderly kissed her cheek.

"Is that lady gone?" she muttered sleepily.

"Yeah," he said quietly. "She's gone."

"She was nice."

He didn't say anything.

"I saw you checking out her tits," she said playfully.

He played along. "No you didn't."

"She had nice tits."

"Yeah, she did."

Sherry half-assedly punched him in the stomach.

Jay pretended to be really hurt and fell back on the bed, fixing his gaze on the ceiling. He'd had a close call today. With one word from Elise, he could've lost everything. Today was the day he needed to start counting his blessings, starting with the one laying next to him. The other one, well—she'd come into his life like a gift from heaven, and she'd left it the same way.

epilogue

Teddy was getting ready to be sentenced for second-degree murder. The story was in all the newspapers about one of the city's most noted ministers, and the scandal surrounding his mistress and her death at his hands.

"I saw the news, Dr. Faye." Renee Turner left a message on my voice mail. I'd refused to take any calls. "Damn! I am so sorry. Really. That shit wasn't cool. Not cool at all."

"Faye," Tess said frantically. "Call me. If you need to talk or just—. Call me."

Elise Clayton said a prayer: "In the name of Jesus, I pray for His continued watchfulness and devotion over you, Dr. Watkins. May he guide you and keep you strong and faithful through this terrible ordeal."

He'd confessed to the crime, so there was no trial. What would happen to the church now was still up in the air. I'd been closed up in the house ever since it happened, confused and lost more than I'd ever been before in my life.

Her name had been Lynette Chambers, and she'd been twenty-seven years old. Her picture was in all the papers and on every local news channel, and yes, I recognized her from church.

I hadn't spoken to him since it happened. Until now, he'd refused to see me. Why I felt the need to see him had more to do with habit or instinct than anything else, I suppose.

I was escorted down a long, narrow corridor with slate gray walls, and white linoleum floors. "In here," the guard said, opening a large metal door for me to walk through. "Number three. You got fifteen minutes," he said gruffly.

I found my seat behind a glass wall, and waited patiently for them to bring him in. Teddy wore an orange jumpsuit, and he reluctantly sat down on the other side of the glass from me. We both picked up the phone receivers, which we held to our ears. Neither one of us said a word at first, but finally he broke the silence.

"How you doing?" he asked, seemingly trying to smile.

"I don't know," I admitted. "You?"

"Oh." He shrugged his large shoulders. "I've seen better days."

"Why did you do it, Teddy?" I blurted out the question before I'd even realized it.

Teddy stared expressionless at me, looking as if he wasn't sure himself.

"Were you in love with her?"

He nodded. "Madly."

His confession hurt me, but he didn't seem to notice.

"Did you stop loving me?"

He never said.

"Why'd you shoot her?" Tears fell down my cheeks. "Why would you do something like that?"

The distant look in his eyes made me wonder if he'd even heard me.

"She was going to leave me," he said finally. "She told me she

didn't want to be with me anymore. Said I was too demanding. Too controlling." He said it, almost as if he couldn't fathom these accusations.

But she'd been right. Teddy was those things. Always had been, only I saw his qualities as those of a strong man, and I loved him for them.

His gaze grew cold. "I couldn't let her leave me, Faye. I just couldn't let her go."

Now that he was gone, my practice was all I had. But the scandal brought more people interested in the freak show than real patients, so I moved to Florida, and went back into private practice. It's been a long time since I've been to church. But that's how it goes with most people. After a big hurt, most of us turn our backs on God.

Teddy got twenty years for killing that girl. I filed for divorce shortly after he was sentenced and went back to my maiden name, Harris. Every now and then, I hear from Tess and Elise, just checking up on me, promising to come visit, but they never do, and I'm relieved. Renee never calls, though, but I'm not surprised.

I have new patients now. And a new attitude to go along with being their counselor. I'm in no position to look down my nose or judge anybody. No matter how screwed up they may be. Present company included.